She started to look back t̶  caught in Daniel's intense g... ... ... a butterfly in a spider's web.

Never breaking eye contact, he said, "What is it about Van Buren that fascinates you?"

All she could do was shrug. She honestly had no idea. She only knew that to her he'd always been Prince Charming, living high on the hill, and she wanted to share his castle with him. She rubbed her knees.

Eileen felt her mouth go dry and her heartbeat accelerate as Daniel removed his glasses and leaned closer, his gaze searching for something in her eyes.

His voice turned soft and sensuously throaty as he said, "The guy's crazy. He doesn't know what he's got. I think you're beautiful."

Was he putting her on? She searched his eyes and saw only truth. She also got the feeling he was about to kiss her.

Suddenly, she wanted to be kissed by someone who saw her as beautiful. So, when Daniel reached up to remove her glasses, she didn't pull away. Her eyes closed, and she sensed him slowly coming closer. His lips stopped just short of touching hers, teasing with an unfulfilled promise of skin upon skin. His warm breath brushed her skin, and her lips tingled with the need to consummate the kiss. But she didn't move.

She needed Daniel to want her, to want and need her so much that he *couldn't* hold back from moving that last millimeter. Her heart drummed in her chest like it was going to burst free, and at the same time liquid warmth suffused her entire body. She felt Daniel's fingers stroke her shoulder, sensuously gliding their way up to her neck. Her breath caught.

At last his lips found hers, possessed hers, and an instant, unbidden response shot through her. Daniel's heated kiss belied the restraint he'd shown only moments before, and Eileen felt herself fall into an abyss of sensations. Daniel told her with his lips and his hands that she was beautiful, desired and sexy.

But this wasn't the man she loved! This wasn't Brock! Roughly she pushed away, forcing her eyes open to break Daniel's spell.

This book is dedicated with love to my mother, Colleen Black, who taught me to look for fairies in the flowers. My husband, Fred, my "happily ever after." My children, Jaimie, Aubrey & Colin, who have shown me what real magic is. And to my father, fellow-writer, fishing buddy and dreamer, Bob Buchanan (1924-1998), for his sense of humor.

GLASS-SLIPPER-DOT.COM

✳✳✳

Rebecca Anderson

GLASS-SLIPPER-DOT.COM
Published by ImaJinn Books, a division of ImaJinn

ISBN: 1-893896-16-1

10 9 8 7 6 5 4 3 2 1

PUBLISHER'S NOTE:
This book is a work of fiction. Names, characters, places and incidents are products of the author's imagination or are used fictitiously. Any resemblance to actual events or locales or persons, living or dead, is entirely coincidental.

Books are available at quantity discounts when used to promote products or services. For information please write to: Marketing Division, ImaJinn Books, P.O. Box 162, Hickory Corners, MI 49060-0162, or call toll free 1-877-625-3592.

Cover design by Patricia Lazarus

ImaJinn Books, a division of ImaJinn
P.O. Box 162, Hickory Corners, MI 49060-0162
Toll Free: 1-877-625-3592
http://www.imajinnbooks.com

Prologue

Senior Good Witch and "Granter," Mirabelle Saintly, studied the image on her computer screen as she sipped hot peppermint tea and enjoyed the evening's balmy California breeze drifting through her open window. The young woman in the picture before her looked like she was trying to smile, but only succeeded in a pensive grimace. Horn-rimmed glasses and a mass of long auburn hair nearly obscured her delicate features.

Mirabelle spoke to her supervisor, Mary, through the PC-linked headset, "So, this is my assignment. What's the young woman's name?"

Mary's usually cheery voice had a worried edge to it. "Her name is Eileen Pringle, and her wish wasn't direct. The child still doesn't believe herself worthy of attaining her dreams. Her wish came as a loved-one's bequest."

Bequests were rare. Considered a special event by the entire Wishmaker's network, they could only be given by someone who had "passed on" without attaining their own wish in this lifetime.

Mirabelle could hear Mary blow out a long breath. "But there's something else. I'm afraid Eileen Pringle's not just another assignment, Mirabelle." Mary paused so long Mirabelle began to worry that the connection had been broken. When Mary finally continued, her voice held a wavering quality Mirabelle had never heard in all the eons she'd known her.

"I hate to put such an awesome responsibility on you, but

the future of our entire organization is riding on your success with this client. Wishmakers is in imminent danger of being disbanded. Forever."

Mirabelle felt the tiny hairs on the back of her neck prickle. "But, didn't Minerva just Grant?"

Mary's sigh was deep. "Her client lost heart. I'm afraid both Minerva and the young woman gave up."

"Oh dear, that's so sad." Mirabelle sipped her rapidly-cooling tea. The breeze through the window brought the distant, mournful cry of a coyote, as if even the animal kingdom knew disaster loomed close.

Mary said, "Sad for Minerva and her client, but devastating for Wishmakers, as well as for future generations of prospective 'Grantees.' Minerva is now on probation, which, you know, relegates her to Helper. That drops the number of active Granters to exactly half what it was at the beginning of the new millennium. Besides that, our recent successive failures have taken our energy reserves down to critical. We have only enough power for one more Grant. If we succeed with Eileen, we'll be on the road to recovery. If we fail ..."

Mary didn't have to finish. Mirabelle knew the Good Witch power structure. It had been close to the critical stage for nearly a hundred years. That's why they had gone all-out to update. They'd even enlisted outside help. If they could only make it through this crisis, she was sure they would prevail in the new millennium with more energy and power than ever. If not, Wishmakers and the entire network of *Granters* would fade— as many other so-called "Fables" had—into oblivion.

Mirabelle studied Eileen Pringle's face again. "You can count on me, Mary." She squinted to look past Eileen's eyeglasses, happy to see clear, intelligent blue eyes. And there was something else. "I see a lot more to this young woman than her solemn demeanor suggests. Eileen Pringle's spark isn't out altogether. A little encouragement, and it could be rekindled, I'm positive."

She leaned closer to Eileen's image, studying every feature as she listened to Mary.

"Do everything in your power to bring Eileen to Granting."

A moment of silence. "But, no shortcuts. I know we're desperate, but we must maintain our integrity. She still must become enlightened before you grant. We wouldn't gain anything if we won the battle but lost the war."

Mirabelle felt a queasy uncertainty wind its way through her stomach. Wishmakers' entire future—or lack thereof—rested on her shoulders. "I'll do my very best, Mary." Now why had that come out sounding hopeful instead of certain?

Mary coughed expectantly.

"I know, I know. The power of positive thinking. *I will do it.*" Mirabelle chided herself for her negativity. Wishmakers' very last seminar had been on the insidiousness of negativity.

"You're quite capable, Mirabelle. Otherwise, you wouldn't have been given this case. Just keep Rule Number One in mind and you'll do fine."

Mirabelle chanted the rule as if it was a mantra. *"Look beyond what the client thinks they want, to what they really want.* Always good to remind ourselves." Although Mirabelle didn't really need reminding, she wasn't put off by Mary's prompt. She knew her supervisor's heart was in the right place. Mary wanted each and every one of their client's dreams to come true.

"Mary, is there anything you can tell me about Eileen that might not be in her bio?"

"For the most part, it's a standard "True Love" case. On the surface she seems to have lost her belief in true love. But deep inside she's cautiously hopeful. Most importantly, she's lost faith in herself, and she'll never be able to recognize true love until she regains that."

Mirabelle lowered the window next to her computer, effectively blocking the coyote's howl, and then quickly checked her printer to make sure it was on. She had no time to lose. "I'll download and get right to work."

One

As Eileen Pringle exited the elevator at Wincomp's fifth floor offices, her sensible Italian loafer caught on what must have been a rogue air pocket. Her wildly acrobatic dismount would have scored a dismal "1" by Olympic judges. By the time she recovered, the gaping mouth of the elevator doors had silently swallowed her shoe. "Damn shoe!"

"Welcome back, Princess Leia, or should I say, Princess Grace." The familiar voice came from behind her. It was kind but held a note of barely suppressed mirth.

Eileen turned, trying to generate a smile for her friend Ray Mitchell but, after the week she'd had, all she could manage was a shaky grimace. Ray was a combination older brother figure and buddy to Eileen. Although there was an age gap of twenty years, they'd hit it off from the first day she came to work for Wincomp five years ago. Many evenings they'd share both dinner and confidences. The confidences mostly revolved around unfulfilled dreams—his for wealth, hers for romance and adventure.

Kind eyes looked her up and down, stopping at her shoeless foot. Ray slowly shook his head. "Start off on the wrong foot this morning, did we?" He quickly breached the distance and engulfed her in one of his characteristic gruff, brotherly bear hugs.

She could feel the deep rumble of his chuckle against her cheek. As good as the hug felt and as much as she needed the comfort of a friend, compassion was still a threat to the raw emotions she'd waged a losing battle with for the past week. Hot tears threatened, and she quickly pushed away from Ray's barrel chest before she made a mess of his starched white shirt.

She sniffed back her tears, finally managing a smile as she gazed around the office. Everything looked exactly as it had when she'd taken her leave of absence to care for her terminally ill father. To Eileen, the computer software company's neat rows of identical cubicles gave her a sense of much-needed order. "It's good to be back. Three months was way too long."

Ray studied the back of his hand, for some reason obviously avoiding eye contact. "I know you've heard the scuttlebutt around here—that you've been reassigned." He looked up. "I'm sure it's just one of those office rumors." Was he trying to convince her or himself? "I'm sure the out-of-towner Brock hired hasn't permanently snagged your job."

That very concern had been plaguing Eileen for over two weeks, ever since her boss, Brock Van Buren, had informed her that her long absence had compelled him to hire someone to "work" on her project list while she was away. Brock had been vague, saying he didn't want her to worry about the office when she had more pressing matters to focus on.

Well, her father had died, and now her job at Wincomp was all she had to focus on. She wasn't about to let someone usurp either the lead programmer or the security director positions she'd worked so hard to achieve.

Eileen straightened, searching for the strength she needed. She didn't need to look far. A ready supply was attached to the anger she felt over the events of the past week. She looked at her friend.

"Snagged my job? No way." She hoped she sounded more confident than she felt. "I'm not letting go. I need this job. Now more than ever."

Ray's thick gray eyebrows dipped in concern. "Something happen since we talked at the funeral?"

She had to snort at the understatement of the year. The past few days had seemed like a lifetime. "Yeah, Jeannette kicked me out." Ray was privy to the long-standing problems she had with her stepmother.

"What! After all you did for your father while he was sick? That witch wouldn't even set foot in his room. You'd think just out of gratitude...The *cajones* on that woman!" He looked like he might explode.

The growing pink hue of Ray's face made Eileen rethink the possibility of sharing the more sordid details of the past week. He tended to be overprotective.

"Don't worry, Ray, I'm fine." She crossed her fingers behind her back. "I've got a darling little apartment and," she presented her crossed fingers to Ray, saying with forced bravado, "a job as lead programmer with the hottest up-and-coming software company in California." She looked over the cubicles, their walls too high to see more than the tops of several bent heads as the people worked. She tilted her chin up. "I'm ready. Just point me in the direction of mine enemy."

Ray's smile didn't reach his eyes. "Go get-um, Princess Leia. May The Force be with you." He looked pointedly at her shoeless foot. "But you might want to rethink your battle armor."

Eileen huffed in frustration as she looked down at her wriggling toes. Could anything else go wrong? She counted off her disaster list for the morning. First off, her glasses had broken, forcing her to wear her old, wobbly standbys. They only corrected her astigmatism, leaving her squinting to see anything more than three feet away. Then her car had decided to have a tizzy fit, resulting in Eileen's experiencing an E-ticket joy ride in a tow truck. Finally, the elevator incident with the missing shoe. Didn't bad things happen in threes? Clinging to that fuzzy logic, she calculated she should be home free for a while.

Ray waved her off with a chuckle and a courtly bow. "M'lady, you go face the forces of the Dark Side. I'll retrieve your slipper."

"Thanks, Ray." She removed her remaining shoe and walked in stocking feet toward what she hoped was still her office at the far end of the room.

When she'd called yesterday to tell Brock she'd be back, he'd seemed unusually preoccupied and rushed their conversation. She never got the chance to ask if the office adjoining his executive suite was still hers, or if she'd been relocated.

Great. Not only had she been tossed out of her home of twenty-eight years, but now she was also in jeopardy of being usurped at work by a stranger. The anger and frustration she'd suppressed for the past week melded with the growing agitation she felt for the unknown man.

Although Brock had made it clear he couldn't hold her senior position open indefinitely, he'd assured her she would always have a job at Wincomp. But, she didn't want just any job. She wanted her job as Brock's right-hand man.

Better yet, she'd like the job as Brock's right-hand *woman*. Unfortunately, in all the years she'd known Brock, she hadn't been privy to that particular application.

Eileen rounded the last bank of cubicles, coming to a screeching halt at the doorway to her office. Her worst fears became reality as she stared at the back of a stranger's pinstriped shirt. He had no right to be sitting at her desk. She hadn't been gone *that* long.

Outraged, Eileen started to step into the office, ready to do battle. But she stumbled over a small box just inside the doorway, doing a repeat of the elevator circus act. Her purse and the remaining shoe flew from her arms.

During her flailing attempt to gain her footing, Eileen noticed in her peripheral vision that the man quickly turned off her computer screen.

He whirled around in his chair—her chair—to look up at her. Intelligent eyes behind wire-rimmed glasses flashed a quick head-to-toe look of scrutiny. The look changed to wry amusement as his gaze met with her stockinged feet.

She picked up her purse while trying to unobtrusively slip her foot into the shoe and still maintain some semblance of dignity. But after several failed attempts, she was forced to bend down and hold onto the darned thing while she put it on. Even then she was compelled to wrestle with the shoe, which had magically shrunk two sizes.

"You must be Eileen Pringle." He glanced at his watch,

reminding her she was two hours late for work. "I figured you decided not to come in today after all."

Looking up from where she'd bent to retrieve her shoe, she realized she was almost eye-level and a bit too close to the stranger for comfort. As close as she was, she couldn't help noticing he had the most sensuous brown eyes she'd ever seen, which did nothing to calm her anxiety. Her stomach fluttered at his shuttered appraisal, and she realized she was physically reacting to him as a man.

She straightened and moved back a step. "Well, I'm here." She didn't bother keeping the accusation out of her voice, and hoped the glare she gave him told the stranger he wasn't welcome.

His eyes didn't break contact as they grew serious yet hard. He gruffly cleared his throat. "Sorry to hear about your father." Obviously he wasn't comfortable with the acknowledgement.

"Thank you." She felt compelled to break eye contact and focus on his left shoulder. Sure, she was embarrassed by the clown act, but more than that, she didn't want to discuss her father's death and the resulting chaos with a stranger who could, at that very moment, be homing in on her weaknesses.

Eileen forced herself to meet his eyes. "And you are?" She did a quick appraisal of her own, doing her best to be objective and reevaluate her initial attraction. He was no Brock Van Buren, but he could be considered handsome, if you liked the nerdy-preppy-with-an-attitude kind of guy. Were bow ties back in style? If so, she'd been gone longer than she thought. With his dark hair, he reminded her of Dean Cain's Clark Kent TV character. Was Superman hiding behind those glasses?

She shook off the ridiculous whimsy, only to have it replaced by another which she couldn't as easily shake off. Her instincts told her that this man was hiding something.

"I'm Daniel Collins. Programming. New Guy at Wincomp. New Guy in LA." His mouth quirked in what she took as a smile, and he got up to offer his hand.

Why was he in her office? Fighting raging territorial impulses, she ignored the feeling she was letting her guard down around the enemy, and put her hand in his. He had a strong, warm handshake, bringing to mind her father's words that a person could be judged by their handshake. Then she had to remind herself that her father hadn't been such a hot judge of character or he wouldn't have chosen Jeannette for a wife.

She pulled her hand from his and tilted her head up so she could look through her too-big frames and into his eyes. They were light brown, almost golden. Too bad eyes that nice were obscured by glasses. She saw a look of speculation in those eyes, and she had the feeling he was sizing her up. Did he consider her a threat? Why, if he already had her job? Maybe it wasn't a done deal after all.

"Daniel," she sighed deeply, not bothering to hide her frustration. "This *used* to be my office. Do you know—"

"Still is. Mine's over there." He jerked his head toward the cubical opposite her office.

Positive it would sound like pistol shots in the quiet, she fought the urge to relieve the tension in her neck by cracking it. "Any special reason you're using my terminal?"

"I've been working back and forth on your projects as well as mine. Mr. Van Buren gave me your password. Said you wouldn't mind since I'd be helping you out."

Helping her out of a job, he meant. Did she mind? Big time. For the first time since she met Brock over eighteen years ago, she was furious with him. How dare he let a complete stranger have access to her program data. What if Daniel Collins wasn't what he appeared to be? One of the programs she'd been close to completing just might be her pot of gold at the end of the rainbow. She couldn't believe it might be in jeopardy because of Brock's unthinking act.

Eileen finally gave in and bent her neck to the side, the satisfyingly resounding pops caused Daniel's eyebrows to shoot up.

"Well, Daniel, it seems I kinda do mind."

Daniel held up his hands. "Bad call, huh? Well, then I'll leave you to your work. The jobs I completed are in your mailbox, and so is Mr. Van Buren's schedule. They're all yours. Sorry to have stepped on your, ah ... toes." She caught the smirk as he glanced at her shoeless feet. He got up and picked up the box she'd tripped over. Then he left, quietly closing the door behind him.

She looked around her office, suddenly wondering why she'd taken for granted that Daniel Collins wanted her job. The office rumors she'd heard from various co-workers had been like acid, slowly eating away at her confidence for the past two weeks. Maybe, like the guy said, he'd only been trying to catch up on some of her work while she was away. She should apologize for her bitchiness. It wasn't like her at all. Just because her life had turned sour didn't mean she had to take it out on a complete stranger.

It didn't look like he'd messed with anything on her desk, so she couldn't fault him for that. The coveted bottle of "fairy dust" she'd gotten from her mother on a childhood trip to Disneyland still sparkled from atop her PC. Her prisms still hung in the window ready to paint tiny rainbows on her wall when the late afternoon sun hit them. And the toy "Magic Eight Ball" sat in its usual spot in front of her manuals, waiting to answer life's more serious questions. She sure could have used it while she'd been gone. If only it really could magically answer the questions fate had thrown her way.

Even though almost a week had passed since her father's death, she still didn't have the answers she needed as to why she'd been left out of his will. She had her suspicions—and they all led to the devious Jeannette and the possibility of a forgery—but she didn't have answers. She wasn't even sure how to go about getting them.

A knock on her door rattled Eileen out of her thoughtful quandary. She tucked a stray hair into her rapidly loosening French braid and ran her tongue over her lips, hoping it would be Brock. When she opened it to find Ray standing there, she tried not to look disappointed. Her missing shoe dangled from one of his fingers.

"Thanks a million, Ray." She took the shoe and put it on, instantly feeling some measure of composure return.

Ray leaned against the doorframe, crossing his arms as he whispered, "How'd it go with the out-of-towner?" He jerked his head, indicating the man in the cubicle behind him.

"Not too hot." She moved closer to Ray so Daniel wouldn't

overhear. "He seems okay. Not too nice, but then I'm sure he doesn't think I'm Miss Congeniality, either." She realized she had most likely taken her anger at Jeannette out on Daniel, and that her fears about losing her job were probably unjustified.

Ray said, "Brock let him use your terminal until Daniel's workstation was ready. But ever since Collins heard you were coming back, he's been hurrying to get his stuff transferred to the new workstation's data base."

Eileen took a deep breath. If Brock had let Daniel Collins use her office, maybe she was directing her anger at the wrong man. "I guess I didn't have to be so bitchy. But still, I have the strong impression he's here under false pretenses."

"Darlin', I've taken you to one too many *film noir* movies. Collins seems like a regular guy to me. Why don't you just ask him what's going on?" Ray glanced back toward Daniel. "I need to get back to work. We on for lunch?"

She really should try to smooth things over with Daniel. "I'll meet you downstairs at noon. Thanks, Ray."

After Ray left, Eileen leaned out her doorway to see if the adjoining office's double doors might be open, as they always were when Brock was in. But his office was closed and, she was sure, locked up tight. Remembering Brock's strong inclination for security in his own office, she began wondering all over again why he'd given Daniel her password.

A glance toward Daniel's cubical told her he was already deep into a programming setup. She walked up behind him, noticing he seemed stymied by what was on his screen.

"Daniel?"

He jerked around to look at her just as he had when she'd surprised him in her office. Why was he so jumpy? Although her instincts still told her he had something to hide, her rational mind said he was probably just a caffeine junkie. Or maybe, like her, he was working on a secret project.

He acknowledged her with a, "Yes?," his expression cautious.

"I'm sorry we ..." She bit back the words, 'got off on the wrong foot,' before they left her mouth. Instead she began again. "I'm sorry *I* was so cross. I'd like to start again." She held out her hand as a peace offering. If they both stayed on, she'd most likely be working closely with Daniel. Tension between them could create an unbearable situation in a job she loved.

Digging deep she found a trace of humor. "Hello. My name is Eileen Pringle, and I'm a slightly paranoid workaholic."

He stood up, towering above her. Why did men always do that? It made her feel so small. And this guy was at least six-four. He took her hand in his, the handshake firm but gentle. Evidently Daniel was a forgiving kind of man.

"Hello Eileen Pringle. My name is Daniel Collins, and I, too, am a workaholic."

***

Undercover FBI agent Daniel Manatucci—alias Collins— had been startled when he realized one of his prime suspects, Eileen Pringle, was standing behind him. That made twice she'd sneaked up on him, and it had him mentally scratching his head. Since her level of grace just about matched her "four" on the "one-to-ten" beauty scale, he couldn't figure out how he hadn't heard her coming a mile away. For some reason his senses were definitely off-kilter when he was around the woman. That meant he'd have to be even more careful and stay alert when she was close by.

Eileen bent to the side to look around him at his computer screen. "Anything I can help you with? Just want to reciprocate, since you've been doing my work."

He stepped aside. Good luck if she could solve a problem he'd worked on for over two days. "Just a glitch. I'm sure I'll ..." His voice trailed off as he watched her step past him, quickly assess the screen and begin clicking through the program.

She seemed like she was in a better mood, and he wondered what had brought about the change. Now might be the time to ask her about the apartment Van Buren had told him about. Daniel wasn't sure when Dr. Jekyll would leave and Ms. Hyde might reappear.

Daniel took notice of her focused concentration as he said, "Mr. Van Buren said you'd recently moved into an apartment close by. I relocated for this job, and I'm staying in a motel until I can find a place. He said he thought there might be an apartment available in your complex."

She seemed to be ignoring him. Maybe he needed to pray on her sympathies. He said, "I know it's only the second week in December, but the thought of spending Christmas in a motel is depressing."

After working over two weeks trying to find out who in Wincomp had hacked into sensitive government files, Daniel realized the assignment would be a lengthy one. He'd need to find a more comfortable place to live, and living in the same apartment complex as one of his suspects was perfect.

"An apartment? Christmas?" She seemed to stiffen as she glanced back at him, and then returned her focus to the terminal. "Then you're staying on." She tapped several keystrokes, thoughtfully moving aside and giving him access to see what she was doing. He noticed she never used the mouse. Daniel was a mouse man all the way. "Voila!" she said and, just like that, the program problem he'd slaved over for two days was solved.

She looked extremely pleased with herself, and Daniel had the feeling she expected him to be upset. On the contrary. He'd heard that Eileen Pringle was smart when it came to computers, and he'd just seen the proof of her techno-wizardry firsthand. There was more to the woman than he'd originally thought. Maybe much more. Even though his background check on her indicated she had been on leave when the hacking occurred, Daniel mentally moved Eileen up a notch on his list of suspects.

She returned her full attention to him. He took a closer look at her as she went on, "Well, I'd better get to work. Do you know when Brock's coming in?"

Either the thought of having Daniel for a neighbor was unpleasant, or her personality leaned toward the absent-minded-professor type. She couldn't possibly have forgotten his question about the apartment so quickly. He realized they'd gotten off to a bad start. That wasn't like him, especially when he was on assignment. Making friends with the suspects was an integral part of his job.

He answered her question first. "Mr. Van Buren said he'd be in around eleven. He had some personal business." He turned on the charm. "About the apartment?"

She chewed the corner of her thumbnail, and he noticed how gracefully tapered her long fingers were. Her, "I don't know if there's a vacancy," held a note of dismissal.

Evidently she couldn't see his charm through her huge, cockeyed glasses. He continued to smile. *Keep it non-threatening, buddy. Keep it non-threatening.* "Brock seemed to think there would be. Could I have the apartment manager's phone number?" He really wanted to stick close to Eileen Pringle, and what better way than to live next door.

"I have to warn you, the place is kinda old. Circa thirties or forties."

Man, she really didn't want him around. He challenged her but kept it friendly. "I was told the whole place had recently been renovated."

Finally, she relented. "Well, okay. I'll get the number." She pivoted, heading back to her office, giving Daniel a nice view of slim calves and ankles. He'd always maintained that clothes like the prim, below-the-knee skirt and white Peter-Pan-collar blouse she wore were a real crime on any woman. So were the practical flat shoes, even if they were expensive. He knew quality when he saw it, and the cashmere sweater said she did, too. But she dressed like she didn't want to be noticed, or like she was hiding out. That thought sparked the question, *hiding from what?*

If he hadn't already researched her background and discovered that, physically anyway, with Eileen Pringle what you saw was exactly what you got, he might wonder if she was working at Wincomp undercover, too. Even in her high school yearbook photo she'd been hidden behind glasses and looked slightly disheveled.

He started to turn back to her office to take a second look, but just then Brock Van Buren walked through Eileen's doorway. Daniel kept them in his peripheral vision. They were talking low, so he couldn't catch what they were saying, but from their body language he could read them pretty clearly. Still, he wished his sound enhancer hadn't stroked out yesterday.

Daniel watched as Brock pushed an errant strand of Eileen's

hair behind her ear, his finger lingering on her cheek a moment longer than either a casual friendship or employer-employee relationship dictated. The way Van Buren squeezed her shoulder was intimate, yet not as if the guy really had a serious interest in her.

Could Daniel be reading too much into what he was seeing? He thought not. In fact, he had the feeling that at last he had his first real lead. Those two were definitely in cahoots. Why else would a playboy like Van Buren cater to someone like her? Eileen Pringle seemed like the last woman on Earth a guy like Van Buren would find attractive. The man was all spit and polish, a hair never out of place. And his body language said he wasn't in love with the woman. For some reason, he was leading her on.

On the other hand, anyone with two eyes could see that Eileen was head-over-heels for Mr. Blond Jock; her look said it all. Daniel had to wonder if the look said she'd do anything the man asked. Like maybe using her considerable computer expertise to help Van Buren hack into government files? Background revealed the guy was attuned to computer technology, but his true forte was business.

As Daniel covertly watched the two, he had to keep in mind that they were both suspect. They could be in on this together, or either one of them could be on their own.

Two

Eileen ripped open the plastic bag holding the new duvet, then shook it out and flung it across the bed. It would be nice to sleep in comfort again. A week of fitful rest on an inflatable mattress had taken its toll on her back as well as her mood.

That morning the delivery of her new mattress and box springs put her one step closer to feeling like she lived in a home instead of a dark, empty cave. Her only other pieces of furniture were her computer desk, a loveseat, and a small entry table she'd found at a used-furniture shop that morning. She'd just painted the table a soft green to match the flowers of the sofa's brocade material.

Besides the computer and small loveseat, the large living room still stood bare—the carved mantle the only ornamentation. The dining room's expanse of polished wood floor echoed and creaked when she walked across it, reminding her each time that it needed a table and chairs.

She still couldn't believe she had, in one short week, gone from living in the opulence of her childhood home in the Hollywood hills to being practically homeless and penniless.

The shock of learning that her father's will left everything, down to the last stick of furniture, to her stepmother, Jeannette, had worn off. Now that she'd had time to think it over, she had to wonder whether Jeannette and her father's attorney, Miles Catchum, had somehow changed the will in Jeannette's favor. She tried not to dwell on it, since she had no proof. Eileen had to consider the possibility that she was just in denial, and that Jeannette really had been given everything.

But, why had Eileen's father convinced her to invest her earnings, leaving her dependent on him for ready cash, and then neglected to make those same provisions for her in his will? He knew he was dying. He must have known the earnings generated from her investments by themselves wouldn't be enough to live on. The whole thing had her baffled and feeling like she hadn't known her father at all.

Even before the reading of the will had been finished, Eileen had seen the satisfaction on Jeannette's face, as if she knew Eileen would be left out. Then, not even a day after the reading, Jeannette told Eileen to move. The woman had said, "Don't think of taking anything with you that belongs in this house. I'll know. And you are now responsible for your credit card bills. Your father wasn't doing you any favors by making you financially dependent on him."

At the time, still reeling from the initial shock, Eileen had packed her clothes and left.

Thankfully, she came upon a place to live, the *Deviazione* apartments, that same day. Stumbling onto the charming apartment had been the only good thing in Eileen's world during the past week. She'd been looking for an apartment listed in the newspaper when she accidentally turned down the wrong street. The cheerful, brightly colored "vacancy" sign on the *Deviazione* apartments seemed to call out to her. Even though it looked too nice to be within her means, she'd gone in.

The moment she stepped into the Mediterranean-style courtyard she'd been enchanted. Small front patios held clay pots with multi-colored pansies. Bright pink bougainvillea climbed the white stucco walls, and a fountain splashed in the center of the tiled courtyard. She felt like she'd stepped into another world, another time. Thinking the rent had to be way beyond her budget, she'd almost turned away. But something drew her inside the rental office where, much to her astonishment, the rate turned out to be exactly what she'd allotted for rent. She could almost believe she'd been led to the apartment by a guardian angel.

She now gathered an armful of empty department store bags and headed to the growing mound of moving debris in the middle of the living room floor. Taking a good wind-up position, she prepared to toss the armful of paper onto the center of the existing pile.

The ringing of her doorbell stopped Eileen's toss mid-air. She wasn't expecting anyone. Her startled, breathless, "Who is it?" was rewarded with a giggle from the other side of the door. Eileen quickly tossed the papers into the pile.

"I'm Mirabelle Saintly, your neighbor from the across the courtyard, dear." The voice sounded old but held a certain vitality. "Could I please speak with you?"

Eileen tried to get a look at the woman through the door's peephole, but evidently the installer of the thing had been taller than five-four. Jumping only gave her a split-second glimpse of the top of someone's head. Wavy gray hair appeared oddly distorted by the fish-eye effect of the peephole's glass. Eileen tightened her topknot, which had managed to slip to the side of her head.

Should she open the door? The downtown neighborhood was new to her. It existed in a completely different realm than the gated community she was used to, and she wasn't sure what the rules were. The almost daily TV news stories about break-ins and murder had definitely affected her.

As wary as she knew she should be of strangers, she didn't like the feeling she was a prisoner in her own home. Besides, the woman said she was Eileen's neighbor, and Eileen was curious as to whom she shared the lovely old building with.

"Oh, bother," Eileen muttered under her breath at her own indecision.

"Are you still there, dear?" Eileen heard the woman's soft chuckle.

Eileen opened the door a crack but left the security chain on. She asked, "May I help you?"

"I've got a teensy weensy problem ... Eileen, isn't it? And I was hoping you could help." The woman looked harmless enough with her tiny, rounded features, the half-glasses perched on her upturned nose, and the porcelain teacup steaming away in her plump hands. Eileen couldn't detect the outline of a concealed Uzi beneath the orange-and-brown crocheted shawl.

"A problem?" Eileen found herself smiling at the little woman.

"I heard from the landlady—Oh, *landlady* is probably politically incorrect, isn't it? Well, *landperson* doesn't quite work, does it?" She sipped her tea as she considered. "*Manager.* That's the ticket. But what she manages besides everybody else's business, is a mystery to me."

The woman peeked over her glasses to look directly at Eileen. "Anyway, Mrs. Johnson told me you looked like you were working for James Bond with all the high-tech computer stuff you moved in. I was hoping you could help me with my new modem."

James Bond? Yeah, right, like Eileen's life had ever been anything close to that exciting. "What kind of problem?"

"I'm getting a 'no modem detected' message, and I've done everything within my power to fix it."

"Sure, I'll see what I can do." Glad of the chance to get her mind off her troubles, Eileen grabbed her key and a sweatshirt.

Mirabelle smiled companionably, carefully balancing her teacup as they walked in silence across the sunny courtyard and entered her apartment.

Eileen had to stop herself from staring open-mouthed at the interior. Simple but elegant, in shades of white and cream with glass and oak accents, Mirabelle's living room was modern-classic. The whole effect was, at first glance, incongruous with Mirabelle's person. But on second glance, Mirabelle seemed to fit in perfectly with her surroundings. She was a comfortable blend of old and new.

The elfin woman waved toward the sleek oak computer table as she went into an open-style kitchen identical to Eileen's floor plan. Mirabelle turned on the heat under the teakettle, saying over her shoulder, "Go to it, my dear. Weave your magic."

Eileen sat down and clicked her way to the system setup. "No magic. Merely computer nerd know-how." She glanced back at Mirabelle and smiled.

Mirabelle frowned. "I've only known you for a few minutes,

and already I can see 'nerd' doesn't fit you at all. You're a beautiful young woman with a face to match your lovely soul."

The tinkle of china from the kitchen gave Eileen goose bumps—it reminded her of one of the few memories she had of her mother. A pretty woman's face flashed through her mind: a pretty woman with a delicate porcelain teacup in her hands.

"Thank you." Eileen had to wonder at Mirabelle's perception of her. She quickly made the needed changes on the screen. Dressed in paint-stained, baggy sweats and with her hair a mess, she was sure she looked anything but beautiful. And what could this woman know about Eileen's soul after knowing her ten minutes? Eileen sighed. "There. You're up and running. Want to go for a test spin?"

When Eileen swiveled around to face Mirabelle, she saw compassion in the woman's gaze as she handed her a cup of tea. "You're in kind of a funk, aren't you? Had some tough knocks? Need some answers? Some guidance? A little magic in your life?"

What did the woman do, work the Psychic Friends Hotline? Eileen thought she'd been keeping her grief and anger pretty much to herself. But, if a total stranger could see through her so easily, she was doing a lousy job. She felt her chin quiver, but fought back the emotions triggered by the woman's words of concern.

Clearing her throat, Eileen admitted half-jokingly, "I guess I'm looking for what every other person is. Riches, adventure ... true love." She found herself chuckling.

Mirabelle nodded sagely, stating, "You do want to find true love, don't you?"

"Sure. Doesn't everyone?" She thought about her father's disastrous marriage to Jeannette, then briefly wondered what her parents' relationship had been like.

Mirabelle's smile was skeptical. "I'm not sure most people would know true love if they tripped over it. They can't get past the superficial. They see an attractive person, and, bingo, that's it, they put blinders on."

Eileen thought back to how she'd felt the first time she met Brock. The moment she saw him, she was a goner. "Don't you believe in love at first sight?"

Mirabelle's eyebrows arched. "Lust at first sight, yes. Infatuation at first sight, yes. Love? The jury is still out. I believe some people have an instant connection with someone they first meet, almost as if they already know the person. But that only means they're kindred spirits. Not," she emphasized, "soul mates. Two completely different entities."

"How's that?" Eileen had heard the two terms and thought they were one and the same. The funny little woman had piqued her curiosity.

Mirabelle said, "Kindred spirits are people we've known in past lives, people who are connected to our spirits because of a past. Soul mates are individuals with whom we can find true love. They're really difficult to spot. What convinced you this guy you're talking about was the one?"

Eileen didn't know why—maybe because telling a complete stranger secrets and dreams seemed harmless—but she told Mirabelle about her first meeting with Brock.

"I was just thinking about a time when I was about ten-years-old. I had gone over to this guy's house with my father while he conducted some sort of business with the guy's father." Images flashed like a movie screen through her mind. "My grand entrance had been to trip up these wide cement steps they had leading up to their house. My knees were a bloody mess."

Eileen looked over to Mirabelle, who seemed genuinely interested, her head bobbing for Eileen to continue. Taking a deep breath, she said, "The guy—Brock Van Buren—helped bandage my knees while our fathers talked. I discovered Brock was as passionate about computers as I was. I thought I'd met the man of my dreams. Well, boy of my dreams: he was thirteen at the time. We talked all afternoon." She had to chuckle as she remembered. "Well, I mostly listened and tried not to cry. My knees hurt so much."

She didn't tell Mirabelle about how she'd felt that way for a long time, sort of ready to cry with wanting him. She didn't say, either, that even now sometimes her knees hurt when she thought about Brock. But she'd become resigned to the fact that Brock didn't return her feelings. Long ago she'd admitted to herself that getting over Brock Van Buren was something she might never be able to accomplish.

"He didn't reciprocate your feelings?"

There went that Psychic Friends thing again. Eileen realized the woman must have been reading her expression.

Eileen said, "No. Oh, we became good friends—computer buddies—but I learned early on that Brock only had eyes for the beautiful girls like my stepsister, Alyssa. He's dated her off and on for years." Eileen knew she could never compete with Alyssa when it came to men. Especially Brock. Alyssa was the kind of blonde beauty that made men drool and ensured television programs like *Bay Watch* would be in reruns forever.

Mirabelle continued her probing. "He sounds near-sighted. I'll bet he hasn't found true love."

Eileen thought about that for a moment. Brock never had married. She hadn't really wondered why before. "No, he's never been married either."

"I take it you still feel he's 'the one'?"

"Well ..." She had to admit, she compared every man she met to Brock Van Buren. "I guess I do." She rubbed her knees.

"And what have you done to let him know?" Mirabelle poured more tea.

"Nothing. Like I told you, I'm not his type."

"Not his type, you say?" Mirabelle stood and walked around Eileen, looking her over as though judging a dog show. She said, almost to herself, "Nice cheek bones, outstanding if somewhat hidden eyes." She stopped, her gaze gently challenging Eileen. "Do you always dress like this?"

Eileen responded in defense, "Of course not. I was painting and unpacking. But when I dress for the office, I dress for work, not for a fashion show. And I never wear more than lip gloss and mascara." Why bother? She wasn't model material.

"That's all well and fine, dear. He needs to see you for who you really are, not fall in love with a false face." She rubbed her chin and squinted at Eileen. "I'm more concerned with how you see yourself than with what Prince Brock thinks. Neither Brock Van Buren nor any other man will be able to see your true self until you do."

"Huh?" Mirabelle was losing her. Eileen could almost hear the zing as the woman's words flew over her head.

Mirabelle patted her hand. "My belief is, we reflect what we think of ourselves. And I get the feeling you aren't your biggest fan. Am I right?

Eileen believed she saw herself pretty clearly. While she didn't consider herself ugly, she knew she'd never be model-beautiful. What she had going for her was above-average intelligence and a fair amount of common sense. Was she her biggest fan? No. She had a way to go before she was the person she wanted to be. She decided she didn't have an answer so responded with another question. "Aren't we all a work-in-progress?"

"Sure, but we can't make progress if we're stuck. Don't you sometimes feel stuck? Confused about who you are? What your purpose in life is? What you're about? Whether you're really sure what true love is?"

All Eileen could do was shrug noncommittally.

Mirabelle said, "Don't worry, we'll get you straightened out quicker than you can say 'Bibbidy Bobbidy Boo.'" She tittered at what Eileen figured must be a personal joke.

"*We*, Mirabelle? I appreciate the thought, but I think I'll handle my self-esteem issues and my love life—or the present lack thereof—on my own. If I get desperate, LA's teeming with shrinks." She realized her words sounded a bit rude, and she hadn't meant to be. The woman was only trying to help. To soften her words she added, "Unless you have a magic wand."

Mirabelle's musical laugh seemed to bounce around the room. "Oh, no, no. Common misconception, that magic wand thing. The wand was just a device—a way for Cinderella's *'Granter'* to get the girl to focus. I'm convinced the poor dear had severe ADD—you know, Attention Deficit Disorder. It's the real reason everyone always yelled at her, to get her attention. She was so easily distracted. Oh, well, that's another story in itself, isn't it? And I'm digressing. We're here to concentrate on you."

Had Mirabelle said *Granter*? What was a Granter? Mirabelle Saintly was sounding more and more like a nut case.

But, Eileen had to admit, she was an intriguing nut case. The eccentric woman was the perfect antidote to Eileen's blues. For the first time in days, she was actually beginning to feel lighthearted.

Pushing aside the nudge of concern about Mirabelle's mental health, Eileen gave in to her curiosity about how far the woman was into her delusion. It seemed harmless enough. "The magic wand was a prop, huh? And what is a Granter? I'm not familiar with the term."

"Yes the wands and talismans are all just props. And our image consultant suggested we Granters—Good Witches, if you will—give up the use of magic props. They're connected with the unfortunate bad image we've gotten over the past several hundred years."

Mirabelle rose to retrieve a long, clear, tapered wand from the desk. She said over her shoulder, "You know, it was Shakespeare's portrayal of the three witches in *Macbeth* that started the whole cauldron-broomstick-hag image."

Mirabelle's delusion was pretty complex. Good Witches? *Granters*? The woman sounded like she really believed it.

Mirabelle went on, waving the wand in a figure eight. "This is no more than a device I use to point to graphics during lectures. I could wave this around until doomsday and no sparkles, no electric charges, no magic at all would come out. But it is cute, don't you think?" She twirled the wand with the expertise of a majorette, then returned it to the desk.

Eileen said, "So, the 'witch' stereotypes are misleading?"

"Correct. Good Witches don't use incantations or props of any kind. We give clear-cut instructions on how to take your wish from its first whispered entreaty all the way to the granting stage." She sighed. "The problem is, few people ever follow instructions, so wishes very seldom get to the granting stage."

Scratch Psychic Friends, Eileen thought. She had Glenda the Good Witch as a neighbor. Sure, Eileen had heard of witches, but what Mirabelle was talking about seemed to be a whole other kettle—or cauldron—of fish.

Eileen's curiosity got the better of her. "Let me get this straight. You're saying that you're a Good Witch? A witch who grants wishes?"

Mirabelle nodded, smiling. "I'm a Granter."

"But—now I'm not trying to be facetious here—but I thought Fairy Godmothers did the whole Cinderella-wish-granting-bit."

"Another unfortunate misconception." Mirabelle puffed up, Eileen's words obviously hitting a nerve. "Popular fiction has erroneously credited Fairy Godmothers with Cinderella. The fact is, a Good Witch granted Cinderella's wish." She shrugged. "It's easy to see, though, what with the bad press the label 'witch' has gotten over the last few hundred years, how writers might shy away from using it."

She went on, "Truth be told, we're very good people who were given a bad image by the storytellers of the frightened Medieval era. Our image consultant suggested we switch to a more user-friendly term, so we now refer to ourselves as *'Granters.'"*

Eileen didn't believe for a moment Mirabelle's claims about wishes, witches, or Granters. But, curiosity made her ask. "You said people seldom get to the 'granting' stage. Why is that again?"

"Because people don't follow instructions."

Instructions? Did these Good Witches put out some kind of manual? "You mean there are specific instructions on how to have your wish granted?"

"Most certainly." Mirabelle sat back, regarding Eileen, then sat forward. "You don't seem shocked. Good, because I've actually been appointed *your* Granter, and we wouldn't get very far if you didn't accept me." Mirabelle appeared delighted; a twinkle of merriment danced in her eyes. "Many people stop talking to me at this point."

"I don't think shocked is the word I'd use." 'Nuts' was one word. Fascinating was another.

Eileen took a sip of tea then set down the cup and moved her chair closer to Mirabelle. "How does one become a Good Witch? How did you become mine? Did you have to go to some sort of special school? Do you get a degree? Don't get me wrong, Mirabelle, I really am curious."

"Let me test your handiwork while I explain." Mirabelle gently motioned Eileen off the computer chair with the wave of her hand. She added, "I'm glad you're curious. Curious and skeptical. They're traits that balance each other out. That's what it's all about, dear, *balance*. Without it you can't be open to the magic, if you will, in the universe."

Eileen positioned a chair behind Mirabelle, so she could see what the woman was doing on the computer.

Mirabelle clicked to her online service. The computer hummed, crackled then whined as the modem connected. "You are a wonder! It works perfectly." She began typing. "To answer your questions; first of all, we're sort of ... appointed. And I'm your Granter because I was next in line for an assignment when your wish came in."

"My wish 'came in'? What does that mean?"

Mirabelle's mouth pursed then quirked to the side, as if she was trying to decide just how much to tell Eileen. "It's difficult to explain." Her expression smoothed and she smiled. "It came in from someone dear to you. But, the 'who' must remain anonymous for the time being." As if she'd said too much, she quickly added, "You did say you want to find true love, didn't you?"

Eileen began to wonder briefly if this was some kind of elaborate practical joke set up by Ray in an effort to boost her mood. If it was, it was working beautifully. "True love? Sure, but doesn't everyone?"

"Heavens no." Mirabelle went on. "As far as Good Witch College goes, we do have to go through extensive training and yearly workshops." The online server prompt waited for instructions. Mirabelle typed in the website. A graphic of sparkles rained down the screen before the words, *Wishmakers International*, appeared, and a lovely voice sang the theme, "*A Dream is a Wish Your Heart Makes.*"

Eileen sat mesmerized. Mirabelle, and evidently others, were really into this *Granter* thing if their group had a state-of-the-art web page.

"In fact, my dear, I will be leaving tomorrow for our annual *Wishmakers International* conference. It's in Anaheim this year, so our local Orange County chapter is playing hostess. You can't imagine the work involved with getting guest speakers."

"Guest speakers?" Images of Merlin and Morgan le Fay standing at the podium—complete with purple robes and pointed hats—raced through Eileen's mind.

"Yes. I finally confirmed the world's top image consultant— the one who suggested our name-change. She's done wonders with Madonna, but she tells me a certain basketball player, who shall remain unnamed, was a dismal failure. A dropout. The bad press we've gotten over the past few hundred years lowered our stats to a critical level."

Mirabelle's chin inched up. "We're determined to make a comeback. Our mission statement for the twenty-first century is to dispel the old stereotypes and let people know we're not associated with the devil or evil. And we certainly can't fly. We're not angels. They're a whole other division. We don't have wings."

The little woman moved her plump shoulders up and down as if to demonstrate. "We've laid low while reorganizing, to give people a chance to forget all the old Hansel and Gretel images. Now we're nearly at the stroke of twelve, so to speak, and we still have work to do. The new millennium just happened to mark a critical shift in cosmic energy. Our stats must reflect our viability, or ... well, they must, that's all."

"Sounds like quite an organization." Eileen couldn't help going along with the fantastic claims. Even though she didn't believe her, Mirabelle seemed to have thought every answer out well ahead of time. And Eileen realized she enjoyed going along with Mirabelle's fantasy. "Can't you just do magic or some kind of miracle to help people? To make them understand?"

"Oh, magic and spells? They used to work with the simple, superstitious medieval mindset to help them toward enlightenment and then granting." Momentarily her eyes clouded with nostalgia, but she blinked it away with determination. "But, those gimmicks aren't relevant in today's world of self-actualization."

"You're disillusioning me, Mirabelle," Eileen teased.

Mirabelle giggled as she read the screen. All Eileen saw was a blurred line of characters. Mirabelle typed several keystrokes.

"What's wrong with your screen? Here, let me have a look." Eileen started to get up.

"No, no, it's fine. On this particular link the characters aren't legible to outsiders. Sorry, dear." She logged off and swiveled around to face Eileen, a look of determination on her face. "Now, to the matter of granting your wish for true love."

Eileen couldn't help leaning back, sure she didn't want Wishmakers International, or Mirabelle, to take her on as a project. "Well, thanks, but ..." What if there was a chance to win Brock? Jeez, was she beginning to believe this woman? She must be desperate.

"You're positive this Brock Van Buren fellow is *the one*?"

"Brock's the only man I've ever felt this way about."

Mirabelle reached beside her desk and fished a pamphlet out of a soft-sided briefcase. "Take this home and look it over. When you're ready to find true love—be it Prince Brock or someone else—let me know. I'll be at the Disneyland Hotel for the next week, but my E-mail address is on the back of the pamphlet, and I'll have my laptop with me."

Eileen took the pamphlet, feeling a little like she'd stepped into an episode of *The X-Files*. Although her, "Thanks," was sincere, it wasn't because of Mirabelle's promises, which Eileen knew the woman would never be able to fulfill. It was because Eileen really did like her eccentric neighbor. She didn't feel right about keeping the woman's beautiful pamphlet, though. Eileen started to hand it back, but Mirabelle's raised palm stopped her.

"You're looking a bit skeptical. If you need references, I'm having a little Christmas Gala reunion of graduates, here in my apartment. You're welcome to come. A week from today, Saturday evening at eight o'clock. Come as you are." She tittered. "Well, come as how you see yourself, anyway."

Eileen perused the cover of the brightly colored, tri-fold pamphlet. A glass slipper logo sat beneath the title, Wishmakers International. "Graduates?"

"Former clients. *Grantees*, if you will."

Mirabelle tilted her chin down and looked at Eileen over the top of her glasses. "I must counsel you, though, this wish-granting business is quite complicated. We don't hand wishes out like candy. You have to earn them. You will be assigned tasks you must complete, which will move you forward to the level required to use the powers—or magic, if you will."

Eileen had visions of grail-type quests, and she was pretty darned sure she wasn't up to the task. She didn't fit into either the King Arthur or Indiana Jones mold. If a movie were to be made about her life, it would be more along the lines of *Perils of Pauline*.

Mirabelle went on, "Even Cinderella had to prove herself worthy—to be able to see things in a certain light. She really did communicate with animals, you know. Maybe not to the extent of the Disney movie, but to an elevated level anyway. More like that Horse Whisperer fellow."

Eileen opened the paper in her hand. It read:

WISHMAKERS INTERNATIONAL,
An organization devoted to helping
the individual reach her/his full potential.
(or, How to get your wish ...)

Three

Eileen closed the Wishmakers International pamphlet, looking at Mirabelle more closely. The woman said to let her know when Eileen was ready. Ready for what, exactly? Ready to find love? Or ready to join the woman's madness?

"Thanks, Mirabelle. I'll let you know." Eileen stood up. "As much as I've enjoyed our visit, I've still got unpacking to do. I want to get as much done this weekend as possible."

Mirabelle looked over her glasses. "Remember, our work together will take time, so you don't want to put it off too long."

"Sure, but, well, sure ... I guess. Thanks, Mirabelle."

Eileen left, looking at the brochure. As she stepped onto the entry patio she stumbled over what looked—as she flew through the air—like a packing box. By the time she'd noticed the box, it had been too late to stop the inevitable tumble.

"Watch it!" Strong arms grabbed her, abruptly stopping her headlong fall. Instead of terra cotta paving tiles, her face smashed against the man's hard chest, sending her loose glasses flying, along with her dignity. Her hands grasped at soft tee-shirt cloth and the firm muscle beneath.

Quickly regaining her footing, she pushed away from the stranger's embrace. She came away with a strong olfactory sense of him; a musky male scent made mellow by a hint of cologne. It was sexy as hell, and her body reacted with a tingling awareness. She realized with vexation that this was the second time in two days her hormones had uncharacteristically raged out of control.

Shaking out the crumpled brochure and rubbing her aching nose, she squinted to get a better look at the man whose musky scent now permeated her nostrils, causing her body to react with sensual heat.

When she finally recognized him, she quickly rejected the unwanted feelings and replaced them with indignation. "Daniel!"

"Eileen!" He mocked her, obviously enjoying himself. "You sound surprised to see me."

She was, since she'd only given him the manager's phone number a couple of days ago. Boy, he moved fast. Searching for her glasses, she squinted, craning her neck toward the hedge border leading to the common stoop. They'd headed in that general direction. "You should be more careful where you put your boxes. This is the second time you've almost killed me."

"You should watch where you're going." His chuckle indicated he wasn't in the least remorseful. "One of these days you're going take a really bad fall and injure yourself."

She looked back at him and tried not to squint. He seemed different, but she couldn't put her finger on what it was. Darn, without her glasses it was like looking through a diffusion filter; all his features had a fuzzy edge to them. It was probably the best way to look at Daniel Collins anyway. She didn't want to analyze his effect on her.

She looked away, continuing to scan the bushes. "You didn't have to set your box right in front of Mirabelle's door. What if she had come out? She's ..." She caught herself before she said "old" in case Mirabelle should overhear. "Well, she could have gotten hurt!"

"Okay, don't have a cow." He moved past her and bent down. "Got'em!" Daniel plucked her glasses from the hedge.

Eileen put her hand out, but he tucked her glasses—as close as she could tell—into the pocket of his white T-shirt. "Better rinse them off first, check for scratches." He flipped his sunglasses down from the top of his head. "So, you're not my next-door neighbor?"

"No, I live across the courtyard, in number seven." She didn't want to let on how desperately she wanted the glasses.

The large frames hid the fact she wasn't wearing a stitch of makeup, although why she cared what Daniel thought of her was a mystery. "Here, give them to me. I'll clean them."

But Daniel had already disappeared inside his apartment, taking with him her only means with which to clearly see the world. She followed, this time carefully scanning the stoop for more obstacles as she went.

Daniel stood at the kitchen sink rinsing her glasses, so she took a seat on one of the two barstools and looked around, taking in her surroundings as best she could with her limited vision. Daniel's apartment appeared to be nearly as Spartan as her own. She could just make out a brown leather sofa, a television and two barstools. There were still several big, unpacked moving boxes.

Although fuzzy around the edges, she saw some kind of angled metal protrusions through the bedroom door. Either Daniel was building a robot or he had a workout bench. In her mind, techno-geeks and weight benches had always been incongruous. She looked back to Daniel.

Daniel set her glasses on the counter in front of her, then bent toward the floor to rip open a taped box. She put on the glasses.

"When did you move all this stuff in?" Her restored vision took in the room.

"Last night. Late." The quizzical look on his face as he looked at the plate in his hand gave Eileen the impression he was seeing the crockery for the first time. Maybe, like her, he'd bought a new set for the move. He went on, "I had some errands this morning and was just bringing in the last of the boxes from my car when you made the '*trip*' over." He glanced up with a smirk.

Adjusting her frames, she gave him her best 'You're a smart-ass' smile. But she really did need to be more careful. Her recent distracted mood had turned her into a dangerous woman. Dangerous to herself, anyway. "So, what do you think of the *Deviazione* apartments?"

He snorted. "I'd like to know who chose the name."

Setting the Wishmaker's pamphlet on the counter, she picked

up a discarded sheet of bubble packing and began popping away. "Why? It sounds lovely." Eileen repeated the name, "*Deviazione*," giving it as much of an Italian inflection as her Irish soul could manage.

"*Deviazione*." Daniel's accent was perfect, without hesitation. "It means, 'detour.'"

"Detour?" That just about summed up her life right at that moment. She'd been happy, secure, headed down a comfortable path, when, wham! the road had disappeared.

Eileen studied him. "Collins doesn't sound Italian, yet you seem comfortable with the language."

"My mother's people." He appeared distracted, looking for markings on one of the boxes. "You don't see anything that says 'coffee maker' do you?"

She had been right. He was a coffee-fiend. She looked at the boxes by her feet, the bold script markings on the sides easy to read. Either Daniel was very much in touch with his feminine side—NOT—or a woman had marked his boxes. Thus far her experiences with the man had her leaning toward the latter option. He might appear mild-mannered, but she'd witnessed definite machismo tendencies in him.

Maybe he'd just broken up with someone. Or maybe his mother or sister had packed for him. Her logical mind took over, trying to fit Daniel into a category. None of the 'family' slots seemed right. For some reason she got the impression Daniel Collins had been on his own for some time. He definitely didn't look as uncomfortable with his new surroundings as she felt in hers. But maybe that was just a guy-thing. Women were nesters; men were gypsies, or something along those lines.

She spotted the box he was looking for. "Here it is." She hopped off the stool to grab it, and her glasses slid down to the tip of her nose.

She placed the box on the counter and pushed her glasses into place. "I'd better go. I've got all this," she indicated the packing boxes, "waiting for me at my apartment." Actually, she didn't have much "this" waiting. Most of her unpacking was of just-purchased necessities. She'd only brought her clothes, several boxes of books, and her computer with her from her father's house.

Daniel set down the wineglass he'd been unpacking and leaned his elbows on the counter. "How about car-pooling to work?" He twisted his head in an attempt to look at the Wishmakers pamphlet she just retrieved from the counter. She put it in her lap, hoping she looked nonchalant. The last thing she'd want bandied about the office was that she was involved with a group called Wishmakers.

"Rideshare? Fine with me." She wasn't really taken in by his charming smile. Besides there was no need to coax her into ride sharing. Negotiating LA's heavy commuter traffic ranked right behind a dentist's drill on her list of favorite things to do, so any break was welcome. She just hoped Daniel didn't have Andretti blood coursing through his veins along with caffeine. "We'll take turns. I'll take Tuesdays and Thursdays."

Daniel cocked an eyebrow. "Okay. But, unless we've gone to truncated math, you're going to owe me a beer come Friday."

She'd give him a whole keg if it would get her out of driving even one day of work traffic. "Deal."

He reached out his hand. "Deal."

Eileen found herself reluctantly putting her hand in his. Not only did she find physical contact with him disconcerting, but Daniel had conceded to her lopsided offer a bit too quickly, leaving her with the unsettling feeling her ruse had just boomeranged.

***

Daniel raised his shoulder to hold the phone receiver as he twisted the cap off a beer. "Special Agent, Daniel Manatucci for Pete Silva." While he waited for the agency operator to locate and connect his boss, he took a swig of liquid. He flipped off the living room lamp and nudged aside the front window curtains just enough to see out. Even though it was evening, the courtyard lighting was sufficient to observe any activity.

He reminded himself that he had to be more careful when he wasn't in disguise. That morning he'd let his guard down for no more than a few seconds only to have Eileen show up out of nowhere to nearly catch him without his glasses. He knew the glasses made a world of difference in the way he looked. They were just preppy enough to take the edge off. And when he added a slightly slouched posture, he knew he came across as nondescript and non-threatening.

Pete came on the line. "Daniel. What do you have?"

Daniel had called in daily and e-mailed reports, so his boss knew most of what was happening—or not happening—with the investigation.

"Sir, I'm circling the drain on this one. Only managed to get two of the employee's passwords, and I don't see how I'm going to get the others without inside help. You already have the report on the two I did manage to get. Both negative so far."

Pete said, "Your report states the Pringle woman has access to all employee passwords. Is that still the case?"

Daniel swirled the beer around in the bottle. He was afraid he already knew what his boss was leading up to. "Yes, but she hasn't been eliminated as a suspect."

"Your report states she was on a leave of absence when the hacker struck."

"But she still had access to the building. And, there's the possibility that she could have coached someone." Like Van Buren.

"Background was thorough. She seems clean."

Daniel knew Pete was right, but for some reason, Eileen Pringle bugged the hell out of him. And until he figured out why, he was going to keep a wary eye on her.

Pete said, "Who else can get you those passwords?"

"Van Buren's the only other person who has them."

The line was quiet for a few moments. "And he's still your prime suspect. You have a real reason to think the Pringle woman is involved?"

"No," Daniel admitted grudgingly. But he wasn't ready to trust her completely just yet.

"Unless you know something about her I don't, work on bringing her in on the investigation."

Daniel drained the last of his beer. All he needed was a damned woman—a klutzy one at that—in on his case. It would be like working with a ticking time bomb. At any given moment she could decide to squeal him out to Van Buren. "You might want to rethink that. The report I'm sending over says the reason she has the passwords is because she's got a," he emphasized the next word, "*real close relationship* with her boss."

"He's sleeping with her? Background didn't come up with that."

"I'm not sure if he's sleeping with her." He thought back to when he'd watched them together and decided their body language didn't indicate *that* intimate a relationship. "But they've definitely got something going."

"So use it. Tell her if she doesn't help us we're gonna toss her butt in jail as an accessory if Van Buren's found guilty. Or if you want to take a shot she's on the level, tell her she has a chance to prove her man is innocent. Hell, tell her anything. Do anything. Just get those passwords. You're the only man available with the computer skills to track the hacker down, and even you can't do it without inside help. You need those passwords, and I think we can be ninety-nine-percent sure the Pringle woman isn't directly involved in the hacking."

"Okay, boss. I'll do what it takes to get them."

Daniel could hear Pete's impatient sigh. "You got anything on the woman? Anything you can use to 'persuade' her?"

"No outstanding citations, no warrants, no overdue taxes. She's so clean, she squeaks when she walks." Daniel watched through the drapes as two of his neighbors—a tall black man and the old lady from next door—stood in the lighted courtyard, talking by the fountain. The man had a funny way of moving his hands when he talked. Not the forceful charades some of Daniel's Italian relatives used to emphasize their words. No, this guy's gestures were more like he'd been to the Vanna White Wannabe School.

"Miss Pringle need any favors?"

Daniel dropped the curtain, snapping his fingers. "That's it." He thought back to what he'd learned about her stepmother during his background check. He put that information together with the office buzz about Eileen believing she'd been cheated out of her inheritance, and his mental gears began grinding. "I just might have a carrot." A carrot the size of Texas.

"Do whatever it takes. So far our guy—or girl—has only

hacked into level-five information. But, if they hack into section-six data, we're in deep—"

"I know, Pete. We need to nail him. Or her. And we need hard evidence. I'm on it." He hung up, walking back to the window to inch the fabric aside.

Eileen had joined the other two at the fountain, and the man had his hand flattened over the center of his chest while he listened intently to something Eileen was saying. Eileen's lopsided ponytail bounced as she spoke.

"Talk about your motley crew," he said out loud, shaking his head as he dropped the curtain, turned the light back on and headed for his workout bench. He had Grandma Moses next door and Vanna directly across the courtyard. Then there was the perpetually muddled Eileen Pringle, who he had to somehow bribe, blackmail, or seduce—an unexpected thrill shot through him—into helping him with his case.

***

Late Sunday night, her body aching from arranging and rearranging what little furniture she had and setting up her apartment, Eileen slipped between crisp sheets and melted into the luxurious comfort of her new bed. She'd just treated herself to a long, hot, lilac-scented soak and indulged in a satin set of hot-out-of-the-catalog Victoria's Secret pajamas as a reward for her hard work. Maybe she didn't look like the sleek catalog model in them, but they made her feel sexy, even if there was no one in her life to notice. She was sure her closet addiction to VS kept stock in the company riding high.

When she leaned over the side of the bed toward the lamp on the floor, she noticed her clock read eleven-fifteen. It would be six o'clock before she knew it. Exhausted as she was, she had to admit she was anxious to get back to work. Mondays, she and Brock usually had lunch together. Of course the subject was always business, but those lunches had become the highlight of her work week.

She'd almost drifted off when a knock at her front door had her jerking the covers up to her chin and her heart racing into warp speed.

"What a little idiot," she said out loud as she jumped out of bed and put on her robe and slippers. "If someone was going to break in, they probably wouldn't knock." She quickly searched the floor for her glasses, but gave up when she couldn't find them. She'd just have to make do with fuzzy vision.

On the way to the door she tightened the belt of her robe. Although she wasn't used to answering her door in her pajamas, the blue satin set was definitely one of her more modest bedtime ensembles.

She turned on both the entry and porch lights then pulled an unpacked box of books to where she could stand on it and comfortably look through the peephole. Her mouth dropped open in shock. Daniel! What on Earth was he doing here so late?

"Yes?" she asked.

His voice was low, as if he didn't want to disturb the neighbors. "I need to talk to you. It's important."

"We'll talk in the morning. It's late."

"No, Eileen, we need to talk tonight. It's about Brock Van Buren."

Brock? Daniel's tone sounded serious. Not serious like, "It's about Brock. He's been in a car accident," or "It's about Brock. He's dead." More, like, "It's about Brock. He's murdered someone." She didn't remember pushing the box aside, unlatching the chain, or opening the door. But there she stood, staring at Daniel.

Or was it Daniel? He'd changed from the jeans and tee he'd had on earlier into sweats, and he seemed somehow taller. And he wasn't wearing his glasses. A quick squint assured her it really was Daniel.

His eyebrows shot up as he looked her up and down. But his demeanor quickly changed to professional and aloof, effectively throwing a wet blanket over the rare, sexy self-image she'd been experiencing. Jerk.

He cleared his throat. "May I come in?"

"Well, I don't know. It's really late." She stupidly looked behind her, as if someone might be there. The truth was, she'd much rather face the potential of dreaming about Brock than dealing with Daniel's mocking zingers at this late hour.

Daniel's eyes sharpened. His words a statement instead of a question, he said, "You're not alone." He stepped back, his gaze taking in her attire and the room behind her in one darting glance.

"Unfortunately, I am alone." She could have bitten back the wry words. Even if they were true, Daniel Collins didn't need to know about her love life, for pity's sake! "Why? What's wrong?"

"I thought for a moment Van Buren might be here."

"Brock? Here?" She had to chuckle. "No." She hadn't gotten that far into her dream world before Daniel knocked.

Daniel looked into her eyes. Her glasses remained somewhere next to her bed, but she forced herself not to squint.

"Eileen, I assure you, this is important. You'll want to hear what I have to say about your ... friend."

Eileen grudgingly motioned him into the room, praying her gut instinct about Daniel was right, and she wouldn't end up in tomorrow's LA Times in a sordid headline like *Psycho Killer Strikes Again*.

***

Daniel wasn't sure what Eileen's weird expression meant. He sat on one end of the only place to sit—a tiny, flowery sofa— and watched as Eileen tried to sit as far to the other end as humanly possible. She held the satin of her robe closed in a death-grip.

She asked, "What did you want to tell me?"

Daniel brought out his FBI identification, flipping it open and handing it to her. "Ask is more like it. I need to ask you a very important favor."

She held his ID close to her face, inspecting it, then looked at him in disbelief. "This a joke, right?"

"I'm afraid not. Someone at Wincomp has hacked into government files. I'm working undercover to find out who."

The startled look on her face quickly changed to one of disbelief, and she shook her head. By the way she stared into the distance he could tell she was searching for answers and going over the ramifications of his accusation. "A hacker inside Wincomp? But who?"

"Someone with heavy-duty hacking experience, I would say. And I need your help in finding out who that individual is."

The grip on her robe loosened as his proposal sank in. He patiently watched her while she sat chewing on her thumbnail, her disbelief waging a battle with indecision.

Tonight Daniel was seeing a different, unexpected side of Eileen Pringle. Gone was the hard-edged, uptight brainiac who seemed doomed to trip over her own feet.

The woman before him was soft, vulnerable and smelled like some kind of flower. Her dark hair, usually tortured to the top of her skull with a rubber band, now hung loose, forming a soft frame to features he'd never before noticed weren't all that bad. It helped that she wasn't wearing those godawful glasses.

Her startled look made him realize he'd been staring. He quickly straightened, but instead of looking away, challenged her with a direct stare. "What do you say?"

"To what?" Her cheeks turned pink.

"My proposal."

She swallowed, turning once more into the unsure, awkward Eileen. Somehow he was more comfortable with this Dr. Jeckyll persona. He still didn't have a handle on what Ms. Hyde was all about.

In a shaky voice she asked, "How do you know I'm not the hacker?"

Her forehead was creased with concern. And he was pretty sure he saw fear lurking in her overly bright eyes. She certainly had the know-how. In fact, periodically hacking into Wincomp to discover and remedy security weaknesses was one of her jobs.

"We have an exact date the files were breached by someone using one of Wincomp's terminals. You weren't anywhere near Wincomp that day. We checked. You were with your father." He wasn't about to tell her he still considered her a long-shot suspect. No one at Wincomp would be one-hundred-percent absolved of guilt until the case was closed.

The lines above her eyebrows disappeared. Her expression grew hard, defensive. Ms. Hyde was back with a vengeance. "I was being watched?"

"The lives of everyone at Wincomp have been thoroughly investigated, and their recent movements monitored."

She stood up, her anger evident in the rapid rise and fall of her breasts beneath the smooth satin. "That's an invasion of privacy. Talk about Big Brother!" She was so incensed she'd forgotten all about her robe, and it now slid open just enough to reveal unexpectedly sexy curves.

"We're talking national security here, Eileen." Why didn't the woman close her robe, for God's sake?

"But, I'm innocent!"

Her *double entendre* opened up a whole new realm of speculation. Being privy to this glimpse of Eileen's warrior-woman side, as well as a generous amount of cleavage revealed by the sexy number she wore, left both counts of her innocence open for debate. Maybe Van Buren wasn't such a dope after all.

Daniel—an avid *X-Files* viewer—put on his best Agent Moulder non-expression. "I know you're innocent." She seemed to accept the half-truth. "That's why I've asked you in on the case."

"Brock is innocent, too!" She cocked her hip, her hand resting against the curve.

He had the impression she thought that by sheer willpower she could convince Daniel of her boyfriend's righteousness.

He said, "Prove it."

Her chin shot up with the force of an uppercut. He detected a slight tremor. "I will."

Daniel began to sweat. He was just no good at interviewing females in sexy pajamas. Not that he'd ever had the opportunity before this. Her rapid breathing moved the satin material, accentuating shimmering curves. Mercifully, she stopped his wayward train of thought when she jerked her robe sash tight. But then he heard grinding gears and the screeching of reversing wheels in his mind as she crossed her arms tightly beneath her breasts, effectively pushing a good deal of them into full view.

Daniel got up and walked around the counter into the kitchen, helping himself to a glass from the sparsely-filled cupboard. Not bothering to ask for bottled water, he filled the glass from the tap and downed it in one long draft. He didn't turn around as he said, "You understand you can't tell anyone about the investigation."

"And why, again, do you think I'm going to do this for you?" Her cynical words came from just the other side of the breakfast bar.

When Daniel turned to face her he kept his eyes focused on hers. "To prove Van Buren isn't involved in espionage."

"I don't have to prove it. I know he's not involved. *Your* investigation will prove that."

Carrot time. "You want us to reciprocate? Give you something in return?"

She looked confused. "What could you possibly do for me?"

"How about giving you ammo to use against your stepmother in contesting your father's will? In case you're interested." Which, if the office scuttlebutt was reliable, she was. "You have grounds."

Her eyes widened in surprise. "Like what?"

"You get me the passwords. I'll get you the information you need to challenge the will. Remember, we investigated everyone at Wincomp. That includes their families."

Eileen pressed her hair back from her face and rubbed her temples. "This is crazy. No one at Wincomp would do this."

He had to nip her uncertainty in the bud. "Well, someone did, and unless you help me, the agency's going to close Wincomp and take everyone in for questioning. We don't want all the employees to be put through that."

Daniel saw the look of terror flash through her eyes. "But I'm working on a special project. I..I..." She sputtered, "I've put every penny into Wincomp's stock. You can't close it down!"

Ouch! That was going to hurt if Van Buren was his man. The company would be a goner. "So, work with me on this. Save your special project." He was curious to find out just what that was. Could it have anything to do with the compromised government files? "Save your investment. And save your *boss*." He couldn't keep the snide edge from his last word.

The quick look she gave him told him she'd caught his

meaning. Their eyes locked as she battled with indecision. Her words, spoken at last, held grim determination. "I'll do it."

"Welcome aboard." He held out his hand, wondering why he suddenly felt like Judas. It's not like he'd never used subterfuge in an investigation before. "Special Agent Daniel Manatucci, at your service."

She reluctantly put her hand in his, shaking her head in wonder, or maybe disgust. Even though her posture was stiff, her hand was warm and soft. Daniel wasn't sure why he held it a moment longer than needed to seal the bargain. Maybe just because her slim, warm hand felt so good in his. Better than good, it was a perfect fit.

"Daniel Manatucci?" Her eyes turned dark as she pulled her hand from his. "I liked Daniel Collins better. And I didn't like him much."

She didn't have to like him, Daniel thought grimly. Hell, the way this thing was most likely going to wind up, he'd have an enemy for life in Eileen Pringle. People tended to get furious when you brought their orderly little worlds down around their ears.

The eye contact she made was unflinching as she asked, "How can I be sure you'll uphold your end of the bargain?"

"You'll just have to trust me."

Trust? Eileen thought about her definition of the word, and it came out as fuzzy as her eyesight. She'd trusted her father to take care of her, and she'd wound up feeling betrayed. She'd foolishly trusted her stepmother, and look what happened. She didn't trust Daniel as far as she could spit. But what choice did she have? No alternative came to mind.

Four

The intimate lunch with Brock that Eileen had anticipated—not to mention her entire day—was doomed from the get-go.

Not only had Daniel, first thing that morning, insisted on holding her to her promise to rideshare, but she'd also discovered he was a bear until he'd had that initial morning cup of java. As soon as she'd gotten in his car, he'd mumbled something about his coffeemaker not working. With a sleepy early-morning look on his face, he'd headed, like a bat-out-of-hell, to the coffee shop, then proceeded to juggle the lidless paper cup while steering with his knees. All he needed was a cell phone in his free hand, and he'd be the poster-boy for the stereotypical LA driver.

After surviving Mr. Toad's wild ride, Eileen had settled in at work and managed to become blissfully lost in the depths of her new security program, when who should walk into her office shrouded in a dark cloud of expensive perfume? Her stepsister, Alyssa.

Alyssa wasted no time in informing Eileen about Brock inviting her to join them for lunch. Sitting across from Eileen's desk, her long legs accentuated by her short leather skirt and stiletto heels, Alyssa said, "Mom wanted me to check up on you, to see how you're getting along."

Eileen was certain her stepmother hadn't given her a second thought since the night Eileen had left. No, Alyssa had her own agenda, and Eileen was afraid she knew what it was. Brock.

Most likely Alyssa had broken up with her most recent—and longest standing—boyfriend, a smooth-talking con man named Devin Hollenbeck. And par for her usual course, she was retreating to safe ground—Brock. Brock had never made a pretense about how crazy he was over Alyssa, while Alyssa seemed only luke-warm about Brock.

Eileen had been so sure Alyssa and Devin were a long-term item, she'd begun to get her hopes up that Brock might see it, too, and she might finally have a chance with him.

Just thinking about the havoc the bleach-blonde, silicon wonder would once again wreak with Eileen and Brock's relationship made Eileen's stomach sink. When Alyssa was around, Eileen became The Invisible Woman.

Eileen turned away from Alyssa and back to the solace of her program. "Tell *Mother* I'm doing just fine. Thanks for stopping by." *Be sure to let the door hit you on the butt on the way out.*

"Mom sends her best."

Eileen stopped typing a moment to shoot her sister a look that said, Y*eah right, give me a break.* "I've got work to do. If you don't mind ...."

Alyssa got up and strolled to the door. "See you at lunch."

As Eileen watched Alyssa walk away, the song, "I'm Too Sexy For My Shirt," went through her head. She couldn't help noticing how Alyssa slowed down to allow Daniel a once-over as she cat-walked by his cubical. Now, *there* were two people who belonged together. Both were devious, manipulative and too sexy for their own good.

Eileen mentally shook herself. What was it about the man that made her physically react? Sure, he was handsome, even in his disguise, but she'd been around many handsome men before and had remained unaffected. Why did her pulse race when Daniel was near, and even more so now that she had discovered who he actually was? She had to admit, on a purely base level, an FBI agent was more intriguing than a computer geek. But, she rationalized, on an intellectual level she recognized Special Agent Daniel Manatucci for what he was—the type of deceitful, macho, overbearing man she detested. She leaned more toward the sensitive, considerate type of man. Like Brock Van Buren.

But, without intervention from Venus herself, Eileen knew

she didn't have a chance in Hades of Brock taking her seriously
as a woman, let alone falling in love with her. At that thought,
Mirabelle Saintly's outlandish claims played cat and mouse with
Eileen's rational mind. If Mirabelle's claims were true—which,
of course, they weren't—could she become sexy enough to break
the spell on Brock cast by her stepsister?

Nah.

Sounds of her sister's irritating laughter mingling with the
deep base of Brock's voice could be heard through the wall
connecting the offices. The tiny hairs on Eileen's arms stood on
end.

"That does it!" Taking her frustration out on her keyboard,
she rapidly jabbed the keys to minimize the screen she was in.
She then logged on to her Internet carrier. The deep breath she
took was a silent prayer.

Having left Mirabelle's pamphlet at home and remembering
the woman was at a conference, Eileen typed in the Glass-Slipper
web site. When she accessed the Wishmakers International web
page she saw the familiar raining sparkles, and she quickly turned
the volume down on her workstation before anyone in the office
walked in and overheard the theme music. The options menu
appeared, and Eileen only hesitated seconds before selecting
"Emergency."

She had to adjust the volume but kept it low, as the image
of a pretty young woman offered, "If you wish to be connected
to your Granter, please type in your name, then you may make
your selection from the drop-down menu."

Eileen typed in her name then tabbed down to *Mirabelle
Saintly*, her mind in a whirl as she passed a long list of names,
some with foreign-looking spellings she couldn't begin to
pronounce. It reminded her of Mirabelle's claims that
Wishmakers was an international organization.

She clicked on Mirabelle's name, and the screen flashed to
a web page with a 'Mirabelle Saintly' heading. Words appeared
across the page. *Welcome, Eileen. I'm thrilled that you're
ready to begin. I'm on my laptop and don't have audio, so
we'll have to type.*"

Eileen, having second thoughts about doing this at all, almost exited the program, but another peal of laughter from the other office had her steaming. She typed, *What do I have to do to get my wish?*

Mirabelle's answer was confusing at first. *The first of seven tasks you will be given is: Balance.*

Balance? The image conjured up was one of herself on a tightrope, and her stomach lurched as her fear of heights kicked in. *How do I do that?*

You are to take a self-defense class.

Eileen sighed. A self-defense class? That would lead to true love? Only if you were in to the kind that included bruises and humiliation.

Eileen saw more words appear on the screen. *Are you still there, dear?*

Yes, she typed. But not for long. She had a lunch date with Brock and her stepsister to get through. A self-defense class somewhere down the road wasn't going to improve her chances of having Brock notice her today.

I told you it would take some time. Patience has wondrous rewards. If you follow my instructions, I guarantee you will get your wish, but it won't happen today.

Eileen gave up trying to figure out how the woman tuned in to her every thought. She sighed again. So, she wasn't going to win Brock today. What did she have to lose in trying Mirabelle's suggestions? She'd be no worse off than she was now. Maybe the older woman's life experiences alone qualified her as a mentor. Besides, Eileen had always promised herself she would take a self-defense class someday. Living in LA was reason enough.

She typed, *How will learning self-defense teach me balance?*

Mirabelle answered, *Attaining personal safety gives you a strong, balanced foothold in the world. And, my dear, we can't begin to fulfill our potential—in this instance, true love— until we feel safe to do so.*

Eileen found herself taking the bottle of fairy dust from the top of her monitor. Even though Mirabelle had told her that props weren't used to achieve magic, she absently shook the bottle as she read Mirabelle's rapidly typed words.

When we are unbalanced, feeling unsafe, all of our decisions are fear-based and made with the approval of others in mind. Until you rid yourself of those fears, you will be unable to get in touch with your inner self.

Fairy dust and magic wands suddenly sounded comfortable and familiar compared to what Mirabelle was saying. 'In touch with her inner self?' She cringed. Not only did Mirabelle sound like one of those New Age self-help books, her statement required a lot on Eileen's part. Eileen gamely read on.

Work on ridding yourself of your fears—find your personal center of gravity—in order to feel the potential within yourself. When you are faced with a decision, ask yourself if your response is fear-based. She ended with, *Have a good day, dear, and don't forget the party at my apartment this Saturday! Bye for now.*

Feeling like she'd come into Greek class mid-semester, Eileen logged off and returned to her programming screen. Personal balance? Fear-based decisions? Personal gravity? She didn't know what the heck Mirabelle was talking about. She thought about how she'd tried most of her life to gain her father's approval. Okay, so she might occasionally seek approval from others. Was that wrong? She didn't see how taking a self-defense class was supposed to change that.

Eileen found herself shaking her head. Mirabelle's heart was in the right place. But as much as Eileen wanted the woman's outrageous vision to work, as much as she wanted a magic spell that could win Brock, she couldn't bring herself to buy into Mirabelle's claims.

The self-defense class itself seemed harmless enough, although she felt deceptive about going along with Mirabelle's suggestion under false pretenses. She'd just have to let the woman know how skeptical she was.

With that settled in her mind, Eileen went back to work. Before long the rumble of conversation from Brock's office had her putting on the headphones to her portable CD player.

***

Daniel had stood in Eileen's office doorway for more than

thirty seconds, but she was so focused on her screen she still hadn't noticed him.

"Ms. Pringle, you have a list for me?"

She didn't answer.

"Ms. Pringle!" he said louder.

She looked perplexed as she glanced around her office. When she saw him, she reached up and removed a set of headphones. "What?"

"Do you have that list for me?"

She quickly looked around as if anyone listening would automatically know what list he was talking about. Her whisper had an edge to it. "Yes, but I don't know what good it's going to do you. Tomorrow is Tuesday."

He raised his eyebrows and opened his hands as if to say, "So?"

"It's policy to change passwords on the second Tuesday of each month."

He blew out a frustrated breath. For a moment, he had forgotten. "So, when can you get me the new list?"

"As I'm sure you know by now, security procedure is that all of us change our passwords at nine-o'clock sharp. Brock collects them at ten, types them into his file, then gives a copy to me by one o'clock in the afternoon."

Daniel said, "Anyone ever change them ahead of time?"

"They're not supposed to. For security reasons, Brock and I are meant to always have the current passwords. In fact, Brock doesn't even change his until he can give me a copy in case something happens to him. Then I'll have access to Wincomp's files. He even couriered them over to me while I was gone."

Daniel mentally rubbed his hands together. He could finally get some real work done. Up until this morning he'd only succeeded in obtaining two employee passwords by means of a little guesswork and the process of elimination. Not an easy job with an office full of people.

He thought about how so many people used their children's or pet's names, or their birthdays as PIN numbers or Passwords. Sometimes it was purely a matter of finding out a little about the person, then trying one guess after another. Now at least that particular sleuthing would be over.

He said, "Bring the list home with you. I'll copy it."
From her worried frown he suspected she wasn't comfortable taking privileged information out of the office, or giving it to him, for that matter. He had to hand it to her. She had a strong sense of ethics—or she was afraid of repercussions from her boyfriend when he found out.
He said, "Mr. Van Buren invited me to your lunch meeting. Hope you don't mind."

Daniel watched as she rolled her eyes. "Join the party. My stepsister will be there, too. She's in Brock's office right now." She gave him a wry look. "Maybe you noticed her?"
Notice the knockout as she walked past his cubical earlier? He'd noticed her all right. He wasn't blind. He'd also immediately recognized her from Eileen's family file. From what Daniel had already learned from the brief background check on Alyssa Barden, the woman might like people to think she was a tad short-circuited in the synapses department, but she'd graduated *summa cum laude* from Berkley. However, it wasn't her brains he'd focused on when she'd sashayed past him. "Interesting," he said. "Are they an item again?"

As his 'again' registered with Eileen, she gave him a quizzical look, then a cynical one. "I forgot, you know everything about my," her snort was dainty, "family." She shrugged, folding her arms. "I don't know, Daniel. Are they dating again? You tell me. I'm sure you know more than I do."

Daniel inwardly cringed. He'd bull's-eyed a couple of raw nerves with that one. Not only was she miffed about him snooping into her private life, he now found himself dodging visual poison daggers. Why had he made reference to her stepsister and Van Buren?

His first thought was, *Give up little girl, you 're out of your league. Alyssa's got it all over you.* But when he looked back to where Eileen stood, vigorously cleaning her glasses with the corner of her sweater, he was incongruously reminded of how she'd looked last night. He tried to see past the pricey but drab work clothes and severe hairstyle, to once again see her as soft, warm and sexy. He couldn't do it. Last night must have been an illusion. He was finding that the more he thought about Eileen, the more he was left speculating.

***

At lunch Daniel got a front row seat for the three-ring circus. It was a great opportunity to watch Brock and Eileen interact. And with the blonde bombshell dropped smack between the two, the fireworks should have been entertaining as hell. But for some reason Daniel wasn't getting the kick out of Eileen's unease that he thought he might.

Alyssa didn't have to work very hard to capture and keep Brock's attention. The guy practically drooled over the pretty blonde. But once she'd wrapped Brock around her little finger, she seemed to be methodically moving in on the only other male at the table—namely, him.

In morbid fascination, Daniel watched as Alyssa placed her hand securely on top of Brock's, looked past Eileen as if she were invisible, and focused the full power of her soft hazel eyes on him. But Daniel wasn't fooled. It was obvious Alyssa's main goal was to prove to everyone, especially herself, that all other females in the room were superfluous. Sure she was sexy, in a cheap, artificial way. But he needed more than that in a woman, and Miss Silicone just didn't do it for him. Besides, he didn't like the way she was treating Eileen, like she could drop off the face of the earth and no one would care.

Brock's cell phone rang, and he went into the restaurant foyer to talk in private. Daniel tried to keep an eye on Brock to see if he could ascertain the gist of the conversation. But Alyssa was making a concerted effort to hold his attention. Besides, a small crowd milling around after their lunch obscured Brock.

Alyssa's voice was breathy and soft, like smooth silk. "Daniel, are you from LA?"

He turned back to her, stating bluntly, "No."

The woman was amazing; her smile never faltered. She tilted her head slightly to one side. "Where are you from?"

"Seattle." Daniel looked at Eileen, whose eyes widened, obviously startled by his sudden attention. He said, "Eileen, are you a California native?"

He could see in his peripheral vision that Alyssa wasn't the least bit happy about the change in focus, so he decided to keep it that way. And once he did, he was surprised to realize he enjoyed the view.

"Yes," Eileen answered, even though they both knew he'd memorized her file, down to the type of toothpaste she used.

As he looked at her, he automatically compared her to her stepsister. He realized Eileen's face had strength of character and honesty, while Alyssa's spoke of wasted intelligence and idle days spent pouring through fashion magazines. He could see from the appreciative smile playing around Eileen's lips that she knew his opinion of her stepsister was anything but favorable.

Alyssa's silky voice frayed a bit at the edges. "I've never been to Seattle. What's it like?"

"Wet." He suddenly noticed how blue Eileen's eyes were, almost gray. And if he wasn't mistaken, her dark eyelashes were mascara-free. "Ever been to Seattle, Eileen?"

"No." Eileen's cheeks turned pink and her eyes bright, but she never broke eye contact with him. He had to hand it to her. Any other woman might have given up the obvious charade by now. But the longer he stared, the more resolute her gaze became. What had started as a tweak to Alyssa had somewhere along the lines turned into a competitive war of wills between him and Eileen. He wasn't sure who was winning, but he was thoroughly enjoying himself.

Obviously, Alyssa's voice had a volume control, because she cranked it up a couple octaves, effectively turning what had been silk into fingernails on a chalkboard. "Daniel, have you seen much of LA yet?"

"No." He wondered what was going on inside Eileen's head at that moment. She had to be dying to look at Brock, who had reclaimed his seat across the table, but she didn't.

Alyssa's tone turned back into seductive silk. "I could show you around."

Daniel almost blinked. Eileen's eyes widened perceptibly, but still didn't break contact.

Daniel said, "Eileen has agreed to show me around, haven't you, Eileen?" He'd already let Eileen know he planned on keeping her as close as possible during his investigation.

Eileen's gaze turned shrewd, and the way her eyelids dipped was sexy as hell. Was she flirting with him? "Oh, Alyssa has much more *experience*." She did break contact then and, as if needing to explain the reference, said, "Experience as an LA tour guide, I mean."

Brock's, "Ahem," brought all eyes to him. "It's almost time to go back to work. And before we do, I need to talk to you both." His glance acknowledged Eileen and Daniel, but he let Alyssa know she was still important by putting his hand over hers. "It seems we have a security breach at Wincomp."

Daniel swore he could feel the whip of air as Eileen's head turned toward him, but he didn't turn to acknowledge the question he knew he would see in her eyes. Brock couldn't be talking about the FBI case—unless Eileen had told him. Daniel continued looking straight ahead, at Brock. "Security breach?"

Brock's thumb absently stroked across the top of Alyssa's hand. Daniel could tell the gesture irritated the woman, but she didn't pull her hand away. She merely kept on smiling, only a bit more stiffly.

Brock said, "I'm afraid we may have a major problem at Wincomp. Although we have the best security system against outside hackers," he smiled at Eileen, "it seems we might have a traitor in our midst."

Eileen shot another look at Daniel, but didn't say anything.

Brock said, "A member of our team has sold us out. One of our new programs—a program scheduled for an initial launch in January—just hit the market under the 'Morgan' label." He looked at Daniel. "Morgan is our biggest competitor." His voice was calm, but Daniel could tell the guy was upset.

From what Daniel had gathered since he'd been at Wincomp, Brock viewed his employees as a family. Brock Van Buren might himself very well be involved in espionage, but evidently, having one of his trusted insiders turn against him was a hard pill to swallow.

Could Eileen have told Brock about Daniel and the FBI investigation? Daniel had to wonder if Brock had set up the software theft as a diversionary tactic to point the finger of guilt away from himself.

Eileen's incredulous tone seemed genuine as she put her hand over her heart. "Which program was it?"

"Michael and Ray's Speech Recognition software."

Eileen said in a whisper, "That was Ray's baby."

She turned to Daniel to explain. "Michael and Ray's program was leaps and bounds ahead of any on the market. We were holding off on the launch until our marketing strategy was in place."

Eileen turned back to Brock. "Are you sure?"

Brock said, "As sure as I can be. The program Morgan released is identical to Ray's. We both know that no two programs are *exactly* alike. The one Morgan released is *identical*, down to the last icon."

Eileen asked, "Do you have any idea who did it?"

Brock shook his head. "The boys are genuinely devastated, so I'm sure it was neither of them."

Daniel couldn't dismiss either of *the boys* as easily as Brock.

Brock continued. "The only other employees I can be assured weren't involved are you two. Daniel, you weren't at Wincomp when this had to have happened. And I'd trust Eileen with my life."

Brock looked fondly at Eileen. "I'm counting on you to beef up all individual workstation security immediately. I'll issue a memo today restating the importance of password integrity. The only people within Wincomp who know about this are the four of us at this table. And the boys, of course. I want the fact that we're aware of the theft kept quiet for awhile, to give us time to find the thief ourselves."

He turned to Daniel. "I'm reassigning Eileen's projects as well as yours, so you can work together on this. You both have the know-how to scan the employee's Internet activities—if, indeed, the contact was made from inside Wincomp. And I want this person stopped before he—or she—steals any more projects. This was a big loss for us. One more software hit, and Wincomp could be in real trouble. With expansion plans already in the works, we really needed that capital."

Daniel caught Eileen's glance. Wincomp might be in trouble

even without their inside trader. Their trader could be the same person Daniel was looking for, or two individuals could be working separately with agendas of their own. Brock wasn't off his list just yet.

Brock continued. "I don't want to cause a panic, or for the person who did this to bolt, so I think it's imperative we keep this quiet. The only way to avoid suspicion while investigating is to do it after regular office hours. Is switching your work hours from day to night going to be a problem for either of you?"

Daniel watched the way Eileen leaned slightly toward Brock and said, "Of course not." Her willingness to comply with anything the man wanted was evident in her face. It was like Brock had cast some kind of spell on her, and Daniel found himself wondering what it would take to break that hold.

Evidently Alyssa was enough of a distraction to Brock that he didn't question why Eileen spoke for Daniel as well as herself regarding their working together after hours. Daniel knew what was going through Eileen's mind. She was well aware Daniel needed to look for the hacker and would work any time, anywhere in exchange for the *carte blanche* Brock was offering.

And Daniel knew Eileen was thrilled with the prospect of uninterrupted time with the workstations, so she could prove to Daniel that Brock wasn't involved with the government hacking.

The only remaining impediment to Daniel's investigation was access to the terminal in Brock's office, which was always locked when he wasn't there. Daniel could break in, no problem, but he was sure Boss Man wasn't going to willingly hand over his computer password.

He looked at Eileen who chewed her lower lip as she watched her stepsister and Brock exchange suggestive messages with their eyes.

Brock smiled at Alyssa but spoke to Eileen. "Eileen, because your time will be taken with this probe, your sister has agreed to take your place as chair of the New Year's Eve party committee. While you were gone, she came up with some great ideas. I don't know what I would do without you two."

Eileen's shoulders stiffened, but Daniel got the impression

she was used to various versions of this particular scenario.

Daniel asked, "Party?" From the tension he saw in Eileen's demeanor, the New Year's Eve party must be a big deal.

Eileen appeared calm, but Daniel's position next to her at the round table allowed him to see her crossed foot going a mile a minute. He could hear an edge of irritation in her voice. "Every year Wincomp hosts a party for its employees. I've been in charge of the committee working on the preparations. At the party, Brock is going to announce the employee winner of Wincomp's software contest."

"A contest?" He was beginning to sound like a parrot. He shifted uncomfortably. As an undercover agent, he should have made it his business to know more about Wincomp's inner workings. He should have known about the competition.

Eileen explained, "A year ago Brock announced an inter-office contest. The person who comes up with the most innovative software program wins. As I said, Brock will announce the winner at the party."

That must be the special software project Eileen said she was working on. Daniel was curious as to what innovative idea she might have come up with. He suspected that whatever it was, it would make her a strong contender. Unlike her stepsister, Eileen used the brain God had given her. "What's the prize?"

Alyssa perked up, announcing, "A big chunk of Wincomp stock." She pouted. "I just wish I knew more about computers. I could use that kind of security."

"Oh, you get by." Eileen's snide expression was either lost on or ignored by her stepsister since Alyssa's falsely adoring gaze remained locked on Van Buren.

Alyssa practically meowed as she turned to Eileen and said, "I'll drop by your office for your party notes, Sis."

Eileen looked out the restaurant window as though she were intently studying the foot traffic. "Fine."

Alyssa looked back to Brock, and Daniel could swear he saw a glint of triumph in her eyes.

***

Eileen grabbed her purse and headed out of her office, almost colliding with Ray, who was on his way in. Ray grabbed her with a steadying hand, but didn't immediately release her. Instead he waltzed her around her office, singing, "Fly me to the moon ...." She laughed for the first time that day.

Ray gave her a final twirl then let her go. "The group's headed for The Grill. You ready?"

"You betcha." She lightly smacked her forehead. Damn, she'd forgotten Daniel. "On second thought, I can't. I'm ridesharing with Daniel." She'd also, for a few blessed moments, forgotten about her and Daniel's shift change. They were scheduled to begin their nightshift at eight that evening so would be pulling a double shift.

Ray said, "Bring Daniel along. It's about time we initiated him into the Monday Night Rowdies."

The small group of Wincomp employees comprising the 'Rowdies' pretty much exemplified the antithesis of rowdy. They were just singles who didn't want to face the boring schedule of Monday night sitcoms alone. So they'd begun sharing dinner at The Grill.

"Count me in," came Daniel's unexpected voice from the doorway.

That's all she needed, Daniel imposing himself on one more aspect of her life. Next thing she knew, he'd be sharing her morning shower. Heat rushed to her neck and cheeks as erotic images tumbled out of left field. She got a firm picture of her and Daniel, naked beneath the spray of hot, steamy water, each sensually soaping the other's body. Her imagination did a good job of letting her know how Daniel's slick, wet skin felt against her fingertips. She took a shaky breath, suddenly feeling a bit lightheaded.

"You okay?" Daniel asked, an amused eyebrow cocked.

She put her hand to her face. The only thing she could think to say was, "Power surge."

Both men laughed, and she couldn't help joining them. Throughout dinner Eileen watched in fascination as Daniel discretely interrogated each of the people at the table. He was a pro at easily joining in the conversations, reminding her he had FBI training, which probably included just this kind of thing.

First he had a regular bull session with Ray about the LA

Lakers basketball team's erratic year. Then he sparked Michael's interest with talk of skydiving. Michael even gave Daniel a couple of tips about playing blackjack in Las Vegas, one of Michael's passions.

She could see that they were all buying—hook, line and sinker—Daniel's guise of amiability. A guise she knew for a fact had to be calculated—and on a personal level, not the least bit interesting to Daniel.

Eileen could tell that, as far as suspects went, he was most keenly interested in Nancy Dace, one of Wincomp's senior and most trusted employees. The way he deliberately made poor Nancy believe he was actually interested in her as a woman made Eileen's blood boil. At least at lunch when he'd looked at Eileen, she'd known he was only doing it to provoke Alyssa, although why he wanted to do that was a mystery to her. With Alyssa all but throwing herself into his arms, he should have been as charmed by her as Brock was.

As Eileen watched him, Daniel cocked his head slightly to one side, as if the only thing in the world that mattered was what Nancy had to say. What a reptile! His hypnotic finesse was working, and had miraculously transformed the quiet, reserved woman into a chatterbox.

Eileen knew firsthand how easy it might be to succumb to his magnetism. She just hoped Daniel the Deceiver would finish his job soon and slither back to his FBI swampland before his poisoned fangs did irreparable damage to someone's heart.

She heard him ask Nancy, "So, programming wasn't your original love?"

"Only one of them." She was flushed, Eileen noted. Maybe the woman should eat some of the food on her plate to help absorb the three glasses of wine she'd had. "I do have a passion for fine art. I've recently acquired a small collection."

She seemed to abruptly sober, although her eyes still looked bleary. "Well, it's not really all that much, come to think of it. Just a couple of paintings I've managed to pinch pennies to buy."

Eileen could almost hear the wheels grinding in Daniel's head. She knew whose terminal they would be working on late tonight.

Daniel seemed not to notice Nancy's discomfiture. "Did you happen to see the Van Gogh exhibit when it was in LA?"

Nancy was off again, chattering about the different pieces, and Daniel listened with what appeared to be rapt attention.

Ray gave Eileen a look that asked, "What's going on?"

She shrugged and took another sip of wine, all the while feeling guilty because she wanted so much to tell Ray about the FBI investigation. She was sure he would be comforted knowing an FBI agent was looking into the theft of his software program. If she hadn't already promised secrecy, she wouldn't hesitate to tell Ray everything. He had always been a wonderful confidant.

Nancy's speech began to slur, her words coming farther and farther apart, and Eileen couldn't help comparing her to the Energizer Bunny finally running out of energy. Eileen watched as, at last, Nancy sighed deeply and then stopped talking altogether.

Ray chuckled. "Nancy, how about I give you a lift home? You can leave your car here and pick it up after work tomorrow."

Eileen noticed the hopeful glance Nancy gave Daniel, a glance he obviously saw coming and avoided. Nancy sighed again. "Sure, thanks. But, you leave your car here. You can drive mine. You've been wanting to since I got it last week."

"Great."

They all headed to their cars, Ray holding Eileen back just outside the restaurant. "Brock told you about Morgan Software snagging my program?"

She put her hand on his arm. "Yes, and I feel just horrible about it, Ray. You put so much into it. You must feel like you've had a child stolen."

Ray shrugged, and Eileen could tell he was holding back emotions, trying to be pragmatic about it. "It's not that bad. It just ticks me off I won't get design credit. Besides, it's not like I was making the big bucks on it, anyway. That would have gone to Wincomp."

Eileen took another look at Ray. Had he just confided in her that he'd been the one to sell his program to the highest bidder?

She said, "You sound kind of bitter about Wincomp."

He shifted irritably. "Look at me, Eileen. At my age, it's not like I'm ever going to start my own software company, or even see any of the money I'm generating for Wincomp. Sometimes it just gets to me."

"What about the bonus program?"

He snorted. "Chicken feed compared to what the programs I've developed are worth, and what they've made for Brock. You must feel the same way. Your programs are some of Brock's biggest sellers."

Neither of them had Brock's business sense, either. Developing programs was their forte, and without a strong business behind them, they wouldn't have had a chance of making substantial money. Unless they made a deal with a competitor to steal completed packages. "So, what are you saying, Ray?" Her heart was beating fast, and she quickly glanced over to where Daniel stood patiently leaning against the car.

Ray took a deep breath then blew it out in a rush. "Oh, never mind me. I've had too much to drink, and I'm whining." He gave her a bear hug. "At my age, I should count myself lucky to be working in this industry at all. And lucky to have such good friends that I can trust."

Was that an emphasis she heard on the word 'trust?' Even as she responded with, "Trust among friends is important," she wondered if she would soon have cause to break that trust by telling Daniel about their conversation. She couldn't believe Ray was guilty of selling to a competitor, let alone the espionage Daniel was concerned about. But then, she couldn't believe Brock could be guilty, either. She had to remind herself they weren't the only two choices. One thing was for sure, at least one person within Wincomp was a criminal, and they were causing her to question the people she trusted most in her life. Suddenly, she was anxious to get back to the office to start playing detective.

She kissed Ray on the cheek. "I'll call you tomorrow, Buddy. Daniel and I will be working late tonight, scanning data, so I'm not sure I'll be in during regular hours tomorrow. Until we discover who sold us out, we may be pulling quite a few night shifts."

Ray looked uneasy. "I hate to say it, but you notice how Nancy has been spending like she won the lottery? You don't think maybe...." He left the accusation unfinished as he jerked his head to where she stood against her recently purchased classic Austin Healy roadster.

Eileen felt sick. Not Nancy. Somehow that would be like finding out the Brady Bunch mom was a mass-murderer. Eileen knew about the new car, but figured Nancy had just saved for it. But Eileen found herself taking Ray's warning to heart, figuring Nancy's computer terminal was as good a place to start as any. She left Ray's accusation hanging in the air. "Good night, Ray."

They both headed toward their waiting companions.

***

On their way back to the office for their first evening of what Eileen was afraid would turn into many, Eileen filled Daniel in on her concerns about Nancy. She was careful not to include Ray's name in the conversation. When Daniel confirmed he'd been keeping a close eye on Nancy, Eileen realized how ambivalent her feelings were. Part of her wanted Nancy to be the one; then this whole mess would be over. Brock and Ray would be off the hook. But another part of her just couldn't believe Nancy was the criminal type. Eileen truly liked Nancy.

When Eileen and Daniel got to the now deserted office, she was surprised to see him make a beeline for Brock's locked office instead of Nancy's workstation.

"Where are you going?"

Daniel pulled his wallet from his pocket and extracted a long, pick-like instrument. "To the source. I plan on starting from the top and working my way down."

She didn't bother telling him she had a key to Brock's office. Let him use his spy gadgets if it made him feel more like James Bond.

She said, "You're not going to find anything."

"Then it will be a quick search and we'll move on."

Daniel eased the door open with a triumphant look.

Eileen suddenly had qualms about what they were doing.

As far as she was concerned, the only thing Brock was guilty of was bad judgement when it came to women. Now she had to prove it to Daniel.

She walked across the room to turn on the power switch. When the computer loaded, she typed in Brock's password. The words "Access Denied" jumped to the screen.

"What's going on?" Daniel looked at her like she had something to do with the message.

She took off her glasses to clean them with the hem of her blouse, which she'd pulled from her skirt. "Evidently, Brock's already changed his password." She hadn't meant to sound so smug, and when she saw Daniel's angry response, she wished her words had a delete button.

She found herself taking an involuntary step back as Daniel came close, a menacing look in his eyes. The desk at her back prevented further retreat. He came toward her, until their bodies were only inches apart, and she could feel his warm, wine-scented breath on her face. Her neck ached with the strain of looking up at such a close angle. For a brief moment she couldn't tell if he was going to strangle her or kiss her, and she wasn't sure which terrified her more. She licked her lips, her breathing labored.

With his arms on either side of her, he braced his hands on the desk, effectively pinning her against it. She felt something deep within her stir to life, something exciting and dangerous. Her face suffused with heat. Her body responded to his nearness as if it had a mind of its own, and she realized there was no denying she was seriously attracted to the man. But that didn't mean she liked him. He might be sexy as hell, and show an occasional tender side, but that didn't remove the fact that he was a threat. Not physically. Even though he pretty much had her pinned to the desk, she realized she felt no physical threat from Daniel. But he was a definite threat to Brock and Wincomp. And, it seemed, he was a threat to her weakening willpower.

Possessing her with a direct gaze she was powerless to break, he said in a seductive voice, "You told Brock about the investigation."

Five

Mirabelle and Mary had just finished an on-line conference with the entire Wishmaker's consortium. Members had focused their remaining individual powers to Mirabelle and Eileen for the task at hand—assuring the granting of Eileen's wish.

Mirabelle said, "I feel strange, being the only member with The Power available to her."

"Our weakened individual energies made it necessary to center all of our reserves to Eileen's granting. Think of it as a vacation for the rest of us."

Mirabelle knew how each spirit constantly exuded and gathered energies—both positive and negative—from the universe. Wishmaker's job was to keep the illuminating powers of positive energy strongly balanced—to keep the dark forces from vanquishing the light. What would Wishmaker's centered energies do to that balance? She wondered aloud, "Will there be cosmic repercussions with the critical energy being dependent on one person?"

Mary sighed. "We don't know. The balance has never been this uncertain. Making one individual the nucleus of the energy does have the potential to cause...a certain *agitation* connected to Eileen's emotions."

"What kind of agitation?" Images of natural disasters rumbled through Mirabelle's overactive mind.

"Perhaps no more than unusual weather corresponding to Eileen's progress. Or..." Mary paused so long Mirabelle's heart began to race with anxiety.

Mirabelle asked, "Or what?"

"Let's just hope Eileen's energy fluxes manifest themselves in positive ways. This is all new to us. We're not sure what meteorological or climatic influences she might have. These concerns are just more reasons to push for an expedient Grant.

"A Grant on the Solstice would be a bonus, but not critical. However, she must get her wish by the stroke of midnight of the New Year, the time when restructuring of cosmic energy takes place. If we haven't re-established our powers by then, we will be vanquished, and what little power we have remaining will be dispersed into the cosmos."

"Of course."

"You must not dwell on the negative aspects," Mary pointed out. "It would put your own energies at risk. Concentrate on keeping your spirit light. Remind yourself to live the rules as well as teach them. We'll deal with any fallout from Eileen's attainment fluctuations when, and if, that time comes. Good-bye for now. I'm sure you have work to do." Mary signed off.

Mirabelle slowly turned from her computer. She would have to use the utmost discretion in using the precious energy bestowed upon her. Not one spark could be wasted when it might be critical to success later.

She got up to look out her window toward Eileen's apartment, softly humming a dreamy waltz.

***

Daniel's natural skepticism prevented him from wholeheartedly buying into Eileen's look of innocence as he held her captive against the desk. It made perfect sense that she would share confidences with the man she loved.

Professional as well as personal prudence told him he should move his arms from around her. Taking a threatening stance went against FBI protocol, as well as personal ethics. But for some reason he liked it right where he was. He liked looking into her eyes. He liked the way her breasts heaved toward him with each rapid breath. The glasses she held in her hand dropped to the carpet with a soft plunk, but neither of them looked down.

He said, "You told me Brock always gave you his password

as soon as he changed it, in case something happened to him."

"He must have forgotten."

"He doesn't seem the type to forget."

She blinked nervously. "I ... I didn't tell Brock about the FBI investigation. Honest."

The "honest" brought back a time when, as a child, he'd tried desperately to convince his mother he hadn't broken her favorite lamp. Daniel couldn't help smiling. The adamant sincerity of her denial rang true with a childlike innocence, totally out of character for the self-assured image he had of Eileen. She must have mistaken his mirth for cynicism, however, because she added. "Really, I didn't." She bit her lip.

Years of experience told him he should remain suspicious, but his gut told him she was sincere. He looked harder into her eyes, trying to discern a hint of deception lurking there. She didn't blink. Then something strange happened.

The light in her eyes changed from that of closed regard to bright feminine awareness, and he felt himself respond. Her body shifted subtly, and thoughts of the investigation took a back seat to the strong physical reaction to the woman he held captive. He clenched his jaw, resisting the urge to breach the distance between them to discover the feel and taste of the moist lower lip she'd just bitten.

Unexpectedly, she stiffened and pushed him away, leaving him more emotionally than physically off balance. Even though she quickly moved halfway across the room, he still felt the warm imprints of her hands on his chest.

With her back to him she said in a shaky voice, "You don't have to bully the truth out of me, Daniel." He watched as she turned to face him and folded her arms across her chest. "Or use your practiced charm to *seduce* me into helping you. I'm telling the truth, and you can either believe me, or you can ...." A derisive smile quirked her mouth. "I'm sure you know what you can do with your doubts." A slight quiver of her lip took the edge off her bravado.

He'd already established to himself that he believed her. So why was he strong-arming her? It was a gentle kind of strong-arming, but strong-arming all the same. He didn't need a cosmic e-mail from Dr. Freud to answer the why of it. He realized that believing she was involved with the hacker made keeping his distance an easier task.

With that barrier down, keeping their relationship professional would be difficult if not impossible. Right from the start, something about Eileen set up an itch within him that his 'Agent' status obliged him not to scratch. "Okay, so I believe you. Let's get to work on Nancy's data." He watched Eileen march stiffly out of the office and head toward Nancy's workstation.

Daniel trailed behind her, enjoying the view, and wondering just how he was going to work so closely with her and keep a professional distance. At first, when he'd approached her in Brock's office, he hadn't intended to put the moves on her. He'd only meant to confront her about telling Brock, and hope for a confession. But when he'd gotten close to the woman, he'd somehow become the one to react.

Daniel couldn't deny the attraction he felt for Eileen, and it left him unsettled. Every minute he spent with her showed him more and more why Brock might be attracted to her. At first, and even second glance, Eileen Pringle came across as prissy and uptight, and she was prone to clumsiness when she got flustered. But her natural, unassuming beauty and intelligence couldn't be contained by the outward appearance, which he recognized was her shield against a world she seemed, for some reason, to be unsure of.

He watched Eileen execute an almost military turn at the entrance to Nancy's cubicle, and he had to shake his head. Images of her with the satin bathrobe gaping open intruded, leaving him more disconcerted than ever.

***

By the time Eileen and Daniel had scanned the volumes of programs and recovered the deleted e-mail files on Nancy's PC, it was nearly two in the morning. For Eileen it had been a challenge to keep in mind both the FBI investigation as well as the internal Wincomp probe. Daniel's presence was a distraction that the late hour and exhaustion only intensified.

She could tell Daniel was as tired as she was. His dark

hair, usually so precisely combed, now looked rumpled after he'd repeatedly run his hand through it as they worked. He'd taken off his glasses, which she realized were only for effect, and which had apparently become irritating. Without his glasses he looked more approachable, not so perfect. She liked that. Immediately she countered that thought. She didn't want to like Daniel.

She noticed he was staring at her and realized he'd asked a question.

"What? I'm sorry. Guess I drifted off."

"We'd better call it a night." Daniel leaned so far back in the chair Eileen wondered if he would flip over, then he stretched his arms above his head and yawned widely. He must have a good sense of balance, because she knew she would have gone over by now.

"But—" She looked toward Nancy's monitor, still heartsick by what they'd found. Nancy was heavy into commodities trading, and from what they'd recovered so far, she'd lost a great deal of money. They didn't know if she'd recovered her loses. "We haven't finished examining her transactions."

Daniel looked at her. "Don't jump to conclusions here. What we have," he held up the discs they'd copied the files to, "isn't proof of Nancy's guilt, only a possible motive. Finding proof— if there is any—is going to take more hours than I have left in me tonight. We'll get back to it tomorrow night."

Eileen felt relief. Maybe it wasn't Nancy after all. Some bad judgements in the commodities didn't make her a criminal. But, if not her, then who? Eileen still couldn't bring herself to believe any of her co-workers were guilty of either espionage or stealing from Wincomp. As she stood to stretch her stiff, sleep-deprived muscles, she looked at the rows of cubicles. "Daniel, the investigations could take forever."

"Yeah. But think about how difficult it would have been without the passwords and unencumbered night access. Don't worry. We always get our man." He looked at her. "Or woman."

After hours of tedious work, they had two vaguely suspicious transactions to trace from Nancy's files. If Nancy proved innocent, which Eileen hoped she would, they still had at least twenty more investigations like tonight's to do. She groaned inwardly at the thought of how many evenings might be spent like this. Then she thought about how it was really the lack of sleep she dreaded. Surprisingly, once they got down to business, she hadn't minded collaborating with Daniel at all. When he wasn't doing his James Bond thing, which always sent her into an immediate defensive mode; or his lady-killer mode—which confused the hell out of her—she occasionally got a glimpse of a different man, an intelligent, perceptive, even sensitive man. Daniel was a man that under different circumstances she might like very much.

His advanced technical understanding matched hers, and she liked that she had to stay on her toes to keep up with him. Other than the fact that she and Daniel were on opposite sides of the fence—he trying to prove guilt, she determined to prove innocence—she had to admit they worked well together.

"The longer we take," she said, "the better chance the— what do we call him, the bad guy?—has to cover his tracks." She knew she was stating the obvious, but she needed to say it out loud, as a confirmation to herself. "If he finds out about the investigation, he could deliberately sabotage his system, possibly all of Wincomp's systems, to wipe out the evidence."

Daniel raised his eyebrows. "Let's hope he doesn't find out."

The pointed look he gave her held a warning. She chose to let it slide, but all friendly thoughts about him flew out the window with a whoosh. As if she would jeopardize her chance to prove Brock's innocence by telling anyone about the investigation!

She blew out a tired breath. "I'm a morning person, Daniel. I don't know how many of these late-nighters I can pull."

"Sleep in. I know I will. I am not a morning person."

He didn't have to tell her. She'd had first-hand experience with his early-morning taciturnity. But she couldn't sleep in. She wasn't about to tell Daniel, but this afternoon she'd phoned in her registration for the self-defense class Mirabelle had assigned her to join. The first session started at six that morning.

The gym offered an evening class, too. But when she'd

signed up, she'd purposely opted for the early-bird session, hoping Daniel's dislike of mornings would keep him away. She'd figured he'd likely never even know she'd slipped away for a couple of hours.

Her response to his suggestion was a vague, "Sleep in. That would be nice."

She sat down and reached over to Nancy's terminal to disconnect the on-line server and back out of the file they'd been in. "We'll finish up here tomorrow?"

"If we find any conclusive evidence against Nancy, the next step is to get a search warrant for her personal accounts and her home."

Eileen said, "You need a search warrant?"

Daniel chucked. "Yes. What did you think? We have legal autonomy?"

She realized she thought exactly that. "Yes, I guess so."

Daniel shook his head. "Bureau agents are bound by the same legalities as all law enforcement."

"You have a search warrant for this computer?" She indicated Nancy's workstation.

"Yes. And, for every terminal, hard drive, all data, and every printer at Wincomp."

Eileen said, "But not our home computers?" Knowing Daniel wasn't above the law gave Eileen a different perspective of him.

"I can only get a warrant for an individual's personal records if there is evidence they are conducting illegal activities from their home. Otherwise, it would be an infringement of an individual's civil rights."

Eileen considered his comment. She already felt like her civil rights had been infringed on to the max by the background check. She couldn't wait for this stupid investigation to be over, so she could regain some portion of her privacy. "So, if you find something on Nancy, you're done here?"

"No, I still need to systematically eliminate the other employees as accomplices."

Daniel's gaze was direct. "I want into Brock's files tomorrow."

She sighed, tired and fast becoming cranky. Daniel still

thought Brock was involved. "I know," she snapped. She realized she wanted that particular search over and done with, too. The sooner she could prove Brock's innocence, the sooner she'd be a happy camper in this FBI prison Daniel had forced her into. And the sooner life could return to normal.

***

Eileen managed two hours of a heavy, dreamless sleep before her alarm jolted her awake at five-thirty that morning. After putting on a jogging bra and sweats, she downed a glass of orange juice and a muffin and headed out the door, her workout shoes and sweatshirt still in her hand.

She tiptoed across the chilly terra cotta tiles of *Deviazione's* dark courtyard, the cold seeping through her socks. She quickly shrugged into her sweatshirt. The timed accent lights had already shut off, and the winter sun was still at least an hour from making an appearance. But the perpetual glow from the surrounding city gave off enough light to make out details.

Pausing a moment, she breathed in the crisp air, enjoying the peaceful quiet. Only the velvet splash of the fountain could be heard, the usual chatter of the resident birds now silenced as they slept. For some reason, this morning she felt a renewed energy. She was sure the sleep-depravation from pulling a double shift then getting up so early would catch up to her soon enough.

The freshness of the morning invigorated her, and Eileen found she actually looked forward to the challenge of the self-defense class. She crept on, enjoying the sensation of feeling like a lone shadow moving silently through the night.

The suddenness of a hand gripping her arm caused her to yelp with a start.

"It's only me." The raspy whisper was close to her ear.

She immediately recognized Daniel's touch and his unmistakable masculine scent.

Somewhere in the back of her mind Eileen had been prepared for Daniel to find out about her class and show up. But she hadn't prepared for him pouncing on her like this, and it both frightened and angered her. First, he had nearly maimed her twice with his well-placed moving boxes. Now he'd tried to cause a heart attack! Was the man out to kill her, or what?

She jerked out of his grasp, whispering a harsh, "One of these days, Daniel!" Although they both knew she was powerless to carry out her threat, the look of speculative surprise on his face gave her some measure of satisfaction.

"Clandestine meeting so early?" Although he'd lowered his deep voice to an intimate level, to Eileen it rumbled like thunder through the sleeping courtyard.

"Shhh!" She looked around to see if any lights went on in the surrounding apartments, but evidently she was the only one disturbed by Daniel this morning. She looked down, directing Daniel's gaze to her sweats. "Does it look like I'm going to a secret rendezvous? Or did you think I was skulking away on spy business?"

She could just make out the quirk of a smile. "Where you off to, then?" The deep gravel of his sleepy voice held a sexy quality that set up a tickle in her lower abdomen. Although she was chilly on the outside, her insides were quickly warming. Damn, she hated being near this man. She hated the way her senses short-circuited, leaving her as jumpy as if she'd touched frayed wires.

She steeled herself. "Nowhere that has anything to do with your investigation, Daniel. And quite frankly, nothing that's any of your business."

He didn't move. "Let me be the judge of that."

She huffed. Did the man need to know everything? She couldn't tell if caffeine deprivation, sleep deprivation, or inherent rudeness caused his gruff mood, but whatever it was, it was wearing off on her. "If you must know—and I want to interject here that I resent the intrusion—I'm going to the gym."

His eyebrows shot up. "Okay, I'll join you. Just let me change and get some—"

She pushed at his chest, trying not to register the feel of warm, hard muscle beneath his shirt. He didn't budge. She pushed harder, and he stepped back. "No, Daniel. This is a special class. A class for women only." As if Daniel needed a self-defense class. He probably had some kind of Rambo combat certificate. She started toward the arched throughway to *Deviazione's* parking lot, whispering loudly, "And, thanks to you, I'm going to be late."

Astonished and relieved by the silence behind her, she hurried to her car, started the engine and left before Daniel had a chance to reconsider.

When Eileen arrived at the gym she was surprised to find two men in the class she'd assumed was for women only. Although she couldn't picture Daniel in the lineup assembled on the large floor mat, the two men in attendance appeared very much at ease among the dozen or so women.

One of the men, a tall ebony-skinned man with a shaved head who towered above the group waved excitedly in her direction.

Eileen looked behind her, and finding only the closed double doors, turned back to him. Then she recognized him as one of her new neighbors, Gus Gustaufson. She remembered being mesmerized by his blue eyes when Mirabelle had introduced them. The blue eyes were a striking contrast to his flawless dark skin. Eileen had also been instantly taken with his open friendliness.

Returning his wave, Eileen went to stand next to Gus. "Hello. I didn't know you were taking this class. We could have driven over together."

He smiled warmly. "Lordy, girlfriend. If I had known you signed up for this crack-of-dawn torture, I'd have snagged a ride for sure. My Bug's been in the shop for over a week—I think the fickle thing is in love with my mechanic—and I hate taking the bus. Let's ride in together from now on, shall we? I'd love the company."

Gus was dressed impeccably in designer sweats, looking like he should be on the cover of a fashion magazine. Eileen felt frumpy next to him. Even though the sweats she wore were of good quality, they were old. She'd been going for comfort, knowing it would help get her though this challenging new situation.

She pushed her glasses up the bridge of her nose, tightened her topknot, and then rolled the waistband of her baggy sweatpants in an effort to tidy up.

The other man, who also towered above the women, walked

to the front of the room. Instantly, the crowd quieted.

"Hello and welcome. My name is Sergeant Mitch Sanders, and for the next couple of weeks I'll be your instructor." He directed his look to Gus. "Mr. Gustafson here is a former student who has generously agreed to be my assistant."

The sergeant, a powerfully built man, put his hands on his hips and walked back and forth as he continued. "By the time you finish this class, you will have learned techniques that will enable you to extract yourselves from almost any physical confrontation. My goal is to help you regain a sense of safety in this dangerous world."

The man's words echoed Mirabelle's. But Eileen had her doubts. Somehow she couldn't even see herself taking on skinny Michael from the office and coming out the winner, let alone being the slightest threat to Sergeant Sanders. Last night's episode with Daniel came to mind, and she just as quickly pushed it aside. She couldn't see herself attacking Daniel, no matter how much he infringed on her personal space. Besides, she'd never felt any physical danger from him—only emotional.

With a concentrated effort to put Daniel out of her mind, she looked around at the assembled group. One elderly, frail-looking woman with alarming purple and green marks on her forearms nodded validation of the sergeant's declaration as she waved her hand. She spoke in a surprisingly strong voice. "I'm proof. I took the sergeant's class several months ago and was, just two days ago, able to fight off a mugger with only," she proudly held up her arms for inspection, "a few bruises." She chuckled. "I'm back now for a refresher course."

A challenging, physically demanding hour later, Eileen and Gus headed out the door into the morning sunshine, Eileen's mind changed forever. She practically bounced to the car.

Gus chuckled. "Feeling pretty good, huh?"

Every nerve ending in Eileen's body buzzed. The adrenaline rush of the class had her talking a mile a minute. "Did you see? Did you? I really hurt him. I hurt the sergeant." Instantly she regretted her words. "Oh, that sounds terrible. But, he did say give it to him with all I had. He did say he'd been doing this for years, and that I couldn't hurt him. But I did, didn't I? You saw the look of surprise on his face, right?"

Gus laughed. "Oh, yeah, I saw. I don't think The Man of Steel will be tossing out challenges like that again real soon. Not with you, at least."

On the ride home, Eileen realized she was talking non-stop, not letting her companion get a word in edgewise, but she couldn't seem to help it. She said, "I feel so liberated, so empowered, and that's after only one class!"

Gus said, "Isn't that how Mirabelle said you'd feel?"

She came to an abrupt stop at a red light and turned to look at Gus. "How did you know?" Curiosity tempered her exhilaration.

He grinned. "I'm a," he hooked his fingers, "graduate."

She was confused. "I know, Sergeant Sanders told us you were a graduate of the self-defense class. But what has that got to do with Mirabelle?"

Gus laughed heartily. "No, I'm one of Mirabelle's graduates."

Eileen knew she was squinting even though she had her glasses on, but she was trying to discern if Gus was on the level. "You mean, as in, she granted your wish?"

"You got it, girlfriend." Gus pulled down the vanity mirror and checked his naked head. Eileen wasn't sure for what. He said nonchalantly, "The light's green."

She accelerated too hard and had to brake with a jerk to maintain a safe distance from the car in front of her. Taking a deep breath, she concentrated on matching her speed with the flow of traffic and found herself shaking her head. She wasn't actually prepared to believe Gus. Was she? Maybe he was just teasing her because he'd heard of Mirabelle's claims.

"You are kidding, right?"

He put up his hand as if to take an oath. "On my dear departed Grandy Gustaufson's soul."

Curious, she asked, "What was your wish?"

Gus gave her a sideways glance. "Don't laugh. Everyone has different dreams, different wishes."

Now she was more curious than ever. "I won't laugh."

When she shot a quick glance his way, she saw that Gus

had turned toward her. "I've always wanted to bring out the beauty in people, to help them believe in themselves. Now I do. I," he waved his hand to encompass all of LA, "make the stars shine." He laughed. "I'm a personal style consultant. Many of my clients are movie stars."

"Exactly what is it you do for them?" She wanted to ask why he needed Mirabelle's help in something that sounded so practical, but held off for the moment.

She saw him smile contentedly. "I help people look their best. I have a passion for finding just the right look for people. Everyone is an individual, and I help them find their 'style.'"

Eileen wondered what his opinion of her 'look' was. "How did Mirabelle help you become a style consultant? Isn't that something you could do without a Granter?"

He sobered. "I could have, if I had believed in myself and been on my intended path. Her magic helped me find myself. Helped me to discover—rediscover really—what I truly wanted." She glanced over and saw him tilt his head, his eyes unfocused, as though remembering. "For a time I thought I wanted fame, that recognition spelled success. I gave acting a shot and did modestly well. But, as Mirabelle helped me see, I'd lost sight of what I really wanted." Then his words became passionate. "I've always loved to create, as well as help people. Mirabelle helped me find my way back to that road.

"Now I find incredible satisfaction in helping people recover themselves. Most of us lose ourselves along the way, you know? I help people recover their hidden, natural strengths, show their natural beauty, the real person behind all the fears and insecurities. And who doesn't want a really kick-butt image? An image that shouts, 'I'm someone special. I love life and life loves me.'"

Eileen said, "It sounds like you've found your *forte*."

"Yes," he said. As Eileen pulled into a *Deviazione* parking space she noticed Gus plucking at his chin and looking at her speculatively. "You know, I don't see you with long hair at all." He rubbed his bald head.

She knew her eyes widened in fright as she looked at his head. "You look great, Gus, but I'm not that adventurous."

He brushed aside her comment with the wave of his hand. "No, silly woman. After what I saw this morning in class, 'sassy' is the image that comes to mind. Yep, the three S's: sassy, smart, sexy."

Eileen couldn't help enjoying the compliment. Although she'd like to think of herself as all those things, she'd never seen herself as sassy or sexy. Sexy was Alyssa's department, while 'smart' seemed to be Eileen's niche. But after this morning's success in the self-defense class, she might reconsider the 'sassy' label.

When Eileen walked with Gus through the archway into the peaceful *Deviazione* courtyard at seven-thirty, it was to a blissfully Daniel-free space. All the way home she had it in the back of her mind that Daniel would be sitting, coffee in hand, at his front patio's wrought-iron table, waiting like a disgruntled father. He must still be asleep. Eileen breathed a sigh of relief.

Mirabelle joined her and Gus as they stopped to say good-bye at the fountain. "Hello, dears. How did your class go?"

"Great," Eileen said. "I'm fast becoming a believer." She realized she meant it. She really was beginning to believe in Mirabelle and Wishmakers. This morning had pumped her up, giving her a new outlook on life, making her ready to believe anything was possible. Maybe she should change her wish from finding true love to making Daniel and the whole FBI investigation disappear. She was ready to settle for being Brock's right-hand-woman—and forgetting her dream of Brock falling in love with her—if it would take the threat away from him and Wincomp.

Eileen watched as Mirabelle's eyebrows dipped. "You must remain on track, my dear. Focus on your wish as you go through the steps toward Granting. Second-thinking your goal is like Snow White taking a bite from the poison apple. It will sidetrack you for far too long."

Eileen was beginning to believe, too, that Mirabelle really could read her mind.

Mirabelle looked at her speculatively. "Would you like to begin step two? You can overlap the steps as long as you give them their due. Don't short-change any of the steps. There are lessons to be learned."

Eileen nodded. "I'd like that. If it's anything like the self-defense class, bring it on, I'm ready."

Mirabelle and Gus both laughed.

"Your next step is," Mirabelle said, "to recover your sense of connection with the universe."

Eileen kept her doubts in check this time, deciding to give Mirabelle's suggestions an open mind, since the last one was working out so well. "Go on."

"Think for a moment, don't answer right away. Have you ever received—or given—unconditional love?"

She knew in her heart that her father's love—although she tried to secure it in everything she did—was clouded by outside influences. She couldn't with certainty say her father's love for her was unconditional, although her love for him had been. Her mother? "Yes," she answered. "Although my mother died when I was a child, what I remember of her, her love always felt unconditional."

Mirabelle's eyes held a moment of sympathy, then they brightened. "Yes, it was, wasn't it? Good. Now hold on to that feeling. I want you to concentrate on giving that feeling to everyone you meet for the next week. No matter how much you've disliked them in the past, or how little you know them, I want you to look at that person and think, 'I love you for the part you play in the universe.' Don't judge what their part is, just accept them for who they are. Can you do that?"

Inwardly she cringed as she thought about Alyssa and Jeannette. "Everyone?"

Mirabelle and Gus said together, "Everyone."

"A whole week?"

The confirming chorus came through loud and clear. "A whole week."

Mirabelle added, "If it's not from the heart, it won't work. Remember, try not to second-guess their place in the universe. Just accept it and give them unconditional love from your heart. After a week of focused thought, it will become second nature."

Eileen said, "Kinda like the whole 'love thy neighbor' thing, huh?"

Mirabelle nodded with satisfaction.

Sleep deprivation was taking hold, and dreamy thoughts of unconditional love took on a surreal quality. It sounded doable. "Okay, I'll try."

Gus said, "You can do it. I did. I forgave my former manager of robbing me blind. I realized his duplicity forced me to take care of myself. I had to thank him for taking on the role of the jerk in order to teach me an important life lesson. I forgave and learned to love my controlling mother. I realized her fears make her who she is."

Eileen could see a vague kind of logic in what Gus was saying, although she couldn't apply it to either her stepmother or stepsister. Maybe she could avoid them for the next week.

Mirabelle said, "This unconditional love must be given in word, deed, *and* thought. Or it doesn't work."

"Okay, I'll give it my best shot." This should be interesting, she thought.

"You get some sleep. When you wake up, refreshed and glad to be alive, remember my words and start giving that unconditional love to the very first person you see. Then keep it up. As I said, after a week, it will become second nature." Eileen started to leave, then looked back at Mirabelle. "And what's the point of this again?"

"Reconnecting with the universe, tapping into its positive power. That power is like an energy source; the more you give, the more it is perpetuated. This energy has the power to transform."

"Unconditional love. Power. Energy. Perpetuate. Transform. Got it." Eileen waved and nodded as she urged her sluggish legs to move, making a beeline toward satin pajamas and her comfy bed.

***

Mirabelle said good-bye to Gus and hurried into her apartment to switch on her computer. She logged onto Wishmakers and accessed Mary's web page. Mary came on immediately, and Mirabelle put on her headset.

"Hello, Mirabelle."

Mirabelle said, "I've just given Eileen Pringle the Second

Step."

"Wonderful."

"Well, yes, but I felt another energy blip. Was that from her?"

Mary sighed. "Yes. It's what we expected might happen. Until you grant, we will most likely all feel Eileen's energy levels fluctuate."

Mirabelle said, "I'm not even going to worry about it. I just know she's on the path to enlightenment—and her wish."

"I know we can count on you. And since granting for Eileen means, well, everything to us all, the network would like to be kept up on her progress."

"Of course. I'll send out daily bulletins."

Mirabelle signed off. Eileen would soon enter a critical stage of the granting process, and Mirabelle was afraid Daniel Collins was going to jeopardize success. Mirabelle had worked so hard to set things up. But Daniel Collins was too smart for his own good, and much closer than he should be at this point to completing his investigation. Mirabelle couldn't let that happen just yet. She needed more time for Eileen to get further into her Steps. What Mirabelle needed was a monkey wrench to throw into that investigation or, she was afraid, all was in danger of being lost.

Mirabelle hummed as she turned back to her monitor and keyboard and began to weave her magic.

SIX

Sleep Deprivation did strange things to some people. Daniel wasn't sure it completely explained Eileen's weird behavior. When he knocked on her door at five-thirty in the evening to see if she was ready to go in to Wincomp, she gave him a friendly smile, and her voice exuded a syrupy, "Daniel, how nice to see you. I hope you slept well."

He gaped at her, speechless. She'd never disguised the fact that she didn't care for him or the investigation, so why the sudden change? He began to wonder if she'd taken a trip to Stepford instead of gym class that morning.

Finally he asked, "What are you up to?"

Momentarily she seemed offended by his accusation, but the frown forming across her forehead quickly vanished. "Nothing, Daniel." She unconsciously touched her nose in what he'd learned in training indicated deceit. "I just thought that this evening it would be nice if we started off on a better foot. I'll get my purse and a coat, then we can go."

"Sure." As he watched her walk to her bedroom, he reached inside the door to switch on the porch light.

He didn't know what she might be up to with the obviously calculated effort to make nice, but he felt certain he could keep up the game longer than she could. Although he'd begun to enjoy being with Eileen, he knew she still considered him the enemy. That made it only a matter of time before her true feelings surfaced. He got a mental image of the creature in *Alien* ripping its way to freedom.

It would, however, be interesting to see how long Eileen could maintain her pleasant attitude toward him since just about everything he did seemed to bring out the beast in her. He had to admit he enjoyed seeing her temper flare, loved the way her eyes flashed and her face became animated, and he provoked her into unleashing her emotions whenever he had the chance.

Once they were in the car and on the road, Eileen glanced toward him as she drove. "Daniel, tell me about your family."

He knew the look on his face showed incredulity. "My family? Why?"

"I'd like to know more about you." With her soft, coaxing voice she reminded him of a psychologist trying to convince a patient he could feel safe in 'sharing.' "I want to know why you became an FBI agent. You know, what makes you...you."

Besides the fact that sharing personal information with someone who was part of his investigation went against Agency policy, Daniel wasn't a 'sharing' kind of guy.

He ticked off some innocuous personal details with as much enthusiasm as he'd have reading a rap sheet. "I grew up in an average kind of family. I've had an average kind of life. I became an agent because it sounded like interesting work."

"How interesting." Could that be an edge of sarcasm in her voice? He looked at his watch. Evidently the Stepford serum had a shelf life of about ten minutes.

"If you say so," he said as she negotiated a left turn.

She took a deep breath, looking like she might be doing a mental cool-down count to ten. "It's okay if you don't want to tell me. I just thought it would be more pleasant working on this investigation together if we knew something about each other."

Her reference to working together made Daniel realize that's just what they were doing. What started out as Daniel asking Eileen for one small favor had turned into a full-fledged partnership. An unorthodox partnership, to be sure, what with them on opposite sides of the fence, but a partnership nevertheless.

And as far as getting to know one another, Daniel knew

more about Eileen than she probably knew about herself. He knew she adored her father, even though the guy didn't deserve it. He knew that Eileen's mother had died when Eileen was a small child, and Eileen's care had fallen to a series of nannies. Then her father hooked up with Jeannette Barden, a woman whose primary focus in life appeared to be promoting her own social status as well as that of her daughter, Alyssa. From that point on, Eileen seemed to become a second-class citizen in her own family. Daniel knew Eileen had basically grown up alone and found solace in computers. He knew she'd been stuck on Brock Van Buren for most of her life, and that, just like her father, Van Buren didn't deserve her.

Daniel went ahead and asked a question anyway, mostly to deflect the focus. "Now it's your turn to tell me about you."

She looked taken aback for a moment, and then seemed to center inward as she focused on the traffic. "Me?" Her shoulder moved in a slow shrug. "There's nothing to tell."

"Come on, how about vacations? Summer camp? Pets? Best friends? College? What do you remember about your mother?" Now who was acting the psychologist? Talking about her mother could be a sensitive subject for her.

Along with a small measure of surprise, he felt a healthy helping of self-reproach when she began to talk in a wistful voice. "I only remember a few things about my mother. I remember thinking she was beautiful, although I can't really get a clear picture of her now."

He looked at Eileen, studying the woman hidden behind the big glasses and the loose-fitting clothes. His pulse raced. Yes, he could believe she had a beautiful mother. "I'm sure she was," he found himself saying. He quickly added, "Anything else you remember about her?"

Eileen gave him a funny glance, as if she suspected his motives, but she went on. "Strange, but even though I can't really remember her face, I do remember her reading me fairy tales. Oh, and she used to sing to me. I remember the song. It was the Kenny Loggins song, 'House On Pooh Corner.' Do you know it?"

Daniel couldn't answer for a few moments. His own mother

used to sing "House On Pooh Corner" to him and his brothers.

He cleared his throat. "I know it."

"I know my mother didn't want to die, but for the longest time after she did, I was angry with her for leaving me alone. I refused to listen to the song, even though my father bought me the CD. It was his big effort to help me sleep." This time her shrug seemed dismissive. "I had trouble sleeping."

Daniel couldn't find stable emotional footing with the uneasy direction of this conversation. But this side of Eileen wasn't in the Agency report, and he wanted to know more. He clenched his jaw and let Eileen continue.

"I thought by refusing to listen to the song I could punish her. I remember thinking that she was up in heaven, looking down, and she would know I didn't need her or the song."

Eileen's soft chuckle surprised Daniel. "Of course, I did need her and wanted more than anything on Earth to hear her sing that song again. My stepmother, Jeannette wasn't exactly the sing-you-to-bed type, so her marriage to my father kind of ended any dreams of 'House on Pooh Corner' bedtimes."

Daniel took a deep breath, relieved they were pulling into Wincomp's nearly deserted parking lot. He could avoid reciprocating or commenting on her openness. Thinking about how Eileen had been deprived of so many years with her mother, he couldn't help comparing her life to his, where he'd grown up with two loving parents. The comparison left him feeling strangely guilty and sad. As she parked the car, he shook off the feeling.

Daniel remained lost in thought as they walked in silence into the impressive glass and steel building housing Wincomp's offices. He'd often noticed that the punctual five o'clock exodus of the building's various companies' employees took on the immediacy of ants pouring out of a burning anthill. Now, at nearly six o'clock, only a few stragglers remained, along with the evening security guard, a man Eileen had introduced the previous night as Jim Stewart.

A short, plump man in his forties, Jim was the antithesis of his movie-star namesake. Sitting at his tall desk, which stood sentinel between the two elevators, a smiling Jim swiveled the sign-in book used for off-hours visitors and employees toward them, opening the book to a fresh page.

Eileen had whispered as they entered the building that during Jim's after-hours shift the man knew exactly who occupied the building at all times. Jim obviously took pride in his work. Daniel made a mental note to get to know Jim better when Eileen wasn't around. The hacker could very well have gone into Wincomp in the evening.

When Daniel and Eileen exited the elevator at the fifth floor, they found Brock still working in his office. Eileen looked briefly at Daniel with concern, and then headed through Brock's office door. For the three weeks Daniel had been at Wincomp, Brock hadn't made it a practice of putting in late hours.

Daniel stood silently in the doorway and watched Eileen walk over to stand next to Brock. The guy seemed distracted but happy to see Eileen.

Eileen said, "Working late?"

"Yes. We ... I've got some catching up to do. I also want to stay on top of this security probe. I've been neglecting Wincomp lately."

Daniel watched Eileen's eyebrow arch slightly. That expression had 'Alyssa' written all over it, but Eileen didn't say anything.

"Eileen, thanks for phoning in this morning to let me know how last night went," Brock said. "I'm heartsick to think Nancy might be our traitor."

Daniel and Eileen had agreed to let Brock know about Nancy's extra-curricular activities. Even though the information might possibly lead to proof in the FBI case, it could also uncover a motive for selling Wincomp's program. Unlike popular belief, it wasn't Agency policy to withhold information potentially crucial to a citizen's welfare merely because that information happened to be gathered during an Agency investigation.

Daniel spoke up. "We don't have proof. Only motive. We should be able to finish scanning Nancy's data tonight, and we'll let you know if we find anything conclusive on the case." Daniel cleared his throat as he realized he sounded like an agent and not like a mild-mannered, computer geek employee who'd been enlisted to help out the boss.

Brock shot him a speculative glance. "You're getting a kick out of playing detective, aren't you, Daniel? Maybe you're in the wrong line of work."

Daniel chose not to acknowledge Eileen's look of alarm as she glanced his way. No need to give Van Buren even the smallest reason to suspect the offhanded comment hit close to home. Daniel also quickly dismissed the idea Brock might be subtly revealing knowledge about the FBI investigation. The man's statement had been said without the slightest ambiguity.

As far as getting a kick out of playing detective? Daniel got more than a little kick out of uncovering hidden tracks left by criminals, then methodically obtaining hard evidence that would hold up in court. He found it the most challenging, satisfying work he'd ever done. But he wasn't about to tell Brock Van Buren that. "Just trying to help, Mr. Van Buren. As is Eileen."

Brock looked at Eileen as he took her hand. "Thanks again, Sweetheart, for being here for me."

Daniel saw the warm smile Eileen gave Brock, and his gut tightened with resentment as he realized the smile Brock returned contained about as much passion as the kind you gave your kid sister. Boss Man might really like Eileen, but he didn't come close to reciprocating the adoration glowing from Eileen's eyes.

Daniel wasn't sure what bugged him more. The fact that Brock had known Eileen most of his life and still couldn't see and appreciate the woman standing directly in front of him, or the fact that Brock remained the focus of Eileen's devotion. Heck, Daniel had only known her for a few days, and he could see she was something special.

Brock surprised them both by squeezing Eileen's hand and saying, "Alyssa is in your office, Eileen, working on plans for the New Year's Eve party."

Eileen squeaked an incredulous, "Now?" She whipped her hand from Brock's. "At my computer? How'd she get access?"

Brock waved off her concern. "I gave her your password. You know as well as I do, Alyssa isn't a threat."

Not to Wincomp, at least, Daniel thought.

Brock continued. "She needs a place to work on the party plans, and most times she'll come over during the day. As soon we find our thief and you go back to working days, we'll make other arrangements. You won't even know she's been here."

"But—my—" Eileen sputtered, obviously too flustered to form a cohesive thought. But the fatalistic resignation Daniel was fast becoming used to in Eileen never came. Instead Eileen squared her shoulders and crossed her arms, giving Brock a squinty look that, Daniel mused, looked capable of shooting lasers. Unfortunately, the priceless look went unnoticed by Brock since he'd already returned his attention to the blue-green glow of his computer screen.

As Brock scanned what looked to Daniel like a statistics page, he said, "Your programs are safe with Alyssa, Eileen. I know you've never gotten along with her, but she wouldn't do anything to hurt you, or," he emphasized, "Wincomp."

Daniel watched in fascination as Eileen made a concerted effort to relax her shoulders and roll the tension from her neck. She took a deep breath, seeming to nod some kind of affirmation to herself.

And when Daniel heard her calm voice, he knew the Stepford version of Eileen had won whatever battle had taken place inside her head. "Brock, I feel I should express my concerns over the fact that security protocol—protocol we set up together and put in place for a reason—has been set aside without consulting me. You did put me in charge of Wincomp's security. I don't think it's prudent, especially now, with what has been going on, to be even the tiniest bit lax about established policies. I have a stake in this company, too. I've put every penny I have into stock options, and I don't want to see it fail."

Daniel watched for Brock's reaction, but the man seemed more bothered than offended by Eileen's subtle attack. "I know this whole stolen-program thing has you upset. Me too. But what could Alyssa possibly do, with her limited knowledge of computers, to hurt Wincomp? She wouldn't know one program from another."

Eileen didn't appear to be placated. "Probably nothing. But I still think you should have discussed this with me beforehand."

Daniel knew Eileen had a valid point, and the fact Brock didn't seem the least bit worried concerned Daniel. Having security-cleared employees check up on fellow employees was one thing. But giving Alyssa, an outsider, privileged information and passwords, even if Brock might be in love with that outsider, didn't sound prudent for a company already experiencing a security breach.

Did Brock have an ulterior motive for letting Alyssa into Wincomp's inner workings? Was Brock giving her access so she could help him hack into government files? No, Daniel was certain Alyssa's lack of computer skills ruled that out. Was Brock, through Alyssa, setting up Wincomp to fail for insurance purposes? That didn't make sense, either. Daniel had read Wincomp's latest financial report and, although they were skating on thin ice because of the recent stolen program, they were still operating in the black. Besides, Brock could accomplish both the hacking and selling of the software without Alyssa's help. Each consideration ran into a dead end as far as a motive.

Still, he had to keep in mind that Alyssa might not know computers, but she certainly possessed intelligence enough to follow instructions given to her by someone else. And, Daniel thought, Eileen was right. It didn't make sound business sense for Brock to be so lax with security at such a tenuous time.

Brock said, "You're right, Eileen, I should have discussed this with you. I apologize. It won't happen again. But, for the record, and to put your mind at ease, Alyssa may soon—" He hesitated a moment, indecision written across his face, but then went on. "If I have my way, she may soon have a very personal stake in Wincomp's success."

Daniel expected to see shock on Eileen's face. Brock had as much as said he planned on asking Alyssa to marry him, if it wasn't already a done deed. Instead, Eileen just shook her head in what looked like disgust or maybe even sympathy, saying, "Daniel and I need to get to work."

Daniel stepped aside as Eileen walked past him and out into the hallway. Her step only hesitated a moment as she passed by her office's closed door and headed toward Nancy's workstation.

As Daniel followed, he realized he might as well give up on Brock having an ulterior motive in letting Alyssa have access to Wincomp files. If Brock planned on marrying Alyssa, the man was simply being the typical lust-sick guy and giving the woman he loved anything she asked for. This time it just happened to be access to her stepsister's computer. And, as Daniel had initially suspected, the only thing deceptive about Alyssa appeared to be certain cosmetic modifications and the intent to outshine Eileen in Brock's eyes.

Daniel expected Eileen to be fuming when he joined her in Nancy's cubicle, but he was mistaken. She seemed to have shrugged off the whole Alyssa fiasco and turned her full attention to Nancy's files. Her unexpected reaction left him feeling like he'd missed something. Why wasn't she more upset? What was going on inside that head of hers?

***

Mirabelle signed on to Wishmakers and connected to Mary immediately.

"Mary, we've made progress."

"I know. I felt the energy surge. What was it?"

"Eileen implemented both of the first two teachings to transcend a situation involving her stepsister and Brock Van Buren."

"Excellent," Mary said. "But, Eileen's handling of one small situation with aerial grace doesn't mean we're out of danger. True, it does restore a certain measure of power, but it doesn't take us out of critical status. Only a Granting can do that. Every day without granting saps more and more of our already meager energy reserves."

Mirabelle knew that Granters worldwide waited in the silent hope that Eileen would grant before time ran out and Wishmaker's energy was depleted forever.

"Mirabelle, you're going to have to give her the remaining 'Steps' ASAP, whether she's ready or not."

"Oh, after today, I know Eileen's ready. She's focused. And she's overcome her initial hesitancy. I believe she's ready and willing to go all the way to get her wish. She's still questioning certain things—not sure which path to take—but I've got plans to straighten her out."

Mary said, "We're all standing by if you need help."

"I've got the new trainee, Gus Gustaufson, who you approved. For now, we're okay."

"Don't hesitate to bring the forces together if need be."

Mirabelle was reluctant to enlist total power, knowing it would be a go-for-broke event. She said, "We don't need total power yet. Just a few 'nudges' in the right direction—not enough to deplete us—and I'm sure Eileen's wish will be within reach."

"I'll sign off, then," Mary said. But before she logged off, she added, "Oh, one more thing. Keep in mind that this year the Winter Solstice falls on a quarter moon."

Mirabelle said, "I know. A time of cosmic renewal. I'm so excited for this spectacular opportunity. I'm already making preparations, in hopes of bringing Eileen to granting that evening. Things will start with my party this Saturday and culminate in a spectacular grant a week later, on the Winter Solstice. The additional power would be such a bonus."

"I know it's a longshot, but if she kisses the man she loves during that evening's energy shift, all energies will be focused on her. Not only will she grant, Wishmakers will be out of danger for at least a hundred years. If she doesn't, we will still have until midnight New Year's Eve to at least Grant her wish and give Wishmakers a reprieve."

Mirabelle said, "I'll give it everything I've got." She didn't add that she still wasn't a hundred percent certain whether Brock or Daniel was the one Eileen should kiss.

***

After booting up the computer, Eileen turned to Daniel who had snagged a chair from the adjoining workstation and rolled it in to seat himself behind her. She kept her voice low even though both Alyssa and Brock occupied offices on the other side of the room, out of earshot. "Doesn't look like you're going to get to Brock's terminal tonight, either."

Daniel gave her a questioning look. She could tell he wasn't buying her effort to be pleasant. Little did he know she was trying her best to see him as a person and give him the kind of unconditional love Mirabelle had talked about. Not the romantic love she felt for Brock, but the simple, uncomplicated love one feels for a fellow human being—a friend.

Continuing to look at her strangely, he said, "I have a feeling Brock and Alyssa will be long gone by the time we finish here."

Eileen couldn't blame Daniel for any suspicions he might have about whether or not schizophrenia ran in her family. Ever since her talk with Mirabelle and the 'unconditional love' assignment she'd been given, her attitude toward Daniel had, out of necessity, been consciously changed.

She found it amusing that putting aside old hurts and angers hadn't been all that difficult. She'd been able to generate some genuine kind thoughts for Daniel, as well as, surprisingly, for Alyssa. On the other hand, her feelings for Brock had somehow shifted, too, but in a disconcerting way.

She still dreamed of Brock falling in love with her. But now, like a puzzle with missing pieces, the unconditional love Mirabelle spoke of couldn't find a snug fit with the love she'd always felt for him. The feelings seemed somehow miles apart. But love was love, wasn't it?

Knowing she didn't have time to analyze the question, she logged on to the Internet and returned to the area they'd left the previous night.

As she scrolled through the data Nancy had stored with her online carrier, she asked, "Daniel, what happens to the rest of Wincomp's data banks when you find the hacker?"

"If Nancy is the lone perpetrator, nothing. The Agency doesn't want to put innocent citizens out of work. We only want to stop the hacker. Wincomp will go on much as before, only with better security in place. I'm sure you'll see to that."

She shivered involuntarily as she felt Daniel's breath against her hair. His closeness radiated warmth.

Forcing herself to ignore the unsettling distraction, she said, "I haven't told anyone, not even Brock, but the project I'm entering in Wincomp's New Year's Eve contest is a new security program. I was hoping to hold off unveiling it until the party, but with our present problem—"

Daniel's voice rumbled from behind her. "Sounds like you'd

be jeopardizing quite a big prize. You can't wait for three weeks?"

"Our 'secret' projects are supposed to remain secret to everyone, except Brock of course, until he announces the winner at the party," she stated. "We're expected to turn them in for judging at the end of this week. But I'm afraid if I don't install the program at Wincomp, and our hacker finds out about the investigation, he could sabotage the entire computer network here, just to cover up his crime. Winning the stock shares won't do me much good if the company goes under because of poor security."

"Kind of a Catch-22, huh? How about we work together on a temporary security system that will get the company through until your new program is launched?"

"Thanks. That would be great. I really need that prize." *'Need' might not be the most accurate word*, she thought to herself. Surely she could live without the added stocks, but she definitely wanted them. For her they spelled independence and financial security. Then she could stop worrying about her father's will and whether or not Jeannette had deliberately withheld money intended for her.

She asked, "Not to change the subject, but when in this investigation do you intend to give me the information you have on my stepmother?"

"Now if you want it," he said, causing her fingers to still over the keyboard.

"Oh, I want it." She gave Daniel her full attention.

His mouth quirked as he looked into her eyes, seeming to search for something, and then he blinked and replaced the look with business-like aloofness. "Your stepmother's attorney, Miles Catchum, is about as shady as they come. He's been accused of falsifying records several times, but he's managed to keep one step ahead of actually going to court. Some plaintiffs dropped their charges. In other cases evidence wasn't substantial enough to go to trial. But, you can be sure if Miles Catchum is involved there's something fishy going on."

Eileen already knew the deceptively charming Miles put the "con" in conspiracy, but what could she do about it without evidence? "That doesn't sound like much of a case."

Daniel smiled. "Not yet. But the courts take a seriously dim view of questionable attorneys. You challenge the will, and I guarantee the court will put the estate in probate and investigate. What they're going to find is that your so called, 'stepmother,' never divorced her first husband."

Eileen stared in disbelief. "I thought he was dead."

"That's probably what Jeannette would like, but the man is still very much alive. And better for you—he's still very much her husband."

"How can that change the will, if Jeannette's name is on joint-property papers?"

"From the one document I saw in the agency report, she signed them under the name of Pringle. The agency wasn't able to obtain record of a marriage certificate. If she and your father were never married, then she signed under a false name, and she did it knowingly. The papers aren't legal. And the quasi-marital, or common-law, statutes don't apply to Jeannette since she's still married to her first husband. Beyond all that, if there is a marriage certificate, bigamy charges alone would kick Jeanette out of the will."

Eileen tried to sort through all he'd said. Jeanette a bigamist? The thought of Jeannette being prosecuted and possibly sent to jail gave Eileen an uneasy feeling. No matter what slights she'd received from Jeannette over the years, Eileen didn't want the woman to go to jail.

"How did you find out she wasn't divorced?" Why would the Agency go into such depth on a suspect's family background? The feeling of violation she'd felt when she'd first found out about the background check now resurfaced. What other secrets did The Agency, and Daniel, know about her?

"You were fortunate I got an Agency trainee doing background checks. She went into much more detail than necessary, partly to familiarize herself with the Agency databases and partly because once you uncover something out of the ordinary, it's prudent to dig a little deeper to find out if it relates to the case."

"Somehow, I don't feel fortunate," Eileen stated. "I just feel violated. My privacy was taken away, too, when your trainee did her digging. Do you know what that feels like, Daniel?"

He said, "No I don't. And I'm sorry, but it had to be done. National security is at stake here."

She didn't feel any less violated, but she did see his point.

"You did want the information about Jeannette, didn't you?"

"Yes," she had to admit.

"Of course, the Agency investigation files can't be used in your petition because this hacking case, even if it never goes to trial, will be ongoing for some time. All of our records pertaining to the case will remain confidential until it concludes. But the information I've given you can get you started. All you have to do is contest the will and, because of Catchum's shady past, the judge will automatically investigate. It wouldn't hurt to let the judge know you suspect Jeannette is legally Jeannette Barden, not Jeannette Pringle."

Eileen felt an uneasy yet excited thrill. Although she didn't want to hurt anyone, she felt vindicated in contesting the will. What she wanted most was to prove to herself her father hadn't intentionally disinherited her. Or if he had, then why? Maybe now she had a chance to obtain access to her father's house and try to find another will, if there was one. The thought lifted her spirits. Things were definitely looking up. And, she had to admit, Daniel was the reason.

She looked at his smiling face, and the words were out of her mouth before she could stop them. "Daniel, I could just kiss you."

His smile faded and his gaze became intense, although his voice held a teasing tone as he said, "You don't want to be accused of sexual harassment at the workplace, but I'm game if you are."

Eileen found herself growing warm under his scrutiny. Could this be just another James Bond move, meant to throw her off guard? Or could she believe the attraction she saw in his eyes?

All she knew was she now understood Nancy's behavior that night at the restaurant. Against her will, Eileen felt herself responding to Daniel's practiced charm.

Her pulse raced as she said, "We'll leave it at 'thank you.'"

She might be responding physically to attention from an attractive man, but her heart still longed to be with Brock.

Eileen turned back to the terminal, but the tension between them remained.

Two awkward, strained hours later, Daniel sighed as Eileen turned off Nancy's computer and swiveled around to face him.

He said, "We can check Nancy off our list. The only crimes she's committed are bad judgement and stealing company time to conduct personal business."

Relief washed over Eileen. She truly liked Nancy and didn't want her to be guilty of either hacking or stealing. But, then, she didn't want to find anyone guilty. "I'm sure an interoffice memo about using company time for personal business will do the trick as far as her extra-curricular activities. So, what now?"

Daniel studied her, his face unreadable. "Why don't we split up? You know what I'm looking for in my investigation, so scan for both the hacker and the thief. I'll do a double search, too. You're under no obligation to work for the Agency, but it would make both our jobs easier. Keep in mind, my hacker and your thief could be one and the same."

Eileen actually felt disappointment at Daniel's suggestion that they split up. But she quickly shook off the feeling. She wanted her life back as soon as possible, didn't she? "Sure. Sounds like a plan."

She got up and craned her neck to see if Brock's door remained open, but found it closed. Her office door, on the other hand, now stood open. "Brock and Alyssa must have left. You want to take Brock's office, I'm sure. Do you have a preference about who I choose?"

She saw a shadow of doubt move across his eyes, but it quickly faded. She felt like she'd said something unwitting, but she had no idea what it was.

"We'd both like to find the right one," he said, and the edge he gave to the words gave them a double meaning. "Put aside your fears, your prejudices and old friendships, and go with whomever your gut tells you is the right one. One thing's for sure, you won't find him, or her, with emotional blinders on."

She had to mentally shake herself to dispel the notion that what he said made reference to himself instead of the investigation.

Before she put more nonsensical meaning into Daniel's words, she hurried past him and headed toward Ray's cubicle. Not because she placed the guilt on Ray, but because his workspace stood far away from Brock's office and Daniel.

***

Daniel had barely gotten into scanning Brock's e-mail when he heard Eileen's shriek from across the quiet room. He hurried out to investigate.

When he reached Ray Mitchell's cubicle he came to an abrupt halt. He found Eileen sitting back in her chair, eyes wide, her teeth clenched hard on the side of her finger. She looked like she was watching a Stephen King movie. He saw her squeeze her eyes shut, and he turned his gaze to the computer screen.

Daniel's jaw dropped open as he watched the nightmare unfold. Scrambled images gyrated across the screen. A computer virus busily ate away at Ray's hard drive and, presumably, all the data contained there. Stephen King would have been damn proud.

The questions Daniel wanted immediate answers to were: How did a virus infect Ray's hard drive when Wincomp ran a daily state-of-the-art anti-virus program? And, could the virus have been intentionally injected into Ray's system from someone inside Wincomp? Or had Ray installed it as a safety net in case someone got into his computer? The virus would destroy any evidence of guilt.

Daniel looked at Eileen. His entire body went rigid. His heart took a dive off a fifty-foot cliff, straight into black, treacherous waters. He clenched his jaw against fears and the inevitable pain he didn't want to acknowledge. But the truth of those fears raced up to meet him. The impact forced the air from his lungs and sent a prickling rush of adrenaline through his body.

And he realized that more than anything in the world he didn't want to believe the guilt he saw in Eileen's eyes.

SEVEN

Eileen couldn't believe what she was seeing. She didn't *want* to believe what she was seeing. Peeking at Ray's screen, she quickly closed her eyes again. She could feel Daniel's tension from behind her, but she couldn't bring herself to turn and look at him.

Quickly she reached over to turn off the terminal and stop the virus, although she knew that was about as effective as halting a runaway train by shouting, "Stop!" She felt like she was standing directly in the path of this particular racing locomotive.

With all the security measures she'd put into place at Wincomp and with all the warnings she'd issued about viruses to every Wincomp employee, how could this be happening? What kind of Security Director was she if something like this could get through?

Only one answer absolved her of the horrible guilt she felt. And the moment the initial shock of seeing the virus began to wear off, her mind quickly deducted that conclusion. Someone had injected the virus intentionally. And it had been directed at Ray's files for a reason. The person who had created this hungry monster to gobble up Ray's files—and any possible evidence of foul play—had to be someone inside Wincomp. In order for the virus to gain access, Eileen's virus-scan program had to have been disarmed, and that meant only someone with first-hand knowledge of the anti-virus program—someone inside Wincomp—could have done it. Her logical mind came up with only one name. Ray. But her heart quickly pushed that thought aside. It just couldn't be Ray. But at the same time, it had to be Ray.

Staring at the dark screen she realized that, until this very moment, she'd been living under the illusion she would somehow be able to prove not only Brock's innocence, but the innocence of all her co-workers as well. In the back of her mind she'd naively held onto the belief that Daniel and the FBI had made a mistake. What an idiot she had been!

Once again, her confidence shaken, she didn't know whom she could trust. Ray was a dear friend, and the faith she'd placed in that friendship became blurred. What if he had done this? And if she could no longer trust her instincts about Ray, then could she be certain of her own judgement when it came to her other friends and co-workers? Anger born of hurt and betrayal formed a painful knot in her chest.

Finally she swiveled her chair around and faced Daniel. The sharp accusation she saw his eyes made her realize he thought she had injected the virus. Something inside her snapped.

A hot flush crept up her neck to burn her cheeks as her righteous anger at the saboteur found a new focus. "Listen, Daniel Collins, or Daniel Manatucci, or whatever the hell your name is, I didn't do this. For all I know, you did it yourself. You had access," she accused, even though in her heart she knew he hadn't done it. But she couldn't help lashing out. "Maybe you're not an FBI agent at all, but some nutcase who gets his jollies by infiltrating and destroying software companies."

Standing up, she paced the cubicle's confining space, her arms folded tightly across her chest. Her tone scathing, she said, "You have the know-how. Why am I a more likely candidate than you? I have more to lose than almost anyone in this company." She put her fingers to her temples and looked back to the silent terminal, her voice suddenly weak. "God, this can't be happening."

And then Eileen did something she hadn't done since she was a child, something she hadn't even done when her father died. She began to cry. After a sharp catch in her breath, the floodgates burst open with a loud sob. With tear-blurred vision she saw the shock on Daniel's face. But no one was more shocked, or mortified, than Eileen.

The more she tried to stop herself, the more violent the sobs became. She knew she should do something—run to the restroom, cover her face, anything—but she couldn't seem to move. She just stood there with her fingers glued to her temples, trying to catch her breath, while an obviously distraught Daniel looked on. As she realized she no longer knew whom she could trust, the sense of betrayal snowballed.

Daniel said, "Hey, okay, so I believe you." He jumped up and grabbed enough tissues from a box on Ray's desk to dry up Niagara Falls. He held them at arm's length, as if afraid to get close. "Sit down. Take a deep breath, or something. Put your head between your knees."

With a loud hiccup her sobs came to an abrupt halt, and she dissolved into giggles. She looked at the frantic Daniel and, between bouts of hilarity, asked, "Since when ... did putting your head ... between your knees help hysterics?"

He shrugged, obviously chagrinned. "I panicked. I grew up in a house full of guys." He still held the fistful of tissues toward her, and his expression became cautious, as if she might relapse into tears.

Taking pity on him, she accepted the tissues, plucking a few sheets from the ball and tossing the rest in the wastepaper basket.

Blowing her nose, she said through a ragged breath, "I'm glad you didn't slap me. I always see that in the movies."

Daniel pulled out the desk chair she'd jumped up from and indicated with a nod that she should sit down. He took the other chair and moved close, a determined frown furrowing his forehead. He took off his glasses. "My initial reaction was that you did it. Don't ask me why. I wouldn't have let you in on the investigation in the first place unless I felt ninety-nine-percent sure you were innocent. But, I have to admit, when I saw you sitting in front of Ray's terminal watching the virus, I could have sworn I saw guilt written all over your face."

Looking directly into his eyes, she said, "You did. At first I thought my security system somehow let in the virus. Daniel, I know for certain it had to be someone in this office. No one could have gotten past my virus scan without intentionally disarming it. That could only be done by someone who has access to my program. Someone operating from inside Wincomp. Someone with access to Ray's password."

Daniel's eyebrows rose as if to say, "Hello?"

It was her turn to look chagrinned. "I didn't want to believe it. But I do now. Daniel, I've just become as determined as you to find this person. This," she shot a glance around the office, "is my life. My future. I can't let it go down the tubes because I'm afraid to accept the possibility that one of my friends has played me for a sucker."

"You didn't seem this upset when Brock told us about the inside trading job."

She said, "That was different. I guess, somewhere in the back of my mind, I began to believe Ray could have sold off one of his own programs. He told me he felt under-appreciated at Wincomp. But I didn't think he was capable of hacking into government files, or of doing anything malicious," she nodded toward the screen, "like this. I thought the whole hacking thing was a mistake on your part."

"It's no mistake, Eileen."

"I know. I just didn't want to acknowledge anyone in my family—" She stopped mid-sentence. Her friends at Wincomp really were the only family she had. "I didn't want to believe I could have misjudged any of them so completely. I guess I've been forced to see I was wrong. Although something inside me still tells me it isn't Ray."

"Ray's got three strikes against him," Daniel reasoned. "Strike one: the guy's program is sold to the highest bidder. Strike two: his computer gets a convenient virus. Strike three: you said yourself Ray's felt under-appreciated as far as his work at Wincomp goes."

She said, "This is a man's life you're playing with here, not a game of baseball. I'm not counting him out just because you think he has three strikes, circumstantial strikes, I might add." She tried to think of another baseball analogy. "As far as I'm concerned it's still the first inning, and it's anybody's ballgame."

Daniel's mouth quirked. "All I'm saying—"

She closed her eyes, held up her hand and shook her head. "I know. It looks like Ray is guilty. But I'm not ready to believe it. I've known him a long time."

"Let's just keep our options open. For all we know, Ray could have been set up by someone who either knows about our investigation, or is trying to cover his tracks because he fears an investigation."

Her head shot up, and she opened her eyes to look at Daniel. "You really think it could be someone else?" But then her heart sank again as she realized that, if it wasn't Ray, the perpetrator still had to be someone she cared about.

"It's possible." He turned back to Ray's terminal, scooting his chair next to hers. "Let's see what's salvageable, and if Ray's backup disks are infected."

She said, "You go on back to Brock's files. I can handle this. It's going to take me a couple of hours to clean up his hard drive and reinstall his programs and data, providing they're okay." She began sorting through the security keys, searching for the one to unlock Ray's file cabinet. Part of the security system she had put in place dictated that each employee did daily backups and locked them in their individual file cabinets. She noticed only a split-second of hesitation before Daniel nodded and got up to leave. He really did believe her. Otherwise, he would never leave her alone with the possible hacker's files. Eileen felt an immense sense of relief, and she realized, it wasn't because an investigating FBI agent believed her. It was because Daniel believed her.

But then, the sudden revelation that it mattered to her what Daniel thought about her scared the hell out of her. What Brock thought about her didn't cause this fluttery anticipation in her stomach. *Get hold of yourself, girl,* she told herself. *Daniel is a dead-end street. Brock is your forever-after.*

***

At noon on Thursday Mirabelle sat with Gus at the small table on her front stoop, looking up at the ominous clouds.

He said, "Channel Five said clear skies for the next week."

"So did Channel Seven. What do they know about cosmic disturbances?" She pulled her shawl closer, watching the leaves blow across the courtyard tiles. "Eileen is upset about something. We need to move fast, or she may lose hope before we've barely begun."

"She should be out pretty soon. She usually sleeps for a few hours after our morning class, but hits the floor running about noon. She's been all over town gathering things for her apartment."

Just then they both turned toward Eileen's apartment as she emerged, dressed in gray wool slacks and a white turtleneck.

Mirabelle said, "She looks like she might be on her way to do just that." She waved Eileen over.

Eileen approached with a tired smile. "Hi you two. How's the Granting business going?"

Although she meant it as rhetorical, Eileen's question had both Gus and Mirabelle looking at each other sadly.

Glad the question didn't need answering, Mirabelle asked, "Where are you off to?"

"The bank, the car wash, and the grocery store. It's one of those run-around afternoons. There are some advantages to working the night shift." She walked up the steps and leaned against the stoop's low wall.

Mirabelle said, "If you have a moment, we need to talk."

Eileen's eyebrows arched. "Sure." She sat down.

"How," Gus asked, "do you feel you're doing with your first steps?"

"Pretty good, why?"

Mirabelle poured Eileen a cup of tea, then handed it to her. "Because it's time to go on to the next two."

"Great. I think I'm ready."

Gus said, "So do we."

Eileen looked at Gus. "I thought you were a graduate, not a Granter."

Mirabelle let Gus give Eileen the good news.

"I'm a trainee."

Eileen's eyes opened wide, then she frowned and quirked her head to the side. "You can do that? What kind of training do you have to have?

Mirabelle said, "Let's just say, it takes ... well, years."

"And years," Gus added. "But, it's what I want to do. I've tried many unusual and varied vocations in my life, and I've finally found my true calling. Of course, I'll include my talents as a style consultant along with it."

The look Eileen gave Gus said she didn't really understand. Thank Heaven she didn't ask, because the whole process—as well as authorization—was more than Mirabelle wanted to disclose.

Mirabelle said, "Are you ready for your next steps?"

"Yes." Eileen sat up straighter.

"You're well on your way to personal balance," Mirabelle stated. "And I can tell by the light in your eyes you now feel a connection with the universe. The next step comes under the heading of, 'Cause and Effect.' In other words, we reap what we sow. Work on learning to make conscious choices."

Eileen seemed to be thinking as she looked, unfocused, toward the fountain. "I thought I already did."

"Only sometimes." Mirabelle caught Eileen's gaze. "Have you ever had some crisis in your life and said to yourself, 'Why did this happen to me?'"

"Sure."

Mirabelle could tell Eileen related strongly to her question. She went on. "Well, what did you do about it?"

Eileen shrugged. "Nothing. I figured it was just fate, or Karma, whatever you want to call it."

"You're on track. Those events are your, for the sake of simplicity, let's use the word 'Karma.' But—and here's the task—how you deal with those events determines how they affect you as well as how you, then, affect others."

"I'm not sure what you mean."

Mirabelle said, "If you look at your crises as seeds of opportunity, or lessons, you can use them to better not only your life, but others' as well."

Eileen leaned forward. "So, take my problem at work—the inside trader. If I see it as a lesson or an opportunity and use it to make my life better, then I'm using the crisis in a positive way instead of a negative one."

"Yes. You become pro-active instead of reactive."

"How will I know what the right course is?"

Mirabelle put her hand over the one Eileen had on the table. "You have to remove yourself from the reactive world, and outside influences. Set aside all your fears and simply listen to your heart when life hands you tests."

"Ok. Become proactive when I'm faced with a problem—a test. Learn from it and then use that knowledge to help others."

"Very good, my dear."

"And the fourth task?"

"Follow the path of least resistance. See where your future is leading you, where your dreams truly are. If you come up against a brick wall, don't waste your energy trying to break it down. It may be there for a reason. Go around it."

"Wait. Getting Brock to love me is extremely difficult. But true love—Brock—is my wish. How do I *go around* him to get *to* him?"

Mirabelle couldn't help laughing. "I know it sounds confusing now. It will all become clear when you've completed your tasks. For now, go on faith."

Eileen's focus seemed to be inward. "Follow the path of least resistance."

Mirabelle said, "It might help to remember to do things for your spirit's sake, not for your ego's sake. The spirit's path is always easier."

Eileen laughed. "You mean, if it feels good, do it?"

"As cliched as it sounds, yes. If it feels good, and if it feels right, follow your heart."

Mirabelle could easily read the indecision on Eileen's face. The girl wasn't sure which man in her life to apply the rules to. A couple of days for Eileen to incorporate her new tasks and Mirabelle would be ready to intervene with a little magic. She crossed her fingers, praying nothing unforeseen happened to set Eileen back.

***

Four weeks into his investigation and a full week of working with Eileen Pringle, and Daniel felt disgusted with himself. Not only hadn't he come up with one clear lead, he also realized his efforts to remain emotionally uninvolved had failed miserably. Where Eileen was concerned, he'd come to accept the fact that he'd lost all objectivity. And that was a dangerous thing on an investigation.

Three times Daniel had walked to the phone on his kitchen counter, and each time turned and walked away again. Jerking open the curtains to the living room picture window, he stared into the courtyard, the tranquil early morning doing nothing to calm his agitation.

He knew what he had to do, but his gut wrenched each time he got close enough to the phone to make it a reality.

Finally, he seated himself at one of the barstools and picked up the receiver, dialing headquarters' number. He took a deep breath, thinking about Eileen as he waited for his boss to come on the line.

A voice said, "Pete Silva here."

"Hey, Pete. It's Daniel.

"*Hola!* friend. How's it going?"

"Not so hot. I want to request a replacement."

"Why, what happened? The virus destroy the rest of Wincomp's system?"

"No, just Ray Mitchell's, and there was no permanent damage done. The problem is, I'm—" He felt the professionalism he'd hoped to maintain during this particular talk with his boss and friend fly out the window. "Pete, I've got a problem."

"Throw it at me."

"It's one of the subjects." He knew his pause was too long, but it took a few moments to spit out what he had to say. "A woman."

He heard his boss chuckle. "From the sound of your voice, she's gotten under your skin. Knowing your aversion to honest-to-God relationships with women, I'm guessing you must be feeling like a cat with a fire cracker attached to his tail."

Daniel pulled the receiver away from his ear and looked at it. How had Pete guessed? He put the phone back to his ear. "I can't seem to keep professionally objective where she's concerned."

"Anything more to it?"

Daniel thought about when he'd almost kissed her. Innocent enough on the surface. He didn't have to reveal how it had messed with his head. He said, "Not yet. But if I keep working with her, I don't know ..." He left the thought unfinished, since he really didn't know what would happen. Although he knew what he'd like to happen, and that was definitely against Agency policy.

When he'd first started working with Pete Silva he would never have dared share such damning information, for fear of losing his job. But he and Pete had become good friends, and Daniel knew he wouldn't get censured.

"This isn't like you, Daniel. She must really be something. Wait, let me bring up the Wincomp file." Daniel heard the click of computer keys, then Pete continued. "We looking at a blonde or brunette?"

"Brunette. Eileen Pringle."

The ensuing moments of silence spoke volumes. Pete must be looking at the unflattering file pictures of Eileen. If Pete only knew the woman behind the big glasses and overpowering hair, he'd know the dilemma eating away at Daniel.

Finally Pete spoke, his words slow and deliberate. "Daniel, I thought you'd never fall in love. Why'd it have to be with someone off limits? Besides, I thought she had something going with Van Buren."

"I didn't say I'm in love with her!" He chose not to reply to Pete's reference to Van Buren. He had daily reminders that Eileen's heart belonged to The Jerk.

Pete said, "My friend, you don't know what love is."

"Let me guess. This is where you enlighten me. Again." Daniel knew Pete would, since he just loved to get sappy about his wife and kids.

The usual hard edge to Pete's voice always softened when he talked about his family. "Love is seeing your woman's head on the pillow next to yours every morning and feeling passion for her even though she's wearing flannel pajamas. Love is babies and laughter and tears and fighting and making up. It's when you can't wait to get home to that whole mess at the end of the day."

Daniel felt his stomach tighten. He didn't want to think about Eileen in that context. "It's not like that."

"You think about it, Buddy."

"I don't have to think about it. The situation here is bordering a protocol breach, that's all. I'd like a replacement."

Pete's sigh was drawn out. "Sorry, Buddy. No can do. All agents with your computer skills are on assignment. Seems everyone and his granny is hacking nowadays. I don't want to sound like I don't care about *el amor* problems, but I know you'll do the right thing."

So much for concerns about Agency protocol. As Daniel dropped the receiver into the cradle, he experienced a sense of relief that Pete hadn't reassigned him. The mixed feelings he had for Eileen would just have to remain his problem. A problem he'd deal with one day at a time.

But he needed to bring the investigation to a close, and fast. The longer he stayed around Eileen, the more difficult it would be when he finally did leave. And leave he would. He'd no intention of letting Eileen get so far under his skin that he couldn't walk away from her. And she was just the kind of woman with the potential to do that.

Even as he made the resolution to keep his distance from Eileen, Pete's words morphed into a picture of Eileen's sleepy face across the pillow from him giving him a sexy good-morning smile.

The picture dissolved like wet, sticky cotton candy. She was in love with Van Buren.

Daniel flipped on his stereo, cranking up the volume just enough to drown out his thoughts. The cheery Christmas music didn't help. He switched to a rock and roll station, then headed toward his workout bench.

***

Eileen had never laughed so hard in her entire life. As Gus sat next to her on their way home from their Friday morning self-defense class, he related hilarious story after hilarious story about his dealings with Hollywood's elite. He had a gift for exaggerated impersonation, while always managing to keep his references kind.

She wiped her fingertips across her wet cheeks. With all the craziness and tension at the office, Gus had become a comfortable, lighthearted refuge. Over the past week, she'd come to know his view on life and people—a view of acceptance and faith he never hesitated to share. He'd shown her a depth to Mirabelle's 'unconditional' love she had never thought possible. Glancing over, she asked, "Tell me what you know about Wishmakers. I'm curious."

Gus studied her. "I think a lot of your questions will be answered at Mirabelle's party tomorrow night. You'll meet quite a few graduates and have a chance to talk to them. There are certain things that *mere mortals*," he joked, "aren't privy to."

Then she asked the question she'd been dying to ask ever since she'd met this man who 'made the stars shine.' "Gus, how much do you charge for your consulting services? I think I'm ready for a change."

He continued studying her. "Oh, I'm not gonna charge ya, Honey. But—now don't get me wrong—I sense you're not quite ready yet. Get through a couple more of Wishmaker's tasks first. You and I both need to peel back a few more layers before we get to the real Eileen Pringle."

He moved his hands around as though sculpting an image of her. "You know, you're like a saucepan full of bubbling fudge. We take you out of the pan too soon, and you'll be all soft and gooey, with gritty little grains of unmelted sugar. No, you need to simmer a while longer. Then we're gonna rock the world with the most seductively smooth, wickedly sensuous, endorphin-inducing kind of delicacy known to man."

Eileen had to laugh. "I don't know about seductive or sensuous, but you're making me hungry. I'm suddenly craving a chocolate donut. You want to stop for breakfast?" She felt light-hearted at the ridiculous image Gus painted of her. But suddenly the picture he painted didn't seem such a long stretch.

He said, "Breakfast? Sure thing."

She pulled into a coffee shop parking lot, and they got out of the car. It was then that she realized they looked like they'd

just come from making an exercise video. Gus wore his usual
spandex body suit with a sweatshirt draped over his shoulders.
And although she had on a new workout outfit with matching
sweatshirt, the high-cut legs and body-hugging material might
be out of place in a restaurant setting. Shrugging her shoulders,
she gave up the critical thoughts and began to accept herself
unconditionally, too.

Once they were seated in a booth and had their orders taken,
Gus asked, "What's going on? All of a sudden, you look like
you're going to sneeze or something."

Eileen smiled and felt the strain creases ease. "I planned on
filing a petition today to challenge my father's will, but I'm
having second thoughts."

"Why should you have second thoughts?"

"Maybe I should just let the whole thing go and leave it to,"
she crooked her fingers, "the universe. You know, like Mirabelle
said, things are happening as they should, and for a reason."

Gus chuckled softly. "On the other hand, maybe there's a
reason you need to challenge the will. The lesson will make
itself known eventually. As Mirabelle would say, 'If the path
opens itself to you, you'll know it's the right one.' Personally,
I'm all for following your heart."

"What if that heart is acting out of bitterness?"

He looked into her eyes, shaking his head as if he heard
more than she had intended from her words. "What is it you
really want from your past?"

She swallowed hard. What did she want? She realized the
two things she really wanted were forever out of her reach. She
wanted her father's love, to know she belonged and was wanted.
But any chance at that had been buried with her father. And she
wanted the time she had been cheated out of with her mother.
She shrugged. "I'd like my mother's things from the attic. If
Jeannette hasn't already disposed of them." She moved the
saltshaker around the table, making invisible circles.

"When Jeannette told me to leave, I was in such shock I
didn't even remember my mother's trunk of keepsakes in the
attic. My father once told me they were there, but I could never
bring myself to look at them. I'm not sure I could now, but I

want to get them if they're still there." She felt the lump forming in her throat again, so she took a sip of water. The hand holding the glass shook.

"Reason enough. Even if you don't get one penny from your father's estate, no court in the land will award your stepmother your mother's keepsakes. You'll have a bit of your mother. That's what you really want, isn't it? I'm thinking that's worth more than the entire Bill Gates fortune. Am I right?"

She only nodded, still unsure of the stability of her voice.

"Looks like you could use a little moral support. Let me go with you."

"You wouldn't mind?"

"It would be a great way to end the week, doing something positive."

She felt her spirits rise. "I planned on going to the courthouse right after I shower and change. Does nine-thirty sound okay?"

"I'll be at your apartment with bells on."

Eileen got a mental image of him in a jester's hat, complete with bells, and she had to smile. "Thanks."

***

By four o'clock that afternoon Eileen's physical and emotional reserves needed replenishing. But the moment she flopped across her bed, intent on a long, luxurious nap, an urgent pounding at her front door jolted her entire nervous system awake. Enough adrenaline shot through her veins to easily match the caffeine buzz from one of Daniel's morning cups of coffee.

She put on her glasses and hurried to the door. The persistent pounding made her wonder if there was a fire in the building.

When she opened the door and found an enraged Jeannette standing there looking like she might explode, her first thought was to call the bomb squad. Her second thought was to call 911. The strange thing was, for some reason, as Eileen looked at the woman she felt no anger. She only felt alarm that her stepmother was so agitated she might have a stroke or a heart attack. "Come in, Jeannette."

"I will not!" She waved a curled piece of what looked like fax paper. "How dare you!"

Eileen's hand automatically went out to calm Jeannette, but the woman stepped back as if Eileen had the plague. "I can't believe you'd do this after all I've done for you. You little witch!" Considering who, or what, Mirabelle was, Eileen took that as a compliment.

Jeanette ranted on. "What do you want? What will it take to drop this? You're putting my entire life on hold. This is emotional blackmail."

She looked at Jeannette. "Why did you keep hanging up on me this morning? If you had listened to me, this might have been avoided."

Jeannette gave her head a frustrated shake. "Never mind that. What did you want?"

"I want access to the house. I still have some things I need to get out."

Jeannette took a shaky breath and seemed to calm considerably, but her face remained bright red and she looked suspicious. "Like what?"

"My mother's things. Are they still in the attic?"

Jeannette said in a snide tone, "For all I know, your mother's in the attic. I haven't been up there in years."

Eileen asked, "Then you'll let me in?"

"I want your promise you'll drop this." She shook the paper.

"I don't know that I can." She avoided the promise she knew she shouldn't make. "I won't know until Monday when the courthouse opens. I want to come over this weekend and get my mother's things."

"Fine! Good riddance! But don't even think about taking anything else." She rattled the paper again. "Thanks to you, a court-appointed attorney has ordered an inventory next week, and the entire estate will go into probate!"

Eileen wondered what items Jeannette would remove to ensure they didn't become part of the inventory. With a feeling of liberation, Eileen realized she didn't care. Aside from a few personal keepsakes, nothing in that house mattered to Eileen. But it didn't seem right that Jeannette and her attorney shouldn't be brought to justice if, as Daniel had suggested, they had willingly falsified the will. Could a copy of another will, a different will, possibly exist somewhere in the house? Or was that just wishful thinking on her part?

Eileen said, "I'll be over at nine o'clock Sunday morning."

Jeannette rolled her eyes, clearly exasperated. "You know I never get up before ten."

"Ten it is." *Unconditional love*, she repeated over and over to herself. *Jeannette is an important part of the universe. She's doing exactly what she's supposed to do. She could be teaching me a valuable lesson.* Although Eileen couldn't think of what that lesson might possibly be, she gave the woman the benefit of the doubt.

Jeannette turned and stormed away, saying over her shoulder as she waved the paper, "I expect you to drop this first thing Monday!"

As Eileen softly closed the door, her thoughts turned to the attic and its contents, and her heart gave a sharp tug. She felt as though she stood with her foot poised over the world's largest, scariest roller coaster. And as terrifying as that was, she knew she must complete the step, get on the ride, and face her fears.

EIGHT

Daniel wanted to question Jim Stewart, Wincomp's night security guard, but he wanted to do it without Eileen present. He'd given her a vague excuse about an Agency meeting so they would have to go into Wincomp in separate cars. She had said she would take the opportunity to catch up on some much-needed sleep, and they agreed to meet at the office at six-thirty.

At five-thirty Friday evening, when Daniel approached Wincomp's sign-in sheet for night workers, Jim's affable greeting from behind the desk suggested he might be open for a bit of friendly conversation. The man's job had to be a lonely one, and Daniel counted on that making him willing to shoot the breeze.

"Hey, Jim, how's it going?" Daniel signed in and kept the book facing him by resting his forearm across it.

Jim beamed at the warm greeting and turned down the volume of the miniature television set he kept on his desk, but not before Daniel heard the *Star Trek* theme. So, the man was a Trekie.

Jim said, "Quiet as usual, Daniel. Where's Eileen this evening? I'm getting kinda used to seeing you two together."

Good. He'd been right on target. Jim was in a talkative mood. "She's not in yet?" He was certain she wasn't, since he'd checked to make sure her car was still in *Deviazione's* parking lot when he'd left. "I'm sure she'll be in shortly."

Now all Daniel needed to do was quickly get the information

he needed without making Jim suspicious. He nonchalantly leafed through the book, scanning the pages for the October date the hacking had occurred.

Jim's smile dimmed. "Sorry, Daniel. Security's policy is not to show the book to anyone besides supervisors. I don't mean to offend you, but you never know who's gonna do what with the information. You'll have to wait for Eileen."

Daniel shrugged as if it didn't matter, then leaned one elbow on the desk to indicate he would just settle in to wait. He looked toward the door. "Eileen said she'd be here by now. Must have stopped for a bite to eat or something." He needed to check out a few dates without Eileen looking over his shoulder. And in his search for anyone who might have come in late to do the hacking, he had to erase the last niggling doubt about Eileen's guilt.

Jim leaned forward conspiratorially. "Hey, why they got you two working graveyard? Some secret project?" He chuckled as if to brush off his question as ridiculous, but Daniel detected a note of hopefulness. And that's all he needed.

The gleam of a Trekie and possible fellow X-Filer he saw in Jim's eyes told Daniel the man was hungry for any morsel of conspiracy, and nothing was too fantastic to be swallowed.

Daniel cast the line, almost hearing it zing high overhead. "Well, it's like this, Jim. It is top secret. This doesn't go past you, right?"

Jim shook his head slowly, swimming toward the glittering lure.

Daniel tugged on the line. "Hell, you're security, Jim. I know I can trust you. But this can't even be discussed with Ms. Pringle. If she knew I was talking to you about this, I'd be kicked off the project."

At that Jim gobbled up the bait, sitting up a bit straighter in is chair. He mimed zipping his lips.

Daniel kept his voice low, glancing over his shoulder for effect. "There've been some strange goings-on up on the fifth floor. Wincomp's been getting some weird transmissions over our computers late at night. The source is, shall we say, out of this world. If you know what I mean."

Jim's mouth gaped open and Daniel gently set the hook.

"Eileen and I are trying to decode the signals."

Daniel reeled him in as he watched the man take a deep breath, seeming to assimilate the enormity of what he'd just heard. Jim whispered, "Just like in the movie, *Contact*."

"If this leaks, Jim, the Feds will come in and take over, and they'll turn it into another 'weather balloon' story. The truth will never come out."

"Same as Roswell, New Mexico," Jim said in awe.

Now that Daniel had Jim reeled-in, he needed to let the guy off the hook without causing any permanent damage. He'd established the trust he'd been after. Daniel was a catch-and-release kind of fisherman when it came to investigation subjects. He didn't want the story he'd fabricated to become too real to Jim. "Of course, there's the possibility the transmissions we're getting could be nothing more than a sub-category quasar anomaly. But it's something we have a duty to find out, don't you think?"

The look of concentration on Jim's face revealed he was searching his "Trekie" data banks for what 'sub-category quasar anomaly' might be. "Oh, yeah, sure," was all he said. Daniel saw the light of interest in Jim's eyes begin to dim.

Daniel said, "I do have some concerns that someone with access to Wincomp's offices could be pulling an elaborate hoax, but ..." He directed his gaze to the sign-in book, "Hey, Jim, you'd know if someone unauthorized came in late at night. Someone, say, who might want to play a practical joke on Mr. Van Buren by messing with his computers?" He wasn't about to let Jim know they were really looking for an inside trader as well as a hacker. Jim might very well be acquainted with that person and might unwittingly leak the fact that Daniel was curious.

Jim straightened in his chair again as if suddenly remembering the importance of his job. "Absolutely no one unauthorized gets past me. And, if they were in the building at night, they had clearance."

"I'd sure like to take a look at the sign-in book, say, for the last two-month period. You never know ...." He purposely trailed off, figuring he'd be better off letting Jim draw his own conclusions. He glanced at his watch, knowing Eileen could barge through the door at any second.

Jim only hesitated a moment before he flipped open the book and swiveled it toward Daniel. "I guess it's okay, since you're working with Eileen, and all."

"Thanks, Jim." Daniel quickly turned to the October section and ran his finger down the row of signatures as he scanned. Not too many people had pulled late shifts. He did see that Brock Van Buren put in several late-nighters, a lot more than in the weeks Daniel had been at Wincomp. He also saw something he knew Eileen wasn't aware of, and wouldn't be thrilled about if she found out. Van Buren had been dating Alyssa Barden as far back as October, since on at least six different dates during that month Alyssa had signed in directly beneath Van Buren.

Daniel realized he didn't want Van Buren to be his hacker. If he were, Eileen would suffer. She would lose the man she loved to prison for a couple of years. On second thought, maybe that would be the best thing for her. She'd forget The Jerk and go out and find a man who appreciated her. But the downside to The Jerk landing in jail and Wincomp closing was that Eileen would lose the money she'd invested in the company. After the debacle she'd gone through with her father's will, Daniel knew that losing the Wincomp stock would devastate her.

He made a mental note of the remaining two Wincomp signatures. Michael Bates and Ray Mitchell had also worked late several nights. Daniel felt like he was back at square one. No one other than his original suspects had signed Jim's book. One discovery, though, made the ploy with Jim worth the effort. Eileen's name was *not* in the sign-in book for October.

He breathed a sigh of relief and gave Jim a negative shake of his head, letting him know his search hadn't turned up anything he could use. At that moment both men looked up to watch Eileen hurry through the doors, a beautiful smile on her lips and a bounce in her step.

Daniel quickly turned from the October section of the book to the present day's page and stepped aside so Eileen could sign in. As he did, he noted she looked different somehow. Her clothes were still drab, shapeless and expensive. She still wore the comical glasses. But, she seemed taller than he remembered. When he looked down at her feet, he saw the same flat, sensible-type shoes she always wore, so the change couldn't be attributed to higher heels. Her questioning look forced him to put his speculation aside.

***

Eileen could hardly wait until the elevator doors closed before she said to Daniel, "I took your suggestion. This morning I filed a petition to contest my father's will."

"Great. I wish you luck." She noticed Daniel's attitude this evening seemed more congenial than it had last night. Even though he still wore his glasses and bow tie, he no longer had that reserved, FBI cloak of superiority.

She said, "I had a visit from my stepmother, Jeannette, the moment she found out the papers had been filed. Boy, was she mad!"

Daniel snorted. "I'll bet. She has a lot to lose."

Eileen thought about Mirabelle's 'second step' and realized she didn't want to hurt Jeannette. She didn't have to like the woman, but she knew now that accepting Jeannette as an important, although irritating, part of the universe gave Eileen a different, more philosophical, perspective. "She agreed to let me get inside my father's house on Sunday and retrieve some of my mother's things."

The elevator doors opened and they stepped out, Daniel's look hesitant. "You okay with that?"

"Yeah, I'm going to ask Ray to go with me. I'm not sure how heavy the boxes will be, so I might need a couple of strong arms. And, besides his muscle and moral support, I was hoping he could help me do some snooping to see if there might be another will hidden somewhere."

She could see Daniel had reservations about Ray, as she knew he would. But Eileen had decided to trust her heart. Ray had always been a good friend to her, and by asking him to do this she was reaffirming to herself that she trusted him.

Daniel said, "I could go with you, too. Snooping is my forte."

Eileen thought about Daniel's offer as they automatically

walked toward Brock's office. Maybe Daniel could be of some help. Although Ray could give her emotional support, Daniel had sleuthing experience. If another will did exist, Daniel might have insights into where to look. Plus he had those handy-dandy spy tools she'd seen him use to pick the lock on Brock's office.

She couldn't figure out why, but she felt overwhelming relief in the prospect of having Daniel along when she faced the ghosts in the attic. "Thanks. I'd like that." She put the key in the lock, noticing the look of consternation on his face as he realized she'd had the key all along and that he hadn't had to pick the lock before.

"Sunday, it's a date." Daniel opened the door and motioned her to precede him. Tonight they'd agreed to work on Brock's files together. Along with wanting to see what progress Daniel had made, she didn't want to be accused of tampering by working on Brock's data alone.

As they sat side-by-side at Brock's terminal, Eileen thought about Daniel's last statement. "It's a date," he'd said, and she relived the thrill his words evoked. Wild sensations she didn't want to feel rushed through her body at the image of them together. A date was such a simple thing, the word itself sounding trite and old-fashioned, yet so rich with intimate possibilities.

A date was a time of shared confidences and dreams, a time to discover common ground and get to know one another emotionally as well as physically. She felt Daniel's nearness and became keenly aware of his every move. Her heart thumped against her ribs, and she fought to steady her breathing.

What were Daniel's dreams? And why was she asking herself the question at all? She didn't want her heart to care about the man, or for her body to respond to his every glance. She was sure he would laugh at the very notion of dating. She inched away from Daniel and let her eyes stray from the screen to study Brock's office.

The elegant perfection of soft leather chairs and warm oak cabinetry were like looking at Brock. *He* was her ideal, and she wasn't about to stray from her goal now that she felt certain it was within her reach.

Even though Brock hadn't yet begun to gravitate toward her, she knew in her heart he would eventually. Mirabelle promised to grant her wish if she followed Wishmaker's directions, and Eileen didn't intend to let anything—or anyone—keep her from "graduating."

She started to look back toward the screen, but found herself caught in Daniel's intense gaze like a butterfly in a spider's web.

Never breaking eye contact, he said, "What is it about Van Buren that fascinates you?"

All she could do was shrug. She honestly had no idea. She only knew that to her he'd always been Prince Charming, living high on the hill, and she wanted to share his castle with him. She rubbed her knees.

Eileen felt her mouth go dry and her heartbeat accelerate as Daniel removed his glasses and leaned closer, his gaze searching for something in her eyes.

His voice turned soft and sensuously throaty as he said, "The guy's crazy. He doesn't know what he's got. I think you're beautiful."

Was he putting her on? She searched his eyes and saw only truth. She also got the feeling he was about to kiss her.

Suddenly, she wanted to be kissed by someone who saw her as beautiful. So, when Daniel reached up to remove her glasses, she didn't pull away. Her eyes closed, and she sensed him slowly coming closer. His lips stopped just short of touching hers, teasing with an unfulfilled promise of skin upon skin. His warm breath brushed her skin, and her lips tingled with the need to consummate the kiss. But she didn't move.

She needed Daniel to want her, to want and need her so much that he *couldn't* hold back from moving that last millimeter. Her heart drummed in her chest like it was going to burst free, and at the same time liquid warmth suffused her entire body. She felt Daniel's fingers stroke her shoulder, sensuously gliding their way up to her neck. Her breath caught.

At last his lips found hers, possessed hers, and an instant, unbidden response shot through her. Daniel's heated kiss belied the restraint he'd shown only moments before, and Eileen felt herself fall into an abyss of sensations. Daniel told her with his lips and his hands that she was beautiful, desired and sexy.

But this wasn't the man she loved! This wasn't Brock! Roughly she pushed away, forcing her eyes open to break Daniel's spell. She felt the trembling of the fingertips she pressed to her swollen lips.

Daniel's gaze searched hers, but she couldn't deny the regret she was sure he could see. He said nothing, only shook his head slowly, and, if she wasn't mistaken, sadly. Then he turned back toward the glow of the computer screen.

What had she done? Eileen hurriedly excused herself and rushed to the ladies room.

The florescent lighting over the mirrors gave her reflection a haunted look. She pulled the rubber band from her hair and messaged her scalp, closing her eyes.

"I don't want Daniel," she whispered to herself. "I want Brock. I've always wanted Brock. Brock is my soul mate. Daniel is my..." Her eyes shot open, and she stared in horror at herself in the mirror. What had she been about to say? Daniel wasn't her wish. Straightening, she said with determination, "Brock is my wish."

She had to splash what seemed like gallons of cold water on her face and re-secure her hair before she felt calm enough to return to Brock's office and face Daniel. And as she walked back, she ran a dialogue in her head. *Pretend it never happened. After all, what really did happen?*

"It was just a kiss," she rationalized aloud. "Daniel doesn't really care 'that way' for you, you fool. It's just that he's been on this investigation—and without a woman—too long. That's it. That's all it was."

She began to feel more like herself. She'd simply made more out of what most people would consider a casual incident than it merited.

As she entered Brock's office and saw Daniel's closed, distant expression, she knew she'd been justified in calling herself a fool.

***

When Mirabelle first felt the electric surge in energy, she

knew Eileen had taken a major step toward granting, and her heart soared. But then the energy changed, becoming confused, and turned into sputtering little sparks. Mirabelle felt as though fallout from a Fourth of July sparkler had just rained down on her spirit.

She wasn't sure which of the two men in Eileen's life had caused the regression, but Mirabelle knew the one responsible was the man Eileen was meant to be with. Only that man could cause a positive change in the energy. If Mirabelle only knew whether it was Daniel or Brock, she would have an easier time directing Eileen down the path to enlightenment and granting.

She shook her head as she sat on her stoop mid-morning Saturday, wrapped in a shawl against the chilly day. And as Mary had said it might, the weather had tuned into Eileen's state of mind. The usually mild California winter weather had turned unstable. One minute the sun would shine, the next, rain threatened. She'd heard two different television weathermen apologize for their balmy forecasts when the weather had changed without warning.

Mirabelle knew for certain Eileen's progress had taken a step backward. And with time running out, Mirabelle must speed up the process. The new plan would put pressure on everyone, and that always risked an energy crisis. But Mirabelle knew it had to be done. Eileen needed to complete the remaining tasks as quickly as possible, for everyone's sake.

As Mirabelle waited for Eileen to emerge from her apartment, she felt the chill wind and once again shook her head. The waiting became unbearable, so she got up and walked across the courtyard to Eileen's apartment and knocked.

When Eileen answered Mirabelle saw that she was dressed in beige slacks and a pretty pink cashmere sweater as if she might be going out somewhere. She had her purse over her shoulder.

"Mirabelle," Eileen greeted her with a weak smile. "I've been wanting to talk to you."

"I'd like to talk to you, too, dear, if you have a moment."

"I'm waiting for my friend Ray Mitchell to pick me up, so do you mind if we talk in the courtyard?"

Eileen glanced at the gloomy sky—which, Mirabelle noticed reflected Eileen's thoughts on the subject of Daniel exactly—grabbing a coat before she locked her door. They walked together to stand by the fountain. Its gentle splashing made a soothing sound.

Eileen seemed to perk up as she said, "Ray and I are going to hit some second-hand stores for furniture; my apartment is so empty. Oh, by the way, I'm really looking forward to your get-together tonight." She adjusted her purse strap nervously, as if she had something on her mind.

"I'm looking forward to the party, too. I love seeing my graduates. I've invited the apartment residents, too. Ray is welcome."

"Thanks. I'll tell him." She exhaled deeply, and Mirabelle could tell she was about to say whatever had been on her mind.

"Mirabelle, there's something I've been wanting to tell you. I didn't really believe in you or Wishmakers at first. I guess you could probably tell. But, I want you to know I'm giving each task my best. They've already made such a difference in my entire outlook on life."

"I had the feeling they had. That's why I want to give you the remaining ones. I'm sure you're quite ready."

Mirabelle could tell Eileen was anxious to complete the tasks. And she could tell by the way Eileen carried herself with new assurance and by her aura of openness that the first four tasks were doing their job.

Eileen said, "I'm ready. What are they?"

Mirabelle said, "Number five is to organize your energy. Conscious change will only take place through careful attention and intention. By actively stating your intention, you open and activate yourself and the world around you to achieving that goal. In other words, write down what you want, and then think about it. Say it out loud."

Eileen said, "Okay, state my desire out loud."

"Oh no," Mirabelle said. "Desire alone is weak. It leaves you open to obstacles. Life-centered *intent*, on the other hand, coupled with the other steps you've learned, will open a path to your purpose—your wish. *Intent* is that which you are determined to do, that which you are firmly fixed to see through to its completion. State your intent, then become focused on present-moment awareness. Your intent for the future will manifest itself."

Eileen said, "Okay, I state my intent. Then focus on present-moment awareness."

"Good," Mirabelle said. "Now, the sixth task is to open yourself up to all possibilities—accept your faith in the universe—in order to find your true dreams. Detach yourself from your search for security. It's an illusion and only leads to a detachment of your consciousness.

Eileen slowly nodded. "I think I've got it. Be open."

Mirabelle nodded. "And when you find yourself closing up or backing away, ask yourself why, then consciously open yourself to the situation."

Mirabelle continued. "The seventh and final step is to find out what your purpose in life is. Why have you been given certain talents, gifts? What part do you play in humanity?"

Eileen's eyebrows knitted. "I know I have a certain knack with computer technology, but I can't see how what I do can benefit mankind. Other than keeping some guy's software safe through my security programs."

Mirabelle smiled. "Keep going with that thought. It will come to you. Try to find out what you have that mankind needs."

"Okay."

Mirabelle saw a cloud pass across Eileen's eyes, and the energy dip she'd felt earlier returned with a gust of wind. "What's wrong, my dear?"

Eileen shook her head as she focused on the dancing water. "Oh nothing. It's silly really. Just something that happened last night. I'm trying to apply it to the step about being open to possibilities."

"I doubt it's silly. What happened?"

Eileen lowered her voice, and her glance darted toward the door adjoining Mirabelle's. "Well, last night Daniel Collins kissed me."

"Intriguing." Was that the power surge she had felt? If so, then Daniel was the man Eileen needed to be with. That figured.

Brock would have been so much easier. Mary had told Mirabelle about Daniel's undercover operation and that he would be leaving. Brock was a constant in Eileen's life and would have been the easiest choice. "How did you feel about Daniel kissing you?"

"I didn't stop him. Well, at first I didn't, but then I pushed him away."

"Did that feel right?"

"No. I mean yes." Eileen sighed deeply. "I'm not sure. Part of me didn't want him to kiss me, but boy, did it feel right when it was happening."

Mirabelle saw the confusion on Eileen's face but knew it was all part of the process.

Mirabelle said, "If the kiss felt right, then why did you push him away?"

"It didn't feel right to let him kiss me, either. I'm in love with Brock. I've known him and wanted him most of my life. Daniel is just...well, I don't know. But Daniel will be gone soon. I only know I don't want him around confusing me."

Mirabelle had seen this before in other clients. "Don't worry. Your heart knows what to do. Maybe your confusion isn't from Daniel. It could be from the emotional fallout of your past. It could be acting like a smoke screen." She straightened and took an energizing breath. "We'll get that smoke cleared out, don't you worry. You work on putting all of the steps together, and you'll be on the right path in no time."

Eileen smiled. "I hope so, because right now I feel really uncomfortable around Daniel."

The door to Daniel's apartment opened, and Mirabelle noticed the immediate change in Eileen. The young woman straightened. Her breath quickened and her eyes darted like a frightened rabbit. Mirabelle felt a soft, almost balmy breeze flutter past, and she smiled, her suspicions confirmed.

Mirabelle turned to get a better look at the man who caused such a reaction in her client. He wore a sweater and jeans, and Mirabelle couldn't help admiring how handsome he was. Usually when she saw him he had on his work clothes and wore glasses.

"Good morning, ladies."

Mirabelle noticed the way Daniel's eyes caressed Eileen. But by the closed look Eileen returned, the poor girl had no idea she was pushing away the very thing she wanted in life. She deflected the energy Daniel sent to her as effectively as if she wore Wonder Woman's magic bracelets. Obviously, the steps she'd just been given hadn't sunk in as well as Mirabelle had thought.

Eileen said a stiff, "Good morning, Daniel," and Mirabelle heard thunder roll in the distance. She looked to Eileen and saw a stormy expression.

Mirabelle needed to get to work. Fast. Eileen seemed bent on pushing Daniel—and her wish—further and further away.

Nine

Eileen was afraid her day of shopping with Ray was going to be strained, to say the least. He'd been unusually distant ever since the virus hit his computer on Tuesday. Even though she'd cleaned up his hard drive and reinstalled the programs from his virus-free backup disks, she'd felt like he'd been avoiding her. Maybe she was imagining his evasion. After all, she'd been working nights, and they hadn't had their usual opportunities to chat.

The distance between her and Ray didn't help or hinder her indecision as to whether Ray was involved in the hacking, the software theft or the virus.

She decided to assume Ray's innocence. She would trust her instincts, just like Mirabelle had suggested. Ray would tell her if something was bothering him.

She was sure Daniel's training would make him suspect Ray's aloofness as a sign of guilt.

Eileen and Ray had a successful day of browsing through LA's trendy used furniture shops. His morose mood had quickly vanished, making Eileen sure he'd just been upset over the virus.

A sturdy but "distressed" farmer's table and four mismatched antique chairs filled the back of his Dodge Ram pickup truck.

As Ray drove up Santa Monica Boulevard toward the *Deviazione* apartments, he said, "Eileen, I'm impressed. There was a time you wouldn't have fought me like you did today about buying those chairs. You'd have caved in to my old-fashioned ideas about order and symmetry in decorating.

Eileen couldn't help smiling. "I know. But I like my chairs. They go perfectly with the table."

Ray harrumphed good-naturedly. "Yeah, they're beat-up and they don't match!"

"They're 'distressed,' and they belong together. They're like lovely old friends with common life experiences, living out the remainder of their lives together."

"So, you've become a commune for aging furniture?"

"No, I'm giving them new life and appreciating their history and craftsmanship."

"If you say so."

Eileen didn't mind Ray's teasing. They just had different tastes when it came to furniture. She was just glad she had her old friend back and that his quiet mood of the past few days had vanished. She went on, "Besides, I feel good when I look at them."

Ray conceded. "I have to admit, they do go together in a weird, eclectic kind of way. At least they're circa the same era, and they're all made out of wood."

Eileen had visited Ray's apartment many times over the years, and she knew his tastes leaned toward modern, functional, no-frills furnishings. A major techno-freak, Ray always seemed to have the latest gadget or toy, be it stereo equipment or computer. Evidently, he chose to enjoy his money instead of investing it as she had. Maybe she should take a lesson from him.

The subject of money reminded her of the investigation into who sold Wincomp's program. "Ray, a while back you told me you didn't feel appreciated at Wincomp. Do you still feel that way?"

Sober disappointment showed in Ray's eyes. "You want to know if I sold my program to Morgan Software."

Eileen knew she had to get past the fear of hurting Ray's feelings and clear up the questions still plaguing her about her friend. She desperately wanted proof she could trust her heart— a heart that said Ray was innocent. "Yes, Ray. I'm sorry, but I do. I wanted to hear the answer directly from you."

His reply surprised her. "And if I did?"

She had to think about that. If Ray had sold out Wincomp—and essentially sold out Brock, the man she loved—how would she feel about him? She realized that no matter what Ray had done, be it hacking or software theft, he was still her friend. And as a friend, he'd been there for her through thick and thin. She knew he was there for her now, no matter what.

Finally she answered, "Ray, it wouldn't matter to me."

The stress lines across his face eased. "Well, I didn't do it, so you can relax. I may not feel appreciated at Wincomp, but I didn't sell out to Morgan."

Immense relief flooded Eileen. She believed him. But what felt best was she'd begun to believe in herself. What Mirabelle had said was true: If she put all her fears aside and listened to her heart, it would tell her the truth.

"Then you had nothing to do with the virus?"

"No. At least no permanent damage was done. As per your very own security dictates, I do backup disks every night and lock them in my file cabinet."

Eileen said, "Any idea who could have done it?"

He snorted, and Eileen remembered Ray had told her about the argument he and Michael had had Tuesday afternoon. Each had accused the other of the software theft. They'd worked closely on several projects over the past three years and now weren't even on speaking terms.

"Michael?"

"Who else had access to my terminal? He knew my password because we work—no, *worked*—on the same projects."

Ray sounded bitter, betrayed. *Okay heart*, Eileen told herself, *it's time to go into action*. Was Ray right, had Michael stolen the program? Had he injected the virus into Ray's hard drive out of anger or as a threat against turning him in as the thief? Her heart didn't answer. Michael as a lone entity—Michael without Ray—became an enigma. She'd almost always seen Michael as part of the team of *Ray and Michael*, and therefore, accepted him on Ray's unspoken endorsement. She would make a point of getting to know Michael better.

"Why didn't you tell us of your suspicions when Brock asked

Daniel and me to investigate?"

Ray turned into *Deviazione's* parking lot, stopping the truck in front of the archway leading to the courtyard. "Because I don't have proof. From what I gather, that's your department. Yours and Daniel's." He turned off the engine. "Any luck on your late-night snoops?"

"Nothing." She didn't feel that sharing the investigation's lack of progress with Ray broke any confidences.

"How long you gonna keep at it? Seems like a lot of time and company money diverted from other projects."

They got out and went around to either side of the truck bed to retrieve chairs. "We'll keep at it until we find out who did it, I guess. You don't want the person who sold us out to have an opportunity to do it again, do you?"

"No. But good luck finding proof even when you do find out who did it. I'm sure he's covered his tracks by now."

"Probably, but we'll keep trying."

They walked to her apartment, each carrying two chairs. But when they went back for the table, Eileen realized she'd overestimated her physical strength. Solid wood, the hefty piece of furniture was too heavy for her and Ray to carry alone.

"I'll see if Daniel's in," she said. "Maybe he won't mind helping." The sun broke through the clouds, which had been threatening rain all day.

"Great. I'll wait here so no one steals the table." Ray leaned comfortably against the truck, turning his face into the sun.

Eileen laughed as she headed back through the archway. As if anyone could grab the heavy table and run off with it.

She hesitated a moment before she rang Daniel's doorbell. For some reason she needed to fortify herself against the physical reaction she knew would come. No doubt about it, when Daniel wasn't playing computer geek, he was a dangerous man when it came to his effect on women. The door opened before her finger left the button, as if he had been waiting. Her heart gave a startled jump, then kept right on pounding as she looked at him. The light in his eyes warmed.

"Eileen." His voice was low, and his glance seemed to take in every detail, making her suddenly glad she'd spent the extra time using hot-rollers and applying a bit of makeup this morning. He opened the door wider. "Come in."

Eileen quickly dismissed the promise of intimacy her wild imagination injected into his offer.

She took a step back, then chided herself for the fear racing through her chest. What was she afraid Daniel would do? Ravage her on his living room floor? Fleeting images of the two of them intertwined caused heat to rush through her midsection. "I was wondering if you might help Ray carry a table I bought today into my apartment." She had to remind herself that last night's kiss had been a fluke—a heat-of-the-moment kind of thing—and it wasn't likely to happen again. "It's really heavy." She wondered why she felt so out of breath. The walk from Ray's truck to Daniel's door couldn't be more than a few yards.

"Sure." He smiled, and she saw a dimple crease his cheek that she'd never noticed before. "Give me a couple of minutes, and I'll be right out."

"Great. Thanks. I'll meet you on the other side of the archway." He probably wanted to put on the weekend version of his work 'disguise' for Ray's benefit.

A few minutes later, seeing Daniel come through the archway, she knew she'd been right. Wearing glasses, a crisp white shirt, sweater vest and jeans, he had reverted to a slightly stooped non-entity. So convincing was his nerd persona that for a moment Eileen forgot the real Daniel hid behind it and wondered if he would be physically able to help Ray move the heavy table. But when he effortlessly held up his end of the piece of furniture, the illusion melted as quickly as a Southern California snowfall.

The two men greeted each other and went to work. Eileen ran ahead to open her door.

Within five minutes of placing the table in the dining room, Ray and Daniel had helped themselves to bottled water from her refrigerator, seated themselves at the new-old table and were deep into sports talk. They had once again found common ground as Lakers fans.

Eileen busied herself, working around the men as she waxed

her new table, all the time covertly watching and listening to the two converse. Daniel seemed more relaxed than she'd ever seen him around Ray, and Ray acted like they'd been best buds for years. Something tugged at a spot beneath her ribs. If things were different, if Daniel didn't have a hidden agenda that could soon upend their lives, she felt certain the two men could become good friends.

Suddenly it seemed important for Daniel to like Ray. And equally important for her long-time friend to respect and like Daniel. Then she had to wonder why it was important to her. She had to ask herself, *What is Daniel to me?* She realized that, although she might fear Special Agent Daniel Manatucci and what he could do to her life, she had reluctantly begun to consider Daniel, the *man*, a friend.

The cloth in her hand stilled as he glanced up during his conversation and gave her a quiet smile. She could almost fool herself into believing that particular smile belonged to her alone. She smiled back. Friends, that's all they were, friends. And she was sure he smiled that way at all women.

A crack Ray made about an outrageous basketball figure had both men laughing so loudly, Eileen almost missed the ringing of the doorbell. Welcoming the distraction from the confusion of Daniel's smile, she went to answer the door, polish and rag still in hand.

"Brock!" His name came out sounding more like a startled chicken squawk than a greeting. At her glance toward the table, she saw that Ray's expression was one of curiosity, while Daniel, after an initial look of hostility, dropped back into a relaxed version of his 'Daniel Collins' mode.

Brock, tall, blond, and perfect as usual, stepped through the doorway with an affable grin. "A party, and I wasn't invited?" He looked over at the two now-quiet men who in unison executed a male head-jerk greeting. It gave her the impression that the casual gesture acknowledged that they weren't working and, therefore, existed on equal terms.

Their macho posturing and the testosterone flying around the room held little interest for her. Mirabelle's dialogue and the lessons Eileen had been learning ran through her head like a stream of cool water, reminding her not to fall apart just because Brock had shown up on her doorstep out of the blue. *Retain balance and be yourself.* "You're always welcome, Brock." She repeated to herself Mirabelle's second lesson, *Give unconditional love. Yeah, like that's going to be hard.* So why had Brock shown up on her doorstep? *Listen to your heart, not your fears.*

As she watched Brock shake hands with the two men then take a seat at the table, curiosity got the better of her. She asked, "What's up?" Circling the table to take the empty seat next to Daniel, she sat with one leg curled under her and then busied her nervous hands by folding the dust rag into a neat rectangle.

Brock directed his comment to her. "I called from my cell phone, but got your machine, so I thought I'd leave a note. Then when I got to your door," his glance flicked to Ray and Daniel, "I could hear you were home." He looked across the table at her. "I thought if you weren't busy tonight, we might go out for a bite to eat. We haven't had much time lately for the two of us to sit down and talk."

Daniel and Ray watched her like she'd just been thrown the basketball for the deciding shot in the game they'd been discussing. Both men knew she'd already committed to the party at Mirabelle's. *Well, hell,* she thought, *I might as well be standing in another stadium for all the chance I have of this shot scoring.*

Butterflies went on a rampage inside her stomach. "Although I'd love to, Brock, I can't. I already have plans." This couldn't be happening. Brock finally asks her out, and she wasn't going?

He coaxed, "I'd really like to talk to you ... alone." The note of flirtation she heard had her doing a quick double-take. In her peripheral vision she saw that Daniel and Ray maintained their spectator status.

As she studied Brock's handsome face—a pastime she could easily indulge in for all eternity—she shook her head, saying a decided, "I'm sorry, not tonight."

Brock looked surprised, then seemed to be waiting for her

to tell him she'd only been kidding.

Her internal voice screamed, "You idiot. He'll never ask you again! What are you doing?" But, Mirabelle's party was something she needed to do, and, darn it, something she wanted to do. Sure, she hoped the end results of gleaning information and wisdom from the graduates would culminate in her "granting," and ultimately, in Brock falling in love with her. But, besides that, she'd been looking forward to enjoying Gus and Mirabelle's company tonight.

Still, her fear-based need to grab the opportunity Brock held out like a carrot tempted her to cave in to immediate gratification. She had to remind herself—quite sternly—that this was exactly what Mirabelle's lesson warned against. Step Number Six ran through her mind. *Step into the unknown; put your faith in the universe.*

Eileen pushed past uncertainty to quiet the nagging voice of fear. She would not rescind her decision, even if they all sat at her newly polished table in silence until the New Year's Eve clock struck twelve.

Ray's glance had an edge of impatience to it, as if at any moment a timed buzzer would go off, and she'd get some kind of game penalty. But she knew in her heart a shot from this distance was doomed to fall short. *Faith*, she said again to herself.

Brock glanced uneasily at Ray and Daniel, then turned a steady gaze on her. "How about brunch tomorrow then? Somewhere with a nice ocean view?"

When those tests Mirabelle spoke of hit, they did so with a vengeance and without warning. This time she felt stronger. She shrugged her shoulders in apology. "Sorry, I'm going to my father's house tomorrow morning." She looked toward the other two men, noticing Daniel's smug smile, and she clutched the dust rag, fighting the sudden urge to smack him. "Daniel," she said his name with reproach, "and Ray are going with me to help move some boxes."

Eileen wondered why Brock seemed to have trouble accepting what he must surely consider an insignificant rejection. Although her refusal had to be a minor defeat for a man like him, it must be a first, she concluded. All she knew for certain was that Brock didn't look comfortable being turned down. She got the impression that the fact it happened in front of the other two men didn't help.

Brock asked in his usual confident voice, "We're still on for Monday lunch?" Their Monday lunches had been a sure thing.

The immense relief she felt came out in a rush of breath. Even though she wouldn't be working at the office during the day Monday, she wasn't about to miss a lunch with Brock. "Of course." She forced herself to stop fiddling with the dust cloth and container of polish, and to rest her hands on the table.

She'd done it. The test had been given, the game had played through, and Eileen knew in her heart, she'd come out a winner. She relinquished the last bit of uncertainty, replacing it with trust that the moment was as it should be. Things would work out. Ultimately she would get her wish. With that thought in mind, she felt the smile she gave Brock turn into a satisfied, maybe even saucy, grin. "I'm looking forward to our lunch on Monday."

Brock took her by surprise when he got up and came around the table to give her a slow, intimate kiss just to the right of her mouth. Then he left.

Swoosh! She mentally heard the basketball go though the hoop.

As soon as the door closed behind Brock, Ray stood up and yelled, "She shoots, she scores!"

Daniel, on the other hand, sat back in his chair with arms crossed and an unreadable look on his face that caused a jolt to her heart. He said quietly, "The game's not over."

***

At six-thirty, wearing a new red-velvet evening dress, the mail-order contact lenses which had finally arrived, and her hair swept up in a French twist, Eileen walked across *Deviazione's* courtyard toward Mirabelle's apartment with confidence and anticipation of a magical evening. She'd taken a chance on a pair of daring—for her—matching open-toed pumps and reminded herself to walk carefully across the uneven paving tiles.

Colorful Christmas lights adorned each apartment archway, and Eileen could hear Nat King Cole singing about, "Jack Frost nipping at your nose." Despite California's usual lack of snow—in fact the evening had turned quite mild—she felt infused with the glow of the Holiday spirit. The filled-to-capacity party had already spilled out of Mirabelle's apartment and onto the patio. Maybe it was the sound of laughter that warmed the evening.

Eileen smiled at the couple conversing by the fountain, nodded a greeting to another small group of people she didn't know, then started up the short path toward Mirabelle's open door.

A tall, still figure at the stoop's top step caught her eye. And her breath. Daniel was dressed in a dark blue double-breasted suit and white shirt. He still wore his glasses, probably because he knew Ray was coming, but at least he didn't have on the usual bow tie. He'd opted instead for a long, Christmas-red tie.

The penetrating, smoldering look he gave her left her breathless. It blocked out the music, and the milling people disappeared. For a brief moment only the two of them existed in a fantasy world of holiday lights. A bubble of fear told her to blink, to break the spell of his gaze. That it was an illusion of her own making, an illusion she shouldn't be entertaining. But something indefinable in his gaze held her entranced.

As he descended the stairs, then reached out his hand to her, his gaze never left hers. She didn't remember putting her hand in his, but the warmth of Daniel's touch on her fingers told her she had. Her entire body reacted with awareness, as though it had been jolted out of a deep sleep. Stupidly, she looked down at their joined hands, sure she would see sparks.

Daniel's gentle tug urged her closer as he whispered, "You're beautiful, Eileen."

Her gaze shot to his face, searching for the truth. She didn't want him to keep telling her she was beautiful, at least not in that slow, seductive way that crawled inside her to melt her very bones. Her heart belonged to Brock. Her wish, her dream-of-a-lifetime, was within her grasp. How dare Daniel, who would surely ultimately wreak havoc on her life then leave never to be seen again, force her to feel what she should only be feeling for Brock.

His thumb intimately stroked the top of her hand, and her insides flashed with heat. She meant to step away, to tell him he had no right to touch her like this, but instead a languid voice which couldn't possibly be her own, murmured, "Thank you, Daniel."

Nat King Cole's lively, "Deck the halls ..." finally broke the spell, and Eileen tugged her hand from his. He immediately put his hands in his pockets and took a step back as if realizing he'd wandered into forbidden territory. She knew he was well aware anything romantic between them remained forbidden.

He looked around with a quizzical expression. "Mirabelle has quite a large and diverse group of friends."

They walked together into the crowded apartment, and Eileen instantly spotted Gus across the room. It wasn't difficult, since he towered above most of the other guests.

Eileen said, "Mirabelle's a very special lady. In her line of work she meets—" Eileen stopped herself, but by Daniel's quizzical expression, she hadn't been fast enough.

"What line of work? I figured she was retired." He studied the people as if searching for clues.

Think fast, she told herself. She wasn't a good liar, and even if she could come up with a good one, surely with Daniel's training, he would be able to read it in her eyes. "She's a mentor, of sorts." Eileen wondered how Mirabelle felt about outsiders learning of Wishmaker's activities. Since the guest list included *Deviazione* tenants as well as graduates Eileen decided it must not be an issue.

Daniel's eyebrows reached up. "Some of these people look too old for mentors. Just what kind of mentor is she?"

Mirabelle rushed toward them, rescuing her from responding. "Daniel! Eileen! You're here! And how wonderful you both look. Our very own Cinderella and Prince Charming to enchant the evening."

Eileen shot Daniel an uneasy glance, responding to Mirabelle with, "Thank you," as she hugged the woman.

"Mirabelle, this is quite a party," Daniel said as he kissed her cheek, eliciting a girlish grin from the woman.

"Just a few of the friends I've made over the years," Mirabelle replied.

A woman with a tray of fluted champagne glasses offered the group drinks. They each took one, Eileen wondering if she'd make it back across the courtyard in her heels after imbibing. She'd always been a lightweight when it came to the effects of alcohol.

"Eileen tells me you're a mentor." Daniel's look of attentive interest reminded Eileen that his charm could be calculated. He was just doing what he'd perfected into an art form no woman seemed able to resist. His direct gaze set out to make Mirabelle feel like the world revolved around her and that his entire focus rested on her alone. Eileen wondered if she was a fool to think the way he'd looked at her earlier held some kind of special meaning.

Mirabelle answered Daniel's question. "In a way. I'm a member of an organization called *Wishmakers*. We help people fulfill their potential in life."

"Just how do you do that?"

Eileen looked at Mirabelle.

Mirabelle answered with a straightforward, "Magic."

Daniel laughed. "I get it. You can't divulge company secrets, right?"

Mirabelle's laugh rang out like sleigh bells. "I have no secrets. You do believe in magic, don't you, Daniel?"

He startled Eileen by turning his smile on her, his searching eyes contemplative. "I guess I do at that, Mirabelle."

There went those butterflies again. Eileen gulped the champagne, the cool liquid easing her suddenly dry throat.

"You two will have to excuse me. I see a new arrival." With that Mirabelle bustled off.

Gus waved and began walking toward them, halting every step or two to greet acquaintances. By the warm reception he got from each and every guest, Eileen could tell they liked him as much as she did.

As her glance flitted around the room again, it got caught in the web of Daniel's intense scrutiny. Because of the crowd, they stood very close, and now Daniel reached out to take her champagne glass and set it, along with his, on a nearby table. Then he took her hands and pulled her close. She couldn't tear her gaze from his. What was he doing? Was he going to kiss her right here in the middle of Mirabelle's party? The notion zinged warmly through her middle. The moment his arms went around her, Glen Miller's dreamy rendition of, "I'll Be Home For Christmas," filled the night, blocking out the world around her.

She couldn't help applying the words, "I'll be home for Christmas, if only in my dreams," to her life, and the resulting melancholy arrested the need to push away from the comfort of Daniel's arms. He felt so good, so right. She placed her left hand on his shoulder as Daniel pressed her other hand to his chest where she could feel his steady heartbeat. Then he began to slowly rock back and forth as their bodies pressed close.

Normally, Eileen would never have dared to dance when no one else in the room was dancing. But this felt right. Mirabelle had said, "If it feels right, go with it." And boy, was she going to *go with it.*

She didn't know if it was her imagination, or the party spirit, but the way Daniel caressed her made her feel cherished and adored. And a little bit dizzy, like she was standing at the edge of a high-dive.

Closing her eyes and resting her head against Daniel's shoulder, she gave in to the dizzying feelings, experiencing them to the fullest as Mirabelle had said she should.

The music ended all too soon, replaced with, Bing Crosby's, "Let it Snow," and she took a step away from the edge of the precipice, gently pushing away from Daniel's arms.

Looking into his eyes, she tried to discern whether what she felt from him had been real or just another one of Special Agent Daniel Manatucci's tricks. What she saw was passion, and her insides did a triple gainer...with a twist. She gulped against the sudden need for air and then ran her tongue over her lips.

Daniel slowly smiled, and she couldn't tell if it was with satisfaction or affection.

Gus joined them, breaking the spell Daniel had become

expert at spinning.

Gus said, "Ohoooo!" as he looked her up and down. "Girlfriend, it's a good thing you paid attention in our self-defense class, with the way you look tonight! You're the Queen of Hearts, right down to your ruby red slippers."

He shook hands with Daniel, who turned to her with an arched eyebrow, evidently recovering from their dance quicker than she had. "I thought you said the class was for women only."

Only after she had said, "Thank you for the compliment, Gus," and was sure she was out of the emotional and physical deep end she'd waded into, did she respond to Daniel. "I'm sure you wouldn't be interested in a beginners' self-defense class."

"I might," Daniel responded.

"Oh, yeah, right." Mr. James-Bond-Wannabe-with-a-black-belt-in-everything. She felt like she'd regained solid footing.

With a smirk on his face, Daniel picked up his champagne. "I'd love to see you in action. Do you wear one of those thong work-out getups?"

She rolled her eyes. "Not in a million years, so it would be a wasted effort on your part." Truth was, she did have one. She glanced at Gus to see if he'd tattle.

Gus rubbed his chin as he scrutinized them both. "I don't know. You two seem to be pretty evenly-matched sparring partners."

Eileen realized she was indeed sparring with Daniel when there was absolutely no reason to. The dance had thrown her off balance. They were friends, she reminded herself. *Think about unconditional love. You love him as a friend, and friends don't need control dramas.*

She said, "Daniel, you're welcome to sit in on a class any time. Gus and I leave at six a.m., sharp, Monday through Friday."

"I just might do that, thanks." He raised his glass to her in a toast, then took a sip.

She prayed the man who'd made it clear he wasn't a morning person wouldn't take her up on her offer.

Just then, to the strains of, *Hark! The Herald Angels Sing,* she saw Ray Mitchell rush through the front door.

Ray seemed out of breath, quickly scanning the room until he saw them, then he waved frantically and hurried over. His eyes looked wild, and he had dark smudges on his face and hands.

He said, "There's been a fire at Wincomp!"

Ten

Daniel watched Ray fight to catch his breath as the man glanced around the gaily-attired crowd.

Ray said between gasps, "Neither of you...answered your phones. I figured you were...already at the party, so I came right over."

Gus appeared with a glass of water and handed it to Ray, who nodded his gratitude and quickly drank it. Mirabelle joined the group, concern on her face.

"A fire? What happened?" Eileen put her hands to her pale face. Daniel put an arm around her shoulders, surprised and pleased when she easily leaned into him.

Ray said, "We don't know. Jim, the night guard, was unconscious when the firefighters found him. I was driving by Wincomp on my way here when I saw the fire trucks and police cars. By then, the ambulance had already taken Jim to the hospital. I don't know how he is."

Mirabelle whispered, "How awful."

"How extensive is the damage?" Daniel needed to get to the evidence before it was completely obliterated by well-meaning local authorities who might not know about the FBI probe.

He'd been around enough to know chances were slim that the fire was an accident. He also had a sick feeling this might, depending on the damage, put an end to his investigation. Without evidence, he couldn't build a case. His assignment would be terminated.

The possibility of never seeing Eileen again left an uneasy knot in his stomach, a knot he forced himself to ignore. From the beginning he'd known any relationships he formed would be temporary. As with every assignment, he would move on. He knew that even if he'd wanted a relationship with Eileen, the nomadic lifestyle he'd chosen, as well as her love for Brock, made it doubly impossible.

Ray said, "The damage? I don't know. From what I could see in the dark—the electricity is out—things are a soggy mess."

Daniel asked, "How is it you were allowed in the building? I assume an investigation was going on."

"In the commotion, I got all the way to our floor before a firefighter stopped me. The door to Eileen's office was blocked by firefighters, cops, and Brock."

Daniel felt Eileen stiffen against him, her body readying to take flight. She was as anxious as he was, if not more, to get to Wincomp.

Ray continued. "Brock asked me to find you, Eileen. The lights are out, so you'll need a flashlight. And you'll have to use the stairs."

Daniel kept his arm around Eileen, urging her toward the door. "Come on, let's go. Ray, are you going back?" Daniel wondered why Ray's hands were smudged. Had he tried to put out the fire? Or were the smoke stains from tampering with evidence?

"Yes, I'm going back. As soon as the cops give me the okay, I want to check out my workstation. It looked like it had pretty extensive water damage."

"Then we'll meet you there."

All three of them said hurried apologies for having to leave Mirabelle's party, then quickly maneuvered through the throng of partygoers, heading across the patio toward the parking area.

Daniel came to an abrupt halt under the archway when Eileen's foot slipped out of one of her high heels, causing her to stumble. When he reached out to steady her, he saw panic in her eyes that had nothing to do with her unsure footing. He wanted to will away the panic. The night had started out so great, only to turn into a nightmare.

He said, "I'm sorry the enchantment's ending before midnight, Cinderella. You want to change clothes then meet me at Wincomp? I'd wait, but I need to—"

"I'm fine," she interrupted. Stepping out of the other shoe, she quickly picked them both up, carrying them as she headed toward his car. "I have to get to Brock." Looking back at Daniel, she admonished, "Hurry!"

He might hurry to investigate the fire, but he damn well wasn't going to bust his butt getting Eileen to her precious Brock. It was beyond him why she still harbored romantic feelings for The Jerk anyway. He obviously had a bad case of the Alyssas, even though he might occasionally flirt with Eileen.

What was it that Brock Van Buren did for Eileen that made her so hung up on him? What missing element in Eileen's life did Brock represent? After a few moments, he gave up. He was admittedly too close to the case to figure it out.

Daniel contented himself with the knowledge that Eileen and Brock didn't go together.

But then the ugly head of the reality dragon reared up. Many people Daniel knew made odd, incongruous couples. But that didn't stop them from being together, many staying in loveless marriages for unknown reasons.

He looked over at Eileen's worried frown as they got into the car. "Take it easy. We don't know how bad it is yet."

She smoothed the delicate velvet of her dress as she clicked her seatbelt into place. Once settled, she took a deep breath, hugging herself. "This is all so crazy. One thing after another. I'm beginning to wonder if Wincomp's jinxed."

"Jinxed? No. The government hacking, the software theft, and the virus were all done by someone—probably the same someone—not fate. And tonight Jim Stewart's injuries and the fire were caused by a human hand."

They sat in silence the rest of the way to Wincomp's offices, Daniel thinking what a shame it was that Eileen's party mood had taken a nosedive. Maybe he felt a little sorry for himself as well. She looked so elegantly beautiful that for him, too, the evening had started out on an enchanted foot.

They pulled into the office parking lot. Several fire-fighting units and police cars, lights ablaze, sat in front.

Daniel got two flashlights out of his trunk, grabbing a pair of rubber gloves and evidence bags and shoving them into his pocket. He and Eileen approached a uniformed officer and, discreetly showing his FBI badge, Daniel briefed the man on the undercover operation.

"Who's in charge?" he asked the officer.

"Arson Inspector Ryan. He's up on the fifth floor."

An arson investigator was in charge instead of the police. That only meant one thing: They'd already established that the fire had not been an accident.

"We'll go on up, then."

The officer motioned them in, signaling another officer at the door to let them pass.

The moment they entered the foyer, they plunged into darkness. Daniel snapped on his flashlight and Eileen followed suit. The beam of Daniel's light danced over Eileen's red dress, giving it a shimmering, ghostly quality in the surrounding dark.

A firefighter with lighted helmet emerged from the stairwell, and Daniel walked over to him to present his badge. He pointed his flashlight at the identification. "Anything I should know before I go up?"

The young firefighter looked surprised by the FBI identification, but didn't ask questions about it. "One injury. A security guard. He's already been transported. The fire was small and quickly contained. Mostly water damage from the sprinkler system."

Daniel heard Eileen's shuddery exhalation. He looked over at her. Although obviously shaken, she looked ready to handle whatever they might find. At least he wouldn't have to worry about her falling apart.

The walk up the dark stairwell seemed an eternity, but Eileen, in stocking feet, gamely trudged on. Daniel had never particularly liked closed-in places, and the five flights up felt like an endless tunnel. The only good thing about it was Eileen's firm grip on his arm, and the feel of her soft body pressed against his.

Once they exited the stairwell, he held Eileen back for a moment. Although in the darkness he could see no evidence of smoke, he could smell the acrid tang, confirmation that there had been a fire. The carpet sloshed beneath their feet. Portable lights had been set up at the far end of the room, where Daniel could see several people. "Be careful. You don't want to disturb evidence."

She nodded and pointed the flashlight toward the back of the room, taking cautious steps in that direction. She didn't seem to notice the wet carpet, even though she was in stocking feet. The red shoes dangled from her fingers, which she'd hooked through the toe openings.

The scene of a fire wasn't the best place to be barefooted. Who knew what kind of debris might be on the floor. Daniel said, "You'd better put your shoes back—"

She took off as if she hadn't heard.

"Damn woman," Daniel said under his breath as he lagged behind, his status as an investigator requiring him to assess the room as he went. The only damage to the front workstations appeared to be from the automatic sprinkler system. The fire must have been contained to the rear offices.

When he joined the small crowd around Eileen's office, he noticed she and Brock weren't there. Evidently they were in his office. Daniel could see people going in and out of Brock's open door.

Daniel recognized the man in charge by the bright orange jumpsuit with the fire department arm patch and the word ARSON across his back. He approached, identified himself as an FBI agent, and told the arson investigator about the ongoing investigation at Wincomp.

Daniel also told him that Mr. Van Buren was unaware of the FBI probe and needed to remain so. Inspector Ryan assured Daniel that his department would help him in any way and would use the utmost discretion. He also said he would let the police officers know about the Federal investigation.

Daniel then joined Brock, Eileen, and another officer in Brock's office. He heard Brock inform Eileen that the fire had affected only her work area.

Daniel noticed the strange look on Brock's face as his gaze raked the evening clothes they both had on. Brock put what could have been either a comforting or possessive arm around Eileen, and Daniel's gut tightened in frustration.

Inspector Ryan came in and said, "So far, our investigation shows a timed incendiary device beneath the desk. Actually, the desk and the immediate area were the only things burned. The desk acted like a shield. The smoke detector tripped the alarm as well as the sprinkler system, so we arrived on scene before the fire ever got out of control."

Eileen chewed on her bottom lip, obviously fighting to control tears. She finally took a deep, ragged breath, asking, "Can I go in? I'd like to see what I can salvage."

The Inspector Ryan shook his head. "Sorry, Miss, not until we've completed our investigation. That'll take some time." He looked down at his feet, then up at Eileen. "I hope you had backup disks of your data and that they weren't in your office. The computer and the adjoining file cabinet were destroyed."

Eileen shrugged, her shoulders slumping. "My backups were locked in the file cabinet." She indicated her office.

The inspector winced. "I'm afraid they're gone, then. The water damage to the rest of the floor's computers will be extensive, too. I don't know enough about computers to know if the damage is repairable."

"Wincomp had an automatic shut-off system, so most of the circuitry should be salvageable," Brock said. "Drying out the motherboards shouldn't be a problem."

A single tear slid down Eileen's cheek. In a quiet voice she said, "My work. My project. Everything's gone." She shook her head. "I should have taken the disks home. But how could I have known? I know none of my friends did this. None of them are cold-blooded or malicious. They would never deliberately cause this kind of permanent damage."

"The inspector said the fire was started by a timed device," Daniel pointed out. "That's as cold-blooded as they come. And whoever set the fire didn't give Jim a second thought, either." He looked at her pointedly, hoping she'd finally get it through that stubborn head of hers that someone at Wincomp was responsible for all the recent troubles. "One of your *friends*, isn't a friend."

Brock tugged on Eileen's arm. "Come sit down while I call the hospital to see how Jim's doing." He pulled his cell phone from his pocket, facing it toward the illumination of the battery-powered lantern so he could see to dial.

Daniel took advantage of Brock's distraction and went with Inspector Ryan and a man introduced as Detective Haden, into Eileen's office. When he saw the destruction of Eileen's workspace, his heart jerked. The charred remains of her monitor and tower looked like so much space junk after a bad re-entry. And the file cabinet stood open, the contents a black heap. He could tell none of it would be salvageable.

A glittering object to the side of the desk caught his eye, and he walked over to bend down, shining his flashlight toward it. The small bottle of what Eileen had called "fairy dust" sparkled, unbroken. He wondered how it could have survived the fire since it had been perched on top of Eileen's monitor.

Taking the rubber gloves and evidence bag out of his pocket, he looked over his shoulder at Inspector Ryan. "How fast are your fingerprint guys?"

"LA's always overburdened. It'll take about a week."

"I'll have my men analyze this bottle then," Daniel said. "They'll shoot both you and the DA a report ASAP."

"Fine," Inspector Ryan said, bending to peer into the file cabinet.

"Detective Hayden nodded as he jotted in his notebook. "That's Special Agent 'Manatucci' with two c's?"

"Correct."

"I'll be back in a moment," the inspector said as he left the office. The officer followed.

Daniel snapped on the rubber gloves, carefully picked the bottle up by the sealed cork lid, and slid it into a clear plastic bag. He slipped the bag into his coat pocket.

Only as Daniel stood did he realize someone was watching him. The bright spotlight set up by the fire inspector made it difficult at first to determine just who stood in the shadowed doorway. Finally Daniel recognized the silhouetted form of

Ray Mitchell. How long had he been there?

Daniel cursed. He had just given Ray reason to suspect Daniel wasn't who he pretended to be. How had Ray gotten past the security officers downstairs? Again.

"Ray," Daniel said, acknowledging the man.

"You know, they don't want us messing around with stuff that could be evidence."

The look on Ray's face didn't indicate he thought Daniel's snooping was anything more than a co-worker's curiosity, and he gave no sign that he'd seen Daniel take the bottle.

Daniel gave Ray his best, "Oh, gosh, you're right," look as he carefully stepped around the debris to join him just outside Eileen's office. He kept his gloved hands in his pockets. "They let you back in. That means they're almost done with their investigation?"

"No. Some fire department guy wants to question me, so they let me come up."

Ray looked toward Brock's office. "I think Eileen's going to need all the support she can get. From what I can tell, all the other stations are salvageable. Hers was the only one hit."

Daniel discreetly removed the evidence gloves as they joined the others in Brock's office. He found himself clenching his jaw at the sight of Brock's arm around Eileen. She leaned into him and had her hand on his chest. And instead of Brock's usual friendly aloofness, his entire focus went to the woman in his arms. He smiled down at her reassuringly, then kissed her forehead. Daniel wasn't too thrilled, either, by the way Brock's hand intimately rubbed the small of her back.

Daniel had to wonder if Eileen's knock-out looks tonight had anything to do with Brock's attention. The Jerk was so superficial.

He noticed that Ray's reaction to Brock and Eileen wasn't too positive, either. The older man's gaze narrowed as he looked at his boss.

Was there something here Daniel had missed in the beginning of his investigation? Was Ray jealous of Brock and the feelings Eileen had for him? That could be motive enough to sabotage Wincomp. But Daniel's probe had already pretty much ruled out Ray as a suspect, and he didn't think Ray's affection for Eileen made all that much difference. All the same, he'd keep an eye on the situation.

He almost chuckled as the irony hit him. Eileen, who usually dressed like she believed herself to be plain and unlovable, had more admirers than she realized. Three men in this very room cared very much about her.

***

Mirabelle saw the last of her guests out, the high mood of the evening still with her. But, even with her immediate energy at a good level, the global energy—the Granter energy—wavered uncertainly. To think, the wonderful people gathered in her home tonight might be the last *graduates*.

Ever.

Mirabelle's heart ached. She needed to do something to insure the continuance of the magic.

Her thoughts turned to Eileen, and she quickly went to her PC, slipping her PC-linked headset on. She typed in Wishmaker's web site address and saw the raining sparkles and heard the musical opening about dreams being wishes your heart makes, which never failed to give her a little thrill.

Soon she had her supervisor, Mary, on the line. "Mary, there was a fire at Wincomp tonight."

"I know. I've been receiving impressions from Eileen all evening. I'm afraid it's bad. We're losing her. *Granting* is further away than ever now. The impact of the fire has already started spreading and building on itself, as if the fire had never been put out. I'm afraid we're not going to be able to stop it from getting out of control unless we act quickly."

"Oh dear. When I saw Eileen and Daniel together tonight— saw the way they looked at each other—I was sure things were going well."

"Tonight's disaster has made her forget your teachings. She's turned her focus away from Daniel and to a man whom she mistakenly believes can give her security."

"Brock. What can I do?" Mirabelle frantically searched for ideas, but, short of all-out magic, she came up with a big zilch. Little fixes weren't going to work this time.

Mirabelle watched the monitor as Mary leaned forward. "You'll have to chance tapping into The Power."

Use The Power when they were critically low as it was? She'd be risking everything. If they were wrong and it didn't help, they would have made the biggest mistake of Wishmakers' existence. There would be no turning back. "There's no other way? I was hoping to put off using it until the Solstice at the very earliest."

"We'll have to use it now and pray that the hope it gives her can carry her through to the Solstice," Mary said. "Then she should be ready to grant. It's our only hope. Let's just pray nothing else happens, or we're doomed. Our resources will have been depleted, and she'll be on her own. If she doesn't grant by midnight of the New Year, our years of helping will be at an end. We will be forced to abandon Eileen, along with every potential future grantee. Negative power will reign. The foretold power restructure will become one-sided."

"What shall I do?" Mirabelle asked.

"The fire destroyed Eileen's backup disks. If she gets them back, she will regain her footing, her emotional balance, and be emotionally open to see her true love again.

Mirabelle asked, "You mean Daniel?"

"Yes. But, to do that, you'll need to use your PC to 'recover' the data. You'll need to download and copy. But you must act quickly, before Eileen gets home."

Mirabelle asked, "Recover the data? I thought it was lost." This was beyond Mirabelle's relatively recent computer training.

Mary chuckled. "Never lost. Are our thoughts and images ever really lost?"

Mirabelle began to see. "No, they remain electrical impulses."

"Same as computer data. The people who worry about their personal data floating around in space for anyone to tap into aren't too far off the mark. Although mortals don't yet have the knowledge to restructure and gather that data."

"You mean, it's as simple as the method we've always used to *gather*?"

Mary said, "Easier. Now we can do it with a keyboard and

monitor, so you won't have to *visualize*. The computer screen will project the visuals."

"And you want me to do this?" Mirabelle gasped, alarmed. "I've had little need in the past to *gather*, and I haven't been taught the latest methods."

"The energy needs to be focused by one person to keep it strong and pure. Don't worry, you're quite capable of *computer gathering*. You'll see. Once you've done it this way, you'll never want to go back to the old way again."

"I'm ready. How do I do it?"

Mary outlined the modifications to *gathering* in the computer age.

Mirabelle listened to Mary's instructions, then prepared for what she had to do. She focused her energy on the computer screen as she went through the lengthy, difficult process to access a Wishmaker's link she'd never before had need to enter. Once she gained access, she intoned the ancient words to call forth the power she needed. With each word spoken into her headset, she felt the surge build. Images flashed across the screen of past grantings and of a time when the force flowed freely through mankind.

At the pinnacle of the power surge she pulled from the universe and into her PC the last remaining ancient power of the Granters and typed in Eileen's name. Then she clicked SAVE.

***

It was nearly four in the morning and pouring rain before Eileen unlocked her front door, feeling every bit the weary, soggy, disheveled Cinderella. She looked down at her clinging dress and her torn nylons. She'd even misplaced her shoes. Her feet ached. She didn't have the strength to object when Daniel followed her inside her apartment.

She flipped on the kitchen light, threw a dishtowel over the chair seat, and plopped down at the dining room table. Her fingers met the smooth surface, finding comfort in the touch of old wood.

Daniel had also grabbed a dishtowel to protect the chair seat from his wet clothing before he sat in the chair next to her. He picked up her feet and rested them on his knees, massaging them as if he somehow knew how badly they ached. She didn't resist. All of her energy had been depleted earlier that night. And for the moment she was glad she didn't have the willpower to stop his touch. His hands felt wonderful, his thumbs expertly massaging the points of tension across her instep. She fought against the urge to moan in ecstasy.

A tendril of dripping hair hung over her left eye and her contacts felt gritty from the initial prolonged use. Her deep sigh filled the room.

"What message am I not getting Daniel?" She thought about Mirabelle's words regarding tests. If she learned her lessons and passed the tests, the lessons wouldn't be repeated. Well, whatever the lesson was, she wasn't getting it, and each subsequent challenge—or test—seemed more difficult than the last.

His quizzical look said she'd lost him.

"Why are these things happening to me?" No, she needed to correct herself. She wasn't the only victim here. "Why are they happening to Wincomp, to all of us at Wincomp? What lesson are we not learning that makes this happen over and over again?"

Daniel surprised her. "Maybe it's not your lesson. Maybe you're just caught in the fallout. Maybe it's Brock's lesson."

The thought had never occurred to her, but it made sense. But then again, maybe she just wanted the lesson to belong to someone else. Then she wouldn't need to face it and learn from it.

"It feels like my lesson. It was my computer and my life destroyed in the fire."

Daniel scoffed, giving her the feeling he held his anger in check. "Your life wasn't destroyed, Eileen. You're not the one lying unconscious in a hospital bed.

"So you've lost an 'innovative' program," he continued. "A program you know from experience will be outdated within a year. You can't create more? Of course you can. We both know you're not a one-shot wonder." His direct look set up a warmth in her chest. "Don't get me wrong. Losing your project was a tough break, sure. But it's not the end of the world.

You've got brains. You've got years and years of creating ahead of you. Years and years of life ahead of you." He sighed sharply. "Maybe your lesson is that Wincomp isn't for you, that you're supposed to be doing something different."

Daniel's words made her realize she had been whining. And he was right. She didn't have one damn thing to whine about. She did have years of new projects ahead of her. And over the past few weeks she'd grown more and more sure that some day she would find a lasting love. That 'some day' might even happen without Wishmakers. Brock might some day see her as his soul mate all on his own. As far as Wincomp not being her life? She'd have to think hard and long about that one.

She smiled at Daniel. "Thanks, I needed that." She stood, catching her sorry reflection in the front room's picture window. Laughter forced its way through her sadness. She looked a sight! "I'm going to get out of these wet things. You'd better go home and do the same."

She wasn't sure if his smoldering look or her wet dress caused the sudden shiver. "Good night, Daniel," she said with finality.

"Good night, Eileen. I'll be over at nine-thirty."

She followed him to the door so she could secure the lock. As she passed the small entry table something caught her eye. Two neat stacks of computer disks sat side-by-side. "Daniel," she whispered. "Look."

Her own neat handwriting labeled the disks as her backups. Daniel smiled. "You brought them home, after all."

She looked at him. "No. I didn't."

His eyebrows rose. "How else would they get there?"

"I swear, I don't know." As she grabbed the disks she was so excited she could have sworn she felt them hum with energy. Hurrying over to her computer, she sat down, not bothering to put a towel on the chair, and slipped the first disk in. "Please, let them be mine."

Daniel stood behind her, his hand on the chair back. "Looks like yours to me."

"How?" was all she could say. This wasn't possible. She was certain she'd left them at the office. Had whoever set the fire removed her backups? But, how could that person have accessed her apartment to leave them on the table? Fatigue and confusion short-circuited any hope of a rational explanation.

"I'm sure you'll find out sooner or later," Daniel assured her. "Just be glad they're safe." Then he teased her with, "You're life isn't over, after all."

She swiveled around in her chair. "Daniel, did you—?"

He shook his head. "No. I had no idea there was going to be a fire. If I had, I would have stopped it. And how could I have broken into your apartment when we spent the entire night together?"

She could tell he'd phrased his words to be intentionally, lightheartedly suggestive.

"And what a night it's been," she responded in kind.

He grew serious, his gaze penetrating. "I just hope it's not our last."

"What do you mean?"

"If the fire and water destroyed enough data at Wincomp, I won't be able to gather hard evidence. That means I'm out of a job. This job at least. I'll be reassigned."

Eileen swallowed. She didn't want to think about that possibility. "We can remain friends." It sounded feeble, weak, and incredibly, stupidly inept.

"Sure."

She could tell by his tone that this was a brush-off—the sort of brush-off you use when you don't want to be unkind. No, once Daniel was reassigned, he'd drive his old FBI-issue, nondescript car off into the sunset, assume another James Bond identity, and move on to the next adventure. It would be the last she ever saw of him.

He walked to the door, turning before he left. "Nine-thirty tomorrow? We're still on to go to your father's house?"

She nodded, her stomach clenching in the usual anxiety brought on by thinking about her past. But after tonight, for some strange reason, she felt strong enough to face both Dragon Lady Jeannette and the memories of her mother.

ELEVEN

At six o'clock Sunday morning Daniel's phone rang. An LAPD detective informed him that Wincomp's security guard had regained consciousness and was ready for questioning.

By seven o'clock Daniel had swung by the FBI lab with the bottle he'd taken from Eileen's office and now stood at Jim Stewart's bedside, ostensibly as a concerned friend.

The detective as well as Arson Investigator Ryan Daniel had met the previous night stood to the back of the room with arms folded, as if waiting for the "friendly visit" to end.

"Jim, old man," Daniel said as he gently high-fived him, then sat down in the bedside chair. "Just came by to see how you're doing. Hope you don't mind."

Jim scooted up further in his bed. "Naw. Glad to see you, Daniel. I hear there was a fire. Anyone else hurt? You know, Van Buren's girlfriend?"

Why would Jim think Eileen was hurt in the fire? "No, no one else. Guess you drew the unlucky straw, man."

He could see the relief on Jim's face. "I'm glad. When I woke up, right off I was worried about Miss Barden."

"Miss Barden?"

"Yeah, Mr. Van Buren's girlfriend, Alyssa. I'm glad she wasn't hurt."

Daniel realized his jealousy over Eileen's love for Brock had colored his thinking. Every one else on the planet thought The Jerk was dating Alyssa, while Daniel seemed stuck on thinking Eileen was his girl.

He refocused on the investigation, making sure the questions sounded like those from any other employee. "Man, what happened?"

"I'm not sure. Miss Barden had just left. We'd been shooting the breeze, and I was still standing by the elevator. I remember thinking how friendly she was...usually she seems like she's got a lot on her mind and hardly says hello. Then wham! Someone hit me from behind."

Daniel glanced toward the other two lawmen, noting they were alert and listening. Ryan, who was out of Jim's field of vision, began writing in his small investigation notebook.

Daniel asked, "Did you hear anything?"

"No, man, I didn't hear a thing."

Daniel had to wonder if Alyssa knew who Jim's attacker was. Had she intentionally distracted Jim? If Alyssa had been unusually nice to Jim, then she had to have some kind of agenda.

Daniel turned his thoughts back to his line of questioning. "What made you think it was a *guy* behind you and not a woman?"

Jim carefully rubbed his bandaged head and with a mirthless chuckle said, "I just get the feeling."

Daniel rose from the bedside chair. "I don't want to tire you." He leaned closer, saying in a low voice as he jerked his head toward the other men in the room, "Besides, looks like someone wants your opinion about what happened."

Jim looked nervous at the thought. "I just hope they don't think I did it."

Daniel said, "Naw. No chance. What? You knocked yourself out?" He started to leave, then turned back. "Oh, by the way, who was Alyssa going up to see? I hope they weren't hurt, either."

Jim shrugged his shoulders. "No one. Mr. Van Buren told me she could have access to the fifth floor any time. Said she was working on Wincomp's party plans and had to do it at odd hours."

Daniel tried to fit the puzzle pieces together but came up with a big hole in the middle of the picture. "Oh, that's good," he said. "I'm glad no one else was in the building and that Alyssa left before the fire started." He shook Jim's hand, careful not to jar him. "Take care, man. See you back at work. The place won't be the same without you."

"Thanks, man," Jim said. He looked tired, like the questioning had sapped him. Well, Jim wouldn't have to worry about too many more questions since Daniel had a confirming nod from both officials that they had all they needed from Jim for the moment.

As Daniel walked out to his car, he tried to figure out if Alyssa's presence had been a coincidence, and if not, then just who Alyssa was helping. Van Buren? No, he had the strong impression he had a mystery man here. And Alyssa was the only one who could enlighten him as to who that was. Had Eileen's stepsister been in on this from the beginning? Her, "I don't know nothin' 'bout computers," *could* be a cover, and she could be actually be a techno-genius. But he had serious doubts about that. Someone else had to be doing the actual hacking. But, who?

Daniel couldn't just haul her butt into jail for the third degree on mere suspicion. No, if she was involved, he wanted hard proof and an arrest. Too many suspects bolted once released after questioning.

Then a thought occurred to him. Maybe the proof he was looking for was in Eileen's backup disks and her online carrier. Alyssa had used Eileen's desk. She could theoretically have carried out the hacking from there. Or perhaps given an accomplice access to the computer.

Daniel had barely begun his initial check for the hacking on Eileen's workstation when she'd returned from her leave. And to be honest, even though he'd put Eileen on his list of suspects, his gut had told him she couldn't possibly have done it.

He made a mental note to get Jim's sign-in logs for the past two months. He needed to know if and when either Eileen or Alyssa had come in. Then he had to figure out a way, without blowing his undercover status, to question Alyssa to find out if she'd been seeing anyone suspicious over the past few months.

***

As Eileen waited for Ray and Daniel, she sipped orange juice and watched the local morning news on her small television. The combination of last night's fire, her confusion about Daniel, and the anticipation of delving into her past had her stomach so tied in knots she couldn't eat anything.

"Mild temperatures," the smiling blonde newscaster said, "and blue skies are predicted. We see no indication of a repeat of the past few days' freak storms."

"From the Stranger than Fiction Desk...," she continued. "Beginning at around one a.m., Pacific Standard Time, unusually strong solar flare activity began wreaking havoc with satellite transmissions. You may see the results of this today as an occasional momentary break-up of your television image, or a static-filled connection on your cell phone. Astronomers haven't yet released their theory about what's going on."

Her co-anchor, a round-face man, chuckled. "I don't know, Barbara. Weird weather. Record solar flares. Is this the beginning of what all those doomsday predictions talked about?"

Barbara scoffed. "Well, I'm not moving to Arizona just yet, Carlos. I feel confident California isn't going to fall into the ocean any day soon. On a lighter note—"

Not only was Eileen's life in chaos, the entire universe seemed off balance. What next? Snowstorms in California? That made her think of what a friend had signed in her high school yearbook, "Yours until hell freezes over and all the little devils go ice skating." This just might be the year.

At the sound of the doorbell Eileen put doomsday thoughts aside by pointing the remote at the television and clicked the off button. Taking a deep breath, she rose from the sofa to answer the door. Today was the day. With Ray and Daniel along for moral support, she would set out to face Dragon Lady as well as the ghosts in her father's attic. Immediately, she consciously retracted the unkind thoughts.

"Jeannette isn't a dragon lady," she said to herself. "She has reasons for what she does. I just don't know what they are. I don't *need* to know what they are. I just need to accept she has a part to play in the universe." Implementing Mirabelle's lessons took a concerted effort today.

When she opened the door, Daniel stood there in an oxford shirt, sweater and tan Dockers. He held a travel mug of coffee. He also wore his glasses.

She looked him up and down as she let him in. "Sorry, Ray's coming with us, and you'll have to go in your undercover persona."

"No problem." Daniel took a seat at the table and settled in to wait. "There's more of Daniel Collins in me than you know." His smile teased, but Eileen had entertained that very thought on more than one occasion.

Daniel Manatucci might intentionally come across as tough, but Daniel Collins definitely had a thoughtful, personable side. It was this side that made her consider him a friend.

"I'm really nervous," she said. "But I think I'm ready to deal with looking though my mother's things. And I feel justified in doing a little snooping to see if another will might exist." Even as she said it, in her heart she was beginning to doubt the possibility of another will.

He nodded, his gaze intense. "I hope you find what you're looking for."

She felt an uncertain smile tug at her mouth as she looked at Daniel. He had only entered her life two weeks ago, but she felt she'd known him forever. She realized that when she was with Daniel her beliefs about what she wanted became blurred and difficult to read, as though the mental page she'd drawn them on had been left out in the rain.

A cadenced rapping on the door caused them both to stand. Eileen went to answer it, feeling Daniel's gaze follow her. Why did he have to look at her that way? It made her knees weak. And why had he come into her life to complicate things? Was he one of the tests Mirabelle had spoken of? Or was he one of the choices? Instantly, she pushed the impulsive thought aside as out of the question.

She opened the door to admit Ray. Her burly friend stood there with a toy battle shield in one hand and a plastic sword in the other. Atop his head he wore a small, horned Viking helmet. She burst out laughing.

"I don't know about you," Ray stated with a straight face.

"But I'm not facing Jeannette without protection."

"Thank God for friends like you," Eileen said, still giggling as she hugged him and then let him in.

When he saw Daniel, the chagrined Ray *harrumphed*, and quickly took off the toy battle armor.

Daniel scoffed good-naturedly, "Dude, don't change on my account. The look suits you."

Ray took the teasing with his usual good humor. "You guys ready to get this over with?"

Eileen felt her hand shake as she picked up her purse and smoothed back her French braid, which was, for once, staying in place. "Sure."

They left. With her two tall friends flanking her, and Mirabelle's words of wisdom to guide her, she felt fortified for battle.

During the twenty-minute drive across town to her father's house, the men seemed determined to keep her mind off the task ahead by a continuous stream of inane conversation. For two habitually taciturn guys, she figured this must be quite a stretch, and she was grateful for their effort on her behalf.

And their efforts paid off. They talked about LA's new proposed sports center, the Lakers, and the price-of-gasoline-conspiracy-theory. They even talked about two recent movie releases they had no intention of going to see. And finally, they wound up with speculation about the unusual weather.

It kept her mind off everything—except to wonder what topic they'd come up with next—right up to the moment Ray turned into the long drive leading up to the house.

Ray's drawn out whistle had all of them looking at the imposing structure as they approached. "I'm always wowed by this place," he said solemnly. "It was definitely built to impress."

Eileen wasn't impressed. Maybe because she hadn't seen it in what seemed a long time, or maybe because of Mirabelle's lesson about giving. But for the first time in her life, her childhood home looked ostentatious and spoke of overindulgence. Who in the world needed a house with ten bedrooms? Bedrooms decorated to perfection, but seldom seen or used? Maybe a superstar who entertained large groups of people, but certainly not her father or stepmother, whose entertaining had mainly consisted of large dinner parties.

As Daniel pulled up to the rounded entry, she noticed his sideways glance and wondered what he was thinking. "What?" she said as she turned to face him.

"Kinda a step down to *Deviazione*, huh?"

She looked back to the structure of cold plaster and glass, and realized *Deviazione* wasn't a step down at all. She already felt more at home at her apartment than she ever remembered feeling here. Friends, serenity, and beauty surrounded her at *Deviazione*, making her feel secure and protected—feelings she'd long ago given up associating with her father's house. She shook her head and smiled in answer to Daniel's question.

The acknowledgement she saw in his eyes spoke volumes, and she wondered what he might say if Ray hadn't been present. She contented herself with knowing Daniel shared her impression.

They all got out of the car and walked up the steps. It could have been because of Ray's silly costume earlier, but as they stood before the large battlement doors, Eileen got the impression they were three warriors. She pushed the doorbell. It felt odd to ring the bell, but with Jeannette's edict, she didn't feel comfortable just walking in unannounced.

Daniel's hand caressed her elbow, fortifying her even further.

When the door opened, much to Eileen's consternation, Jeannette's attorney, Miles Catchum, stood there. He looked down his straight nose. "Sorry, but you're not going to be able to come in after all. And taking anything is out of the question."

The bubble of the calm, accepting attitude she'd been maintaining popped with the emotional report of a firecracker.

"I'd like to see you stop me!" She roughly pushed past Miles, surprising herself with how easily she had thrown him off balance. Her *entourage* followed in her wake as she stormed toward her stepmother's study, where the woman usually took her morning coffee.

Who she saw in the study had her screeching to an astonished halt just inside the double doors. Scuffled footsteps sounded behind her with Daniel and Ray's arrested progress. She turned to see she wasn't the only one with an open mouth. She looked back toward the room's occupants.

Not only did Jeannette hold court from a rigid, throne-like antique chair by the fire. But Alyssa sat on the French settee, intimately close to—of all people—her ex-boyfriend, Devin Hollenbeck. They were an item again? Her heart headed for the clouds, and then just as quickly plummeted to earth, as she realized how this must be affecting Brock. If he even knew. Alyssa wasn't averse to juggling two men at once.

Alyssa jumped up, a startled look on her face, and quickly walked over to stand next to the fireplace. "Eileen, what are you doing here?"

Eileen couldn't catch Devin's eye—he seemed intent on looking everywhere except in the group's direction—so she had trouble discerning his reaction.

Secure with the might of the two men behind her, she put her hands on her hips. "I arranged with Jeannette to come over this morning and get some of my mother's things." Her gaze shot back to where Devin sat. "Seems you weren't expecting me to make it past your guard." Then she blurted out, "Does Brock know about this?"

"This?" Alyssa's gaze flitted toward Miles as he entered the room and sat down across from Jeannette. It seemed to give her the needed moment to recover her composure, her spine stiffening. "What 'this' are you talking about, dear sister? Devin and I are still friends, and he just happened to stop by to say hello. Brock won't have a problem with it. He knows I'm devoted to him."

Eileen wondered which *him* she was referring to, Brock or Devin.

A shuttered, non-committal look passed across Devin's eyes.

Eileen decided to let it go for the moment. After all, it wouldn't be the first time Alyssa had changed her mind where Brock was concerned.

Taking a deep breath and turning to Jeannette, who had remained uncharacteristically silent for the entire exchange, Eileen said, "I've brought friends to help with the boxes." She began to introduce Daniel, but Jeannette held up her hand.

Her stepmother's expressionless face gave Eileen an uneasy feeling. The woman said, "I'm afraid things have changed since we spoke. Your impulsive act in contesting the will has resulted in the court issuing an order stating that nothing is to be removed from the house. Miles has counseled me that it wouldn't be prudent to go against the order and let you take your mother's things. An inventory will be conducted on Tuesday."

Eileen could tell Jeannette was fuming beneath that cold exterior. Jeannette went on. "It seems you've not only inconvenienced us, you've tied your own hands as well."

Eileen turned to the two silent men behind her. Daniel's eyes said the call was hers, and she felt he'd back her up on whatever she wanted to do. Ray's large shoulders shrugged.

Her gaze darted toward the stairs, then back to the two men. The urge to dash up the wide expanse and make a run for the attic overwhelmed her. But what good would it do to? Jeannette was right. She had tied her own hands. "I'll get a court order, then," she heard herself say in a surprisingly strong voice.

Jeannette rose from her chair and crossed her arms. "You bring me a court order saying you have access to the attic, and I'll let you go up. Until then, you are not welcome in this house. Please leave." She turned her back on Eileen, facing the fire.

Eileen had to smile. For the first time since Jeannette had become her supposed stepmother, Eileen wasn't affected by the woman's intentional rejection of her. She even felt stirrings of empathy for the woman who seemed so uptight and unhappy. Without a word, Eileen turned and, walking between Daniel and Ray, headed for the door.

Once the three were in the car, Daniel said, "I'm sorry. I should have thought about the inventory restricting your access."

She shrugged. "I'm not giving up. I'll do whatever it takes. Getting this close and having to turn back has made me more determined than ever. I'll find out what I have to do."

She recalled Mirabelle's words about letting go of her fears and trusting in her destiny. When the time was right, the attic doors would swing open for her, and her past would be revealed.

A thought occurred to her. Maybe the Universal Power

Mirabelle always spoke about intended for her to accept Brock's invitation to brunch, and that's why this path had been closed. Then, again, she could be reaching. She'd call Brock as soon as she got home and see if his invitation was still open. One thing was for sure; he wasn't with Alyssa this morning.

She felt Daniel's hand take hold of hers. He gave it a reassuring squeeze, and her pulse raced. She concentrated on not reacting to the feel of his touch. Nothing could come of it, and she was making too much of the gesture. She forced a smile and then looked out the window to watch the passing traffic.

***

Daniel drove Eileen and Ray back to *Deviazione*, said a hurried good-bye then headed to his apartment. He put a call in to Inspector Ryan, glad to find him in his office.

"You have plans to question Alyssa Barden?"

"Thought we'd wait until we heard from you," came Ryan's reply.

"If I question her I blow my cover, so I'd appreciate it if you would handle it."

"No problem. I already did a DMV and have her address right here."

"I just left her at her home not more than twenty minutes ago, so you might be in luck." Daniel added, "I have reason to believe her accomplice might be a man named Devin Hollenbeck. He was with her this morning. Would you question him, too?"

"Sure thing. I'm on it. I'll shoot over the results as soon as I'm finished."

"Great. Thanks." Daniel hung up, every nerve buzzing. His gut told him this was it. Now he needed Eileen's backup disks and some luck, and he'd have the case tied up.

He sat on the sofa, Eileen the only dark cloud to rain on his parade of success. He knew the investigation would soon be over. But he also knew he didn't want his relationship with Eileen to be over.

"What are you?" he said out loud to himself. "Chicken? Just ask her to drop The Jerk and go away with you." Even as he said it, he knew his chances of getting her to care for him as much as he cared for her were next to impossible. A voice inside his head told him to persuade her. Friendly persuasion was one of his specialties. *But*, another voice warned, *she still thinks she's in love with The Jerk.*

***

Other than the unexpected stormy weather, Sunday was fast turning out to be one great day, Eileen thought as she looked across the starched white tablecloth at Brock. His efforts to secure the ocean-view table were lost on her. Her gaze couldn't get past the view just this side of the window.

Brock's smile was the only thing she wanted to look at.

He said, "I'm glad you changed your mind and agreed to have brunch with me. I've missed you."

They'd already talked about the fire when she'd called him to say she could go to brunch after all. Brock had made arrangements for the cleanup of Wincomp to be done by Monday afternoon, and now they had only each other to concentrate on.

She hadn't told him about the fiasco with Jeannette, and she wasn't about to bring up Alyssa to break what seemed to be turning into a romantic mood.

Eileen chose to reply with a non-committal, "There's no place else I'd rather be."

The server approached their table with a carafe of orange juice and a bottle of champagne. "Mr. Van Buren. The usual?" At his nod, the waiter looked at her, "A mimosa for the lady, also?"

"No, just champagne, thank you."

He poured champagne for her and a combination of champagne and orange juice for Brock. Evidently, Brock's preference for mimosas was well-known at this restaurant. The fact that he came here so often took the edge off the feeling this was a special occasion. It was just another Sunday brunch for Brock. He'd probably only asked her because Alyssa was busy.

Brock discounted her self-pitying thoughts by setting his glass aside and reaching across the small table to clasp her hand. "I really meant what I said, Eileen. I've missed you. There's no place I'd rather be, or no one else I'd rather be with."

She swallowed hard, then with her free hand took a sip from the fluted glass. The chilled bubbles soothed her throat but gave her little help in coming up with a response to his flattering words. Could they be trusted? The warmth of his hand caressing hers told her they could.

Brock had never talked to her in this *you're-as-sexy-as-hell* kind of tone before. And, for as long as she'd wished for it, she didn't know how to respond now that it had happened. Was the magic starting to work?

"Cat got your tongue?" Brock chuckled as he rubbed his thumb across the top of her hand. "That's got to be a first."

She cocked her head to the side, looking into his eyes. Above all else, Brock had been her friend for most of her life. She felt she could be honest. "This Sunday brunch is a first, too." She studied his eyes, but saw no hesitation there.

He said, "But definitely not the last. I'd like to see more of you. Away from the office. Away from everyone. Just the two of us."

She felt lightheaded and knew it wasn't the champagne, which she'd only sipped. The silly thought, *Gee, like, dating?* Had her feeling like a teenager. She tried to keep her voice even. "I'd like that."

The relief she saw on his face surprised her. Then she surprised herself by asking, "What about Alyssa?"

His, "Alyssa who?" had her wondering if Mirabelle's magic involved an amnesia spell. He smiled at her like she was the only woman in the room, or in the world, for that matter.

This is what you wanted, you idiot, don't over-analyze it. Just enjoy!

An awkward silence filled the space between them. During their lunches they'd mostly talked about Wincomp. Now s h e wasn't sure which direction to head the conversation.

She looked up when the server came for their orders, grateful for the interruption. Now that she had Brock's full attention, she wasn't sure what to do with it. She took a big gulp of champagne.

Three glasses later, she felt more relaxed. She only had to give an occasional confirming nod to keep up her end of the conversation. She'd never realized before how one-sided their 'discussions' had always been. Brock talked about Wincomp, about his vision for its future, and about how he'd never realized how much of that vision included her.

Once she opened her mouth to tell him she'd always dreamed of adventure and intrigue, but he was already off on a tangent about marketing strategies. He didn't have to convince her he leaned toward genius when it came to marketing Wincomp's programs.

Suddenly he stopped talking and looked at her. "You know, you've changed." He rubbed his smooth chin, a speculative look narrowing his eyes. "But I can't put my finger on what it is."

She shrugged. "I'm still the same old me."

"No," he insisted, "you're not. Lately I can't get you out of my mind. And then last night, when I saw you, I suddenly knew—" He left the sentence unfinished.

"Last night you knew what?" Her voice came out sounding breathless.

"Last night I realized we had something special. You've always been there for me. I guess I just couldn't get over feeling like you were Alyssa's *little* sister. But you're not, are you? You're all grown up."

For Eileen, Brock's reference to her stepsister hit her as if the woman herself had just walked up, pulled out a chair and sat down to join them. Her heart plummeted. He must have broken up with Alyssa. And just like Alyssa rebounded from failed relationships back to the safety of Brock, Brock was doing exactly the same thing with Eileen. Well, she didn't want to be his rebound girl. She deserved better.

She said a decided, "You're not over Alyssa." He couldn't be, could he? Just last week he'd as much as said he was going to ask Alyssa to marry him.

He never broke eye contact as he said, "Yes, I am. Once and for all, I am. It's as if I was under some kind of spell. But I'm awake now and seeing clearly for the first time in my life. I want you beside me."

Should she tell him that his reaction to her was because of a spell, too? Only this was an honest-to-gosh magic spell. Mirabelle might have said she didn't use spells, but Eileen could see no other explanation for Brock's abrupt change. Sure, she'd changed, but was her new self-confidence and her new outlook on life enough to open Brock's eyes?

There she went, over-analyzing it again. The very thing Mirabelle had cautioned against. This time, she took his hand, feeling free to trail her fingers across his skin. "I'm glad."

It was time to implement Mirabelle's fifth task: her statement of intent.

As Eileen looked at Brock, she said to herself, *Good-bye, Daniel, who constantly throws my life into turmoil. Good-bye to an uncertain future. Good-bye confusion. I know what my wish is, what it has always been. The man sitting in front of me.*

Then she said in a whisper, but still out loud, as Mirabelle said she should, "True love."

"What?" Brock leaned closer.

She said, "Oh, I just said, I want to be with you, too."

A sudden, sharp rush—as if hundreds of tiny pebbles had been whisked into the restaurant's expanse of windows—caught Eileen as well as the other diners off guard. Several gasps could be heard as the entire room leaned away from the windows as if they might break.

To Eileen's astonishment, the storm's wind had suddenly whipped up, and now hail battered the windows.

Twelve

Mirabelle and Gus watched from Mirabelle's apartment as the biting wind gusted small hailstones against the building. They both shook their heads. A hailstorm in Southern California was bizarre enough, but this one had lasted more than an hour. Mirabelle knew it had to be the result of Eileen's emotional confusion.

Gus asked, "Is this it? A sign Wishmakers is ended? You said you used up the last of the remaining magic to recover the disks, and that you thought it would bolster Eileen's spirit enough to move her forward."

"Wishmakers isn't finished yet. I still feel using the magic to restore the disks was the right thing to do. It just may take a little while for the effects to change things." Mirabelle had eons of experience with matters of the heart, and she'd come to know things could change at a moments notice. "True, we've run out of magic we can use. But Eileen has the resources of the universe at her fingertips."

"And why, again, can't you just tell her?"

"She has to become enlightened to use the power. My telling her isn't going to enlighten her. Remember when you were so confused? Your fears and need for approval kept getting in the way of your enlightenment. Same thing with Eileen."

Gus said, "Yeah, I had to learn it by going through the tasks, one-by-one. I remember the moment of my epiphany. It was like, 'Wow, why couldn't I see that before?'"

"Eileen hasn't yet found her Dharma, or her purpose in life," Mirabelle said. "She's had truths revealed from all the other teachings except that one. And it's holding her back from incorporating the other lessons. That, in turn is keeping her from the full power to grant."

Gus leaned against the back of the sofa, looking out the window at the battered courtyard, and the little white drifts of ice. "What about Daniel?"

"Daniel is the key. With our individual powers gone, all we've got left is the good old-fashioned mortal way of urging her toward her goal. Motivation. We need to keep Daniel and Eileen together as much as possible. So destiny can work its magic. Gus, we have to become her coaches for this. To use a football analogy, it's the biggest game of the season."

"You be the coach," Gus chuckled. "I'll be the cheerleader."

They both laughed. Mirabelle loved the positive energy Gus exuded and knew that if Wishmakers survived this crisis, Gus would be an asset.

She walked over to close the curtains and lock the door, sensing Eileen approaching *Deviazione*. She motioned Gus to peek through the curtains. They saw Eileen make a dash from the courtyard's archway, where she'd evidently come from the parking area, to her front door. But when she got there, her key didn't seem to fit. Of course Mirabelle knew it wouldn't since Mirabelle herself had jammed the lock.

They both watched as Eileen dashed to the manager's apartment. Mirabelle knew the manager was at her sister's for the day, so Eileen wouldn't find help there. Eileen glanced at the other apartments, then headed toward Mirabelle's.

"Don't let her see you, and keep really quiet."

Gus carefully replaced the curtain, and whispered, "Why? The hail's gotta hurt."

If I'm not home, she'll go next door to Daniel's."

Gus nodded. "And then?"

"Destiny. I figure the more they're together, the better chance they have to realize they can't live without each other."

Gus shrugged. "Why didn't you just lock them in a room together in the first place?"

They heard the knock at the door but ignored it.

She whispered, "She has to see every aspect of her life in a true light before she can be open to true love. She's almost there, but that darned Brock keeps trying to drag her back to square one. She still has issues with Brock she hasn't addressed."

Mirabelle pressed her ear to the hard wood of the door, hearing the knock on Daniel's door. The deep bass of Daniel's voice blended in harmony with Eileen's higher one. "Even their voices go together," she said, her ear still pressed to the wood. Soon she heard the squeak of Daniel's door closing. Mirabelle checked through the curtains and saw an empty patio.

"If you didn't have any magic left, how'd you do the door-lock thing?" Gus asked. "It was you, wasn't it?"

Mirabelle smiled as she opened the drapes wide to reveal the courtyard. "Oh, I know it was wicked of me, but I put chewing gum in her lock. It will be a bother to have the lock replaced, but with Eileen's and Wishmaker's futures—not to mention the balance of power in the universe—at stake, the end justifies the means."

"How'd you know Daniel would be home?"

"I had one of our members call him, telling him they had news about the fire last night, and that they would call back at exactly two o'clock. Of course, they won't."

"Can't Daniel trace the call? He's probably got every spy gadget known to man."

Mirabelle giggled, "No one could trace a call from Wishmaker Central."

Gus shook his head. "That would definitely be untraceable."

Mirabelle began to hum, nodding toward the windows.

Gus looked shocked, then raised his eyebrows, nodding in satisfaction.

The hailstorm had stopped. The wind calmed and the clouds parted, leaving the courtyard washed clean.

Gus said, "We have exactly fifteen days left to make sure Eileen realizes Daniel is her true love, right?"

"Right. And with no help, we've got a big job on our hands."

"More like Mission Impossible. You want Tom Cruise's phone number?"

Mirabelle said, "Oh, we're hardly down for the count yet, Gus. Not by any means.

***

Daniel handed Eileen a dishtowel to dry off the melted ice. "Weird weather, huh?"

Eileen blotted at her sweater and hair. "Weird. If you ask me it's been a surreal day all around. The streets are practically deserted. You can tell no one knows how to deal with this kind of weather in Southern California. It feels unnatural—kinda scary."

"Have a seat." He motioned her to the sofa. "It's about to get weirder."

"What now?"

Eileen took a deep breath, then held it, and Daniel had to concentrate not to stare at her breasts. The sweater did wonderful things for her figure. He focused on her eyes, which showed fear. "I'm pretty sure I've got my hacker. I need your disks and your online carrier."

Her breath came out in a whoosh. "Who? Me? You think I did it?"

"No." Daniel held up his hand. "Hear me out. I know you do a backup of your programs every night. But how often do you do a backup of your hard drive?"

"Once a week."

"I think someone used your terminal to do the hacking while you were gone. If I can get the proof of those transmissions from the backups, check them against who was in the building at the time, then check the fingerprints we were able to lift from your office doorframe as well as the elevator, I think I'll have my man or woman ... or both."

Eileen's eyes lit up like someone had just flipped the switch to a Christmas tree. Then they darkened with confusion. "You suspect two people?"

"You ready for this? I think it's your stepsister and her boyfriend, Devin Hollenbeck."

Eileen's reaction surprised him. Instead of jumping up and raging against the woman, Eileen just sighed heavily and shook her head.

Almost to herself she said, "I've been trying to figure out an equation without the most important variable—Devin Hollenbeck. No wonder I could never come up with an answer. I came up short every time I tried to work Alyssa into the equation. So I gave up, chalking up my suspicions to jealousy."

Daniel had to admit that Alyssa hadn't worked easily into his equation either. "Do you think she has the computer knowledge to hack into government files?"

Eileen winced. "I really don't know. She's extremely smart, but she's always led everyone to believe she's an idiot when it comes to computers. I've never seen anything to prove otherwise."

"I have someone checking into Hollenbeck's background now. We'll see what turns up. He may have taught her how to do it or even talked her though it over the phone. Or, she could have fooled everyone and done it on her own. I snagged the sign-in books from Wincomp, and Hollenbeck has never signed in. But Alyssa was a frequent visitor in the weeks before your return."

Eileen bit her thumbnail, shaking her head. "What a family."

Daniel said, "At least they're not yours."

Eileen's expression brightened. "Oh, yeah, I forgot. They're not my family." She got up and began to pace. "Daniel, this means Brock is off the hook, right?"

"Not yet." He hated the luminous look just the thought of Brock brought to her face. "But, I'm hoping my suspicions prove out, and then everyone working at Wincomp will be vindicated. You'll all be able to go on with your lives, and," an inadvertent mocking tone slipped in, "pursue your dreams." And he would leave.

Eileen stopped pacing and came over to sit next to him on the sofa. "What's your dream, Daniel? I feel like all my dreams are coming true, and I want everyone to be happy, too."

He looked into her eyes, willing her to be open to what he was about to say. He knew it was a long-shot, but if he didn't take this chance, he would never see her after this assignment. "This is probably my last FBI assignment. I've been offered a position to head a government team exclusively involved with computer security."

"Wow, how exciting." Her gaze broke with his to focus outward. And from the spark he could see within her eyes, hope remained she might find the job appealing. He continued. "I'll be able to choose my own staff."

Her gaze jerked back to his with a questioning look.

Daniel took her hands, relieved she didn't pull away. "I'm offering you one of the positions."

She never broke eye contact, and her voice held a note of pleading. "But, Daniel, I have my work with Wincomp. And I have ... Well, you know how I feel about Brock. I couldn't leave him or Wincomp."

He moved closer. "You once told me you've always dreamed of adventure in your life. With the job I'm offering you'd be free to create the world's best computer security programs. Our programs would make critical government files safe from nutcases who could use that information to cause chaos and destruction in the lives of innocent people. I think I know you well enough to take a good guess that's more exciting than the money you might make at Wincomp."

"Yes, but ... Brock." Indecision floated like clouds across her eyes, and she started to pull her hands from his.

Daniel held tight, urging her toward him. Even though she came of her own accord, he saw uncertainty in her eyes. "Daniel, you're confusing me."

"That's my intention." He moved toward her lips. "Maybe if you're confused enough, you'll come away with me before you realize what you've done. The evil spell will be broken and you'll be free to live happily ever."

He pressed his lips to hers and put all the tenderness and passion he felt for her into the kiss. Suddenly the space between their bodies was much too great. Releasing her hands, he took her in his arms. The feel of her arms going around him made his heart race, and the subtle, sensual movements of her body against his let him know she wanted him as much as he wanted her.

He deepened the kiss and felt her tongue caress his in response. He broke away, needing to taste her skin, to feel the pulsing satin of her throat against his lips. Her sultry moan injected a shot of adrenaline through his veins. His hands found their way under her sweater to caress the silky skin of her back. He wanted her closer still.

The feel of Eileen's teeth and tongue against his ear surprised him. Her bold movement was all the encouragement he needed to unbutton the top buttons of her sweater and move the trail of kisses to the rounded curves of her breasts. The scent of a light, flowery perfume rose up from the heat of her skin, inflaming his senses.

The need to confirm his belief that they belonged together gave his passion free-rein. He moved up to possess and be possessed by her lips. He broke the kiss only long enough to whisper, "Marry me. Work with me. I love you."

Her lips stilled on his. She pulled away. Her breath came in short gasps. Daniel saw anguish and confusion written across her face as she clutched the front of her open sweater.

"Daniel, I'm sorry. I shouldn't have ... This shouldn't have—

"Yes," he interrupted, "it should have happened. Look me in the eye and tell me this wasn't right. That we don't belong together."

She stood and walked to the window, looking out at the courtyard. "Daniel, I've loved Brock for eighteen years. At last I feel the relationship I've wanted and needed for so long is becoming a reality. I'm not about to jeopardize a future I've wanted for most of my life, for someone I've only known a couple weeks."

Daniel's heart sank. This was crazy. She couldn't kiss him like she had, yet love Brock. "It doesn't matter how long you know a person. It only matters how well you know them. We understand each other. And when it's right, it's right."

Eileen kept her back to him. "What I feel for you is ... well, I don't know what it is. But I shouldn't have kissed you. I'm committed to someone else."

Tension stressing every muscle in his body, Daniel got up and walked over to stand behind her. But he didn't touch her. Trying desperately to control his frustration, he whispered close to her ear, "You're right, Eileen. You shouldn't kiss me like I'm the only man you've ever loved. You shouldn't touch me like you want to memorize the feel of my skin. And if you're so damned committed to someone else, you shouldn't be thinking about how good we'd be together."

***

By Monday afternoon all the terminals at Wincomp except Eileen's were up and running again. Everyone had pitched in to salvage what they could and to set up new terminals where needed. Fortunately, no one's backups were damaged, and Eileen retained the mysterious backups someone left in her apartment.

Daniel looked at his watch. Four-thirty. The meeting time Brock had scheduled with him and Eileen. He turned off his monitor and went to Brock's office.

As he entered the office he became aware of the tension in the room. Brock looked uncomfortable as he talked quietly on the phone. Daniel took a seat on the leather couch next to Eileen. "What's up?"

Eileen sat with her arms folded across her beautiful chest. She remained focused on Brock, but she leaned toward Daniel and whispered. "Alyssa. Seems she wants to see Brock again."

Daniel looked back to Brock. Although he couldn't hear the low words from this far away, he could read Brock's body language. The man was talking to someone he cared very much about. He could also read Eileen, and the ramrod straight way she held her body said she wasn't too happy about Brock talking to Alyssa. He also had a hunch her reaction had nothing to do with Alyssa's suspected involvement with Wincomp's espionage.

Eileen had agreed with Daniel not to tell Brock about their suspicions regarding Alyssa's involvement with Wincomp's troubles until they had proof. Now Daniel wondered if that decision might complicate matters. Eileen said Brock was no longer seeing Alyssa. What if she was mistaken? Daniel hoped the meeting wouldn't take long. He needed to get hold of the fingerprint results and get started on Eileen's backups as soon as possible. He wanted proof, and he needed to get it before Alyssa and her boyfriend decided a little fire wasn't enough to cover their tracks.

Daniel leaned closer to Eileen, inhaling her scent, all the

while steeling himself not to react. "After we're done here I
need to get your backups and get to work."

"They're still at home. I didn't want to bring them here until
my office was up and running." Eileen looked at him.

"I can work from home then. It's probably better. I can
work all night if I need to."

"Can I help?" Eileen asked.

It might be the last time they worked together. "Sure. I'd
like that."

Then she tilted her chin down and gave him a warning look.
"No funny business, though. Promise?"

If she was referring to the passion he had for her and their
kiss last night, nothing about that struck him as funny. He was
dead serious. He slid his arm to the back of the couch, reaching
out to touch the tendril of hair, which had escaped her ponytail.
"No, nothing funny. I promise." He saw her try to subdue a
quiver as his fingers brushed her neck.

Although the quick look she gave him shot daggers, her
voice held a note of pleading. "I mean it, Daniel. I really do."

Who was she trying to convince? Him? Or herself?

***

Eileen decided the best thing to do would be to let Daniel
have the backups and work on the investigation alone. She
couldn't seem to think clearly when she was with the man.

So Tuesday evening, she found herself in Mirabelle's kitchen,
cutting up vegetables and throwing them into the steamer, while
Mirabelle fried tofu cakes for their dinner. Gus, who stood in
the dining room, seemed determined to set an award-winning
table even though it was just for the three of them. Bright purple
and red flowers stood in stark contrast to the white tablecloth.
Crystal and china made the simple dinner feel like an occasion.

Since she and Daniel had worked all day on restorations at
Wincomp, they had the night off.

"Mirabelle," Eileen said. "I'm more confused than ever.
I've really given the seven tasks my best effort, and I'm more
conflicted than I was three weeks ago." After the passion she'd
shared with Daniel Sunday night, her Monday lunch with Brock
had been strained and awkward. On her part at least. Brock

didn't seem to notice anything unusual.

"You didn't wish for inner peace. You wished for true love." Mirabelle chuckled as she slid one of the breadcrumb-coated patties into the peanut oil. "No, I'm just kidding. Of course inner peace will come with true love." She turned to Eileen. "I told you that if you were on the wrong path, you'd find barriers and confusion."

She had to be talking about Daniel. Eileen had been so tempted by his offer. His offers, really. He had wanted her to go away with him and become his life partner as well as his business partner. The temptation to give up her original dream for this new one had to be a test of some kind.

Eileen said, "I need to re-focus." She put the lid on the steamer and flipped the switch.

From where he stood surveying his handiwork, Gus said, "Make sure you're focusing on the right goal."

"I guess I'm still confused. Oh, I know it's true love. But that doesn't make anything clearer. Any ideas?"

Eileen looked at her friends. Gus started to say something, but quickly shut his mouth after looking at Mirabelle. Then Gus nodded some kind of affirmation to Mirabelle before saying to Eileen, "Think about the changes the tasks have made in your life. See if you notice a pull in one direction."

She saw Mirabelle nod her satisfaction. "Yes. And remember—you haven't completed the tasks yet. All will fall into place once the first six tasks become second nature, and once you've found what gift you have to share with mankind. The balance you want can only be attained if the scales are equal. If you give, then you receive."

Eileen leaned her elbows on the tiled counter, her chin cupped in the palm of her hand. "I've been thinking and thinking and I can't come up with one darned thing I can do to benefit mankind."

"What about—"

Mirabelle interrupted Gus with a hurried, "Only you can determine what that will be." The woman then looked at Gus. "Oh, I'm sorry, did I cut you off? What had you been about to say?"

Gus gave the woman an impish but contrite smile. "That

she needs to find it on her own."

"Not to change the subject," Mirabelle said to Eileen, "but how are you feeling about your stepmother and stepsister? Are you finding some good in them? Are you accepting them for the part they play in the universe?"

Eileen didn't feel she could share Daniel's suspicions just yet. She'd hate to accuse Alyssa, only to discover she was innocent. She would just have to wait to see if Daniel came up with what he'd called *hard evidence*. Daniel had said he needed enough tangible proof to insure conviction before he had anyone arrested.

Pushing those thoughts aside, she concentrated on seeing Jeannette and Alyssa as people. She realized she had been able to detach herself emotionally from them, and to accept that she would never understand them. She'd also put in a request with the probate judge to allow her to take her mother's things from the attic. She still wasn't sure the path she'd headed down with Jeannette was the right one.

"I think both Jeannette and Alyssa have made me a stronger person," she said carefully. "By watching them while I was growing up, I knew what I didn't want in life: to be so concerned with money, position and power."

"The need for money is an important fact of life," Mirabelle pointed out.

"But they let it run their lives, like they're afraid to be without loads of it." A nagging thought sneaked up on Eileen. Hadn't she done exactly the same thing, but on a smaller scale? Hadn't she let her own fears dictate her actions? Was she placing too high a priority on her Wincomp stock and her financial security at Wincomp? Was that fear putting up a smoke screen to other possibilities?

The timed steamer bell dinged. "Dinner!" Mirabelle announced.

When Eileen left Mirabelle's later that evening, she noticed a light in Daniel's window. He had a long night ahead of him, and while part of her still desperately wanted to be involved with the exciting investigation, another part feared being alone with Daniel. Fear won. Even as the thought went through her mind, and she knew that reacting to fear went against Mirabelle's teaching, she couldn't overcome it. She must remain committed to her dream, to Brock.

She paused by the fountain to look at the courtyard's colorful Christmas lights, then turned her face up to the clear sky. Cold, crisp air stung her cheeks and seeped through her light, California-winter jacket. She'd given up trying to figure out what the heck was going on with the unusually cold weather. That was the least of her problems. She shivered.

Christmas was only a week away. What would it be like for her this year? Would she be sharing it with Brock? Or would Alyssa once again turn his head? She guessed it pretty much depended on whether or not she completed the seven tasks. Or if Daniel's suspicions proved to be true. One last breath of crisp air, and she moved toward her apartment.

Letting herself in with her new key, Eileen flipped on the light and looked around. A warm, cozy apartment welcomed her; an apartment that she, all by herself, had turned into a home.

She walked over to the fireplace and lit the fire she had prepared earlier. It was a perfect night to initiate the huge fireplace, even though she had no one with which to share the ambiance. Only two things were missing from her mental picture of what she wanted for the Holidays. A Christmas tree and her friends.

Eileen picked up the phone and dialed Ray's number. When he answered she said, "How about coming to a tree-decorating party on Saturday night?"

"Sure," Ray said. "Do I come in a Santa suit?"

She laughed. "It wouldn't hurt."

After making party plans, they said goodnight.

Wanting to keep the warm feeling of anticipation going, Eileen went to her bedroom and put on a long red silk nightgown and robe she'd bought for Christmas, then went back to sit by the fire.

Letting a little Christmas spirit into her life was long overdue. So what if her father's idea of a Christmas gift had been to give her a check, and that Jeannette had professionals decorate the house? It was time to begin her own traditions. Thoughts of her future and how those traditions might play themselves out became fuzzy. Brock didn't exactly seem like a traditions kind of guy. That didn't mean he couldn't change.

Thoughts of Daniel intruded, and she hugged the robe closer, the silk a sensuous reminder of how his kisses had burned across her skin. She tried to banish the feelings but they'd already begun winding their way through her body, igniting points of sensation.

Be reasonable, she told herself. *It's just because Daniel is such a practiced lover. Any woman would react.* Surely she would respond even more intensely to Brock's kisses.

Determination made her sit up straighter. Suddenly she knew exactly what she needed to do to get Daniel out of her head. She needed to kiss Brock!

Thirteen

Daniel looked at his laptop screen while he waited for the operator to patch him through to his boss.

Pete came on the line with, "Hey, *amigo*, how's it going?"

"We've got it, Pete. I'm looking at the proof we need to file charges."

Pete said, "So, is it Barden and Hollenbeck, like you thought?"

"Yeah. I've got the transmission records of the hacking. Alyssa's the only one who could have done the actual hacking, but I'm sure it was under Hollenbeck's direction. I just got a search warrant for Hollenbeck's home, bank, phone and office data, and have a team moving in at midnight tonight to confiscate. I'll be questioning Alyssa Barden as soon as she's booked. I have a feeling she's the kinda girl who'll cut a deal and give us everything we need on Hollenbeck. This thing should be wrapped by Monday at the latest. I'm sure we'll find she's the one who sold Wincomp's software, too."

"Great. I never doubted you for a minute," Pete said. "You have something else to tell me?"

Daniel knew Pete was referring to the offer of the national computer security job in Washington Daniel had been considering. Pete had recommend Daniel for the job in the first place. "Yeah. I'm ninety-nine percent sure I'm gonna take the job."

"It doesn't start until January. You have plans until then? It's too close to give you another assignment."

"I've got vacation time coming. I need some time off." He didn't tell Pete that his final decision to take the job pretty much rested on whether or not he could convince Eileen that they belonged together. If she said yes and wanted to stay in LA, he would. He'd come to realize that a life with Eileen was more important than the job, and if that meant changing his plans, then he would in order to have her with him.

"I've got that place in Vermont if you want to use it. Maggs isn't exactly in the mood for skiing this year."

Pete's wife, Maggie, was due to have their third child in two weeks. "Thanks, Pete, I might just take you up on that." Being snowbound with Eileen in Pete and Maggie's cozy cabin sounded like a dream.

"The end of your assignment changes things between you and Eileen Pringle? Kinda turns your concerns about a breech of protocol into a moot point, doesn't it?"

The man was pushing, Daniel was certain. "Yes, Pete." He chuckled. "I get where you're going with this. I'm doing my best, man." During their routine updates, Daniel had shared his feelings for Eileen with his friend.

"Maybe a hometown Christmas in Vermont, with all the schmaltzy trimmings could persuade her. You might even find you like it. Crackling fires every night, a Christmas tree, sleigh rides through the snow—"

Daniel cut him off. "Okay, Pete, not everyone sees life through Norman Rockwell glasses."

"Don't tell me it doesn't sound good to you. I know where you come from, man. You got Mother-freakin-Earth and Father Christmas as parents. You don't come away from that without a sliver of holiday sentimentality embedded in your soul, even if it is buried so deep you'd need an earthquake to shake it loose."

"Yeah, right, that's me, Mr. Sentimentality." Daniel's chuckle was dismissive even though Pete's words hit home. His family did always make Christmas an occasion, with tons of food, thoughtful gifts, and, of course, his mother playing the guitar and singing. It reminded him of what Eileen had said about her mother singing "House On Pooh Corner" to her, and his gut tightened, once again imagining her loss. He'd gotten away from his family's tradition over the past several years and now regretted his push for autonomy. People weren't meant to live alone.

"You think about it, man." Pete interrupted Daniel's thoughts. "I say chance it; go for the brass ring with this Eileen woman. You never know when the merry-go-round might stop altogether, and you won't get another chance."

"Maybe," Daniel said, not committing to anything.

One major obstacle still kept the brass ring out of reach: Eileen's infatuation with Brock. And time was running out. His job here was wrapping up. In a few days, he would be leaving. The question was, with or without Eileen?

***

Wednesday Eileen returned from a disappointing lunch date with a distracted Brock to find Daniel standing in the middle of her empty office, a folder in his hands. Her new furniture was supposedly stuck in a snowbound truck somewhere and still hadn't arrived, so the room seemed strangely cavernous. It smelled of fresh paint.

"Close the door, Eileen. I need to talk to you."

But she didn't want to talk to him. Not face-to-face, anyway, and especially not alone. She wanted to focus on the seven tasks and on Brock, and Daniel spelled distraction with a capital 'D.' She set her purse down against the wall, closed the door, then stood with her back against it. *Face your fears*, a voice said in her head. "I hope this is about our ... your investigation." She tried to keep her voice neutral, all the while remembering the feel of his lips on hers.

She could see his jaw working, and he took a deep breath before he stated, "That's not what I wanted to talk about, but I do have news regarding that." He held up the folder.

Already pretty sure what he did want to talk about, she remained silent, hoping she could altogether avoid the subject of what had happened between them.

Daniel continued. "The fingerprints came in. Hollenbeck was definitely in your office and in the elevator some time before the fire. Warrants has been issued for him and Alyssa." He went on to explain the evidence incriminating Alyssa he'd found on Eileen's backups.

Her glance shot to the wall connecting her office with Brock's. "Does Brock know?"

"Not yet. Since you were in on the investigation, I would like to tell him together, if you don't mind."

Mind? Mind telling Brock that someone he thought he'd loved had been playing him for a fool? She found she did mind. She didn't want to see the hurt look on his face. But Daniel was right. They needed to talk to Brock together, to tell him about how she'd been in on the investigation. He didn't need two deceitful women in his life.

"I don't have much choice." She risked making eye contact. "You ready?"

"Let's go for it." Daniel's gaze held hers with both a question and an accusation.

She fumbled behind her for the doorknob, then opened the door, her hand shaky and her heart racing as she turned to go. Daniel's footsteps were sure and steady behind her.

Brock smiled as she entered, then he looked surprised when Daniel followed. "I hope the look of serious intent on both your faces means you've discovered our inside trader." Brock nodded toward the chairs.

They sat down, and Eileen turned to Daniel, only to see his resolute gaze directed at her. Quickly she turned her eyes back to Brock and with great difficulty gathered the composure to speak. "Daniel and I have something to tell you. Daniel..." She purposely left the rest to him. It was his investigation. Besides, her voice had suddenly developed a quaver.

Daniel opened his FBI identification wallet and set it on Brock's desk.

Forty-five minutes later, Brock sat in stunned silence as Daniel finished telling him about the investigation. Eileen had never seen Brock so pale, his perpetual tan fading before her eyes.

After a few moments he shook his head. "I can't believe it. Alyssa? She couldn't have."

Without hesitation, Daniel said, "We have proof."

Eileen could tell Brock didn't want to believe it, and she wondered if he still loved Alyssa. Brock asked, "Will she be arrested?"

"It's probably a done deal."

That upset Brock more than anything, and he nervously drummed his fingers on the desk, indecision written across his face. The sick feeling Eileen experienced just thinking about Alyssa in jail had to be ten times worse for Brock. He asked, "You think she stole our software program, too, don't you?"

"I'm not sure," Daniel said. "I'm hoping that comes out during the questioning. I'll let you know."

Brock stood up and uncharacteristically ran his hands through his hair, mussing its perfection. He looked around the room, but the focus of his gaze was inward. "I've been such an idiot! Again." He paced the area behind his desk. "Eileen tried to warn me against letting *any* outsider have access, but I wouldn't listen."

Brock looked at Eileen, and she saw a glimmer of admiration along with the speculation in his eyes. "And you were in on the investigation? This whole thing just blows me away." Then he looked back to Daniel, straightening as though he'd mentally regrouped. "Wincomp is cleared of any wrongdoing?"

Daniel said, "Yes. And since my investigation is coming to a close, I'd like to say good-bye. Sorry about the subterfuge, but it was necessary. Working at Wincomp has been," Daniel hesitated, giving Eileen a look of such soul-wrenching intensity, she felt her face flood with warmth, "life-changing."

Brock still looked stunned. "Oh, I guess you will be leaving. This is all so strange. One minute you're an employee, the next you're an FBI agent. It's going to take me a few minutes to process it all."

Daniel stood and shook Brock's hand. Then he turned and put his hand out to Eileen.

This was it? Daniel was leaving? She put her hands behind her, away from the finality of the handshake. Her heart hammered against her chest. She would never see him again?

She found herself saying weakly, "Aren't you coming to my Christmas tree decorating party Saturday night?" She'd told all of her friends, except Daniel, about the party. And she suddenly recognized her reasoning for leaving Daniel out. Fear. She was afraid to be with him. Mirabelle had said not to let her fears control her, and she'd done just that.

She added, "It would be a good time for you to say good-bye to everyone."

Daniel seemed to be considering the invitation as he put his hands in his pockets. "Sure, I'll try to make it."

He left, and Eileen went back into her office to get her purse, wondering if she'd ever see him again. The thought that she might not made her feel sick.

Since her new office furniture hadn't arrived, Brock had told her to take the rest of the day off, and she was going to do just that. She couldn't face work any longer. It wasn't just that her old 'home' was gone, either. All of her keepsake treasures had been destroyed in the fire, too. She turned in a circle, looking at the room. It definitely no longer felt like home.

Ray showed up in her doorway, leaning against it with a look of concern on his face. "Hey, Princess Leia, what's wrong? You the last one to find out Darth Vader is really your father?"

Her laugh felt hallow. For some reason she couldn't bring herself to tell Ray that Daniel was gone. "It seems so strange. I don't feel like I belong here anymore. All my 'stuff' is gone. My crystals, my magic eight ball. And worst of all, the bottle of fairy dust my mother gave me. I know it's silly, but I always felt like my mother was near when I held it."

"Speaking of mothers," Ray said, "how'd it go with the judge this morning? He gonna let you into the Deathstar to get your mom's stuff?"

She retrieved two pieces of paper from her purse, holding them in front of her. "This," she separated one of the sheets of paper from the other, "is, my passport to the attic." She fanned the other paper to the side. "And this is my passport to peace of mind. I'm no longer contesting the will."

Ray looked surprised. "What if Jeannette forged it?"

"Then that's her bad Karma. I'm making a good life for

myself, and I've come to the realization that I don't need my father's money to be happy."

Ray pushed away from the doorframe and came into the room. "But, Eileen, that money would mean security for the rest of your life."

She shook her head. "No, it wouldn't. I have to find security within myself. Money isn't going to do it for me. If it turns out I get a portion of the estate, fine. But if I don't, that will be fine, too."

"Well, I wouldn't be as gracious about it as you."

"Ray, I'm working on happiness from the inside. My issues —my fears—about money were holding me back from doing what I really want in life. I'm trying to let go of those fears by letting go of the money."

Ray raised a cautious eyebrow. "You do what makes you happy. But I hope you don't mind if I hold off buying into what you're saying until I see if it works. You be the guinea pig."

She smiled. She hadn't really been trying to convince Ray to change, but she could see that he was actually considering what she'd said. Mirabelle told her that effecting change in her own life would perpetuate changes for the good in others. Could it really be this simple? "Follow your dreams, Ray."

Ray smiled. "I'm going to stop calling you Princess Leia. I think Yoda fits you better." He cocked his head to the side. "Except for the ears. Yours are a little bigger," he kidded.

She laughed, her heart suddenly lighter. Now all she needed was to take her own advice. She needed to follow her dreams. Her thoughts turned to the man in the office next door. It was time to get serious about making Brock Van Buren fall in love with her.

***

Friday evening, Eileen quelled the moment of fear as she watched Gus. They were at his apartment—she sitting on a high stool in his dining room, and he walking around her, snipping stylist scissors in the air as if he were cutting imaginary puppet strings.

She'd given herself over to his expertise and had to forcibly push aside the last thread of residual fear. "Go for it, Gus.

Make me into Wonder Woman."

He squinted, assessing as he moved his head back and forth, looking at her from different angles. "I'm thinking more along the lines of a combination Meg Ryan and Venus." Picking up her long hair, he measured its weight. He took a small section, twisted it, and then chopped it off about two inches from her head.

She gasped as the long auburn strands spilled to the floor.

"Just close your eyes, girlfriend. Let me unshackle the woman you are."

Eileen closed her eyes tight, reminding herself over and over to breathe. *It will be okay*, she thought. She could feel the rapid pull-jerk-twist-snip motion repeated over and over as Gus hacked away. As far as Eileen could tell, he had no plan other than to grab whatever caught his eye, then cut it off.

Words from Mirabelle's teachings ran through her head. *Let go of your fears.* She thought about how quickly hair grows, and suddenly what Gus was doing became an adventure. *Give unconditional love.* She concentrated on giving positive energy to Gus, accepting his gift as inspired. *Make a conscious choice.* She told herself to relax, to enjoy, to step away from her fear, and experience the sensations. Immediately, she realized how light and airy her new haircut felt. *If it feels right, do it.* This did feel right. She felt energized by the prospect of a new look.

"*Voilá!*" Gus exclaimed as the scissors halted.

Eileen felt Gus ruffle and scrunch her hair. She pried open one eye, giving a sideways glance at the large mirror he had propped on the bar.

She turned to get a better look, not recognizing her own reflection. Hair, which had always been hard to control, now went every-which-way. Only, for the first time in her life, it somehow worked beautifully. The cut let the slightly-moussed curls find their own direction, and absurdly, their wildness only enhanced the style. They framed her face and brought out her eyes.

"Wow!" was all she could say.

Gus put the scissors down and took her hands to pull her from the stool. He brushed hair from the towel over her shoulders as he stood her before the mirror. "Eileen Pringle, I'd like you to meet ... the real you."

Finally, she found her tongue. "Gus. I don't know what to say. I love it."

As if to confirm their existence, her hand moved of its own accord toward the short curls. The chaos she had fought for years to control still existed. Only now Gus had turned that chaos into something synergetic.

"Smart, sassy and sexy, didn't I tell you?" Gus said from behind her. She could see his reflection in the mirror and could tell he was pleased with his creation. He scrunched another handful, pulling a curl here and there.

"How'd you know this would work?" She couldn't take her eyes off her reflection, still trying to accept the new look as real.

"I just let your hair tell me what it wanted. I didn't try to change it or confine it. I just cut away the excess, so it could be free to dance in the wind." He scrunched some more, leaning his head to the side in critical satisfaction.

"All I can say is, you've worked magic," she said.

Gus laughed. "No. I'm still in training."

She joined in his laughter, the reference to his training with Mirabelle only part of the merriment bubbling through her. This is how she'd always dreamed of looking. She had to admit it; Gus had made her beautiful.

"I only showed you what was there all the time. It was just hidden," Gus said, eerily answering her unspoken thought just like Mirabelle had so many times.

She looked in the mirror again, telling her reflection, "It's definitely time to stop hiding, Eileen Pringle."

Gus said, "You go girl!" and they both laughed.

***

Daniel splashed on after-shave, finished tying his tie, and then slipped on the dinner jacket. It was Saturday night—the night of the party—and anxiety over seeing Eileen twitched through his chest like a caged cat.

Paperwork and questioning Alyssa and Hollenbeck had prevented him from seeing Eileen since Tuesday, and each time he'd called her he'd gotten her answering machine. He wanted desperately to see her, to somehow prove to her that they belonged together, that they would have a wonderful life as husband and wife working together on the project he'd been offered.

Tonight he could attend her party as himself. Completely. No more intrigue. No more disguises. Daniel Manatucci was going to try to convince the woman he loved to marry him.

As he walked across the festively-lighted courtyard, he noticed the evening had turned balmy.

Gus Gustaufson answered the front door, and the sound of instrumental Christmas music and laughter spilled out.

"Eileen's not quite ready," Gus stated. "So I'm playing host. Isn't it just like a woman to be late to her own party? Come in and make yourself a drink. I'm sure you know everyone better than I do."

Daniel could see Nancy Dace by the fireplace, intently listening to something Brock Van Buren said. Michael Bates stood on a ladder next to the tree, taking a strand of Christmas lights from Ray.

As Daniel entered the apartment, he looked around, amazed by the transformation Eileen had managed in so short a time. Granted, his apartment was temporary, but it still looked exactly the same as when he'd moved in—functional but dull. Eileen's, on the other hand, had metamorphosed into a reflection of the woman who lived here.

Warm woods, subtle lighting, and classic fabrics were accented with whimsical, creative touches of holiday decorations.

A richly-robed figure of Father Christmas stood in the middle of the dining room table, surrounded by food and an eclectic assortment of Christmas china and crystal. He found himself chuckling. Eileen had obviously raided the second-hand stores again. Somehow, just like her mismatched dining room chairs, her odds-and-ends tableware appeared to comfortably coexist.

Mirabelle Saintly came out of Eileen's room, closing the door behind her with a conspiratorial smile. When she saw him, she waved and came to where he stood next to the table.

"Daniel. What an enchanted evening! And Eileen's gone all out to make it special." She leaned closer. "Don't let this opportunity of a lifetime pass you by." The look of excited expectation on Mirabelle's face had him taking a closer look at the enigmatic woman. It was as if the woman knew of Daniel's intentions.

"I don't plan to, Mirabelle." He smiled. Just as soon as he could get Eileen alone, he intended to persuade her to marry him.

Mirabelle took hold of his arm, her voice turning serious. "Do everything in your power to convince her."

What was the woman talking about? She couldn't really know what he was thinking. He opened his mouth to ask for clarification, but she turned from him, saying, "Oh, here she comes."

The woman he saw emerge from the bedroom took his breath away. He realized his mouth had dropped open, and he forced his jaw into place.

To the strains of soft Christmas music, Eileen walked into the room looking every bit a princess out of a fairy tale. Her, simple, off-the-shoulder dress was short, the silver lace hinting of enticing curves beneath. High-heeled sandals glittered on her feet. Her unruly hair had been cut short, and a sparkling jeweled headband of some kind looked enough like a tiara to complete the illusion. Christmas music played softly in the background.

She smiled at him, and he was lost. Their gazes held for long moments. But a figure cut between them, blocking her from his view.

Brock.

The Jerk took Eileen's hand, threading it possessively through his elbow. And from what Daniel could read by the lecherous gleam in The Jerk's eyes, the guy very clearly found this new Eileen to be his kind of woman all the way.

Daniel couldn't stand the way Van Buren looked at Eileen. And he felt sick at the way Eileen looked back. Deciding he'd had enough, Daniel walked over to the couple. "Eileen, you look fabulous."

Her eyes sparkled like the jewels in her hair. "Thank you, Daniel."

He put out his hand. "Will you dance with me? I think this is our song."

***

As Eileen put her hand in his, she recognized the strains of "I'll Be Home For Christmas." They'd danced to it at Mirabelle's party. Heedless of the reluctant tug from Brock's hand, as well as the stares of her friends, she went with Daniel to the middle of the living room and moved easily into his arms. It was as if she moved through a dream with no control over her actions.

Relief flooded her when she saw Ray and Nancy, then Gus and Mirabelle join them on the makeshift dance floor.

What am I doing? she asked herself over and over. The only answer was the feel of Daniel's arms around her, and his warm breath against her hair. Her body ignited like a lightning-sparked wildfire, but she felt powerless to pull away from the heat. She felt his hand at her back pressing her body against his.

Daniel murmured in her ear, "We belong together, Eileen. You know we do. Mind, spirit, and, body."

She tried to pull away then, but he held her tight. "I love you Eileen. Come away with me. Marry me."

Her breath came in short gasps, and she looked into his eyes. His words sent an excited thrill through her entire being, threatening her resolve more than ever. He was the only thing standing between her and her dream of a lifetime. Then why couldn't she tell him no and move away from his arms? Why couldn't she tell him she loved Brock? Because she was no longer sure.

Daniel moved her around the floor, his voice hypnotic. "If you don't want the job in Washington, I'll get a job here in LA. Whatever it takes for us to be together. Don't be afraid to love me."

Afraid? Mirabelle's words came back to haunt her. Eileen realized she was afraid. Afraid what she felt for Daniel wouldn't last. Afraid that if she said yes to her attraction to him, she would find herself years down the road in a loveless marriage like her father and Jeannette's. So what happened if she let go of those fears? The word *happiness* seemed to float through the room. But she had to be sure Daniel was the right path. *Trust your heart*, came the whispered words. She glanced toward Mirabelle, but the woman was facing the fireplace.

The music ended, and the other couples moved apart.

"Let's get this tree decorated," Gus said.

People gamely began taking ornaments from their boxes.

Daniel wouldn't let her move from his arms, obviously still waiting for her answer. Still stunned by the fact that she wanted desperately to say yes to his proposal, she couldn't respond. Could Daniel be the man she was meant to be with? Her wish had been for true love, after all. She realized what she felt for Daniel went beyond passion. It was love. But was it a love to last a lifetime? They'd only known each other a few short weeks.

Breaking the hold Daniel's gaze had on her, she looked to where Mirabelle had Brock cornered by the fireplace. She had to exorcise herself of the last thread of doubt concerning whether or not the man she had believed herself to be in love with all these years was the right one. But, how could she know? The phrase, *Trust your heart*, repeated in her mind.

Trust her heart? She couldn't even think straight with Daniel close by. Turning back to him, she put her hand on his arm and looked into his eyes. She felt her mouth curve into a smile, and her heart soared. "Daniel, I'd like to answer you after everyone else has left ... when we're alone."

He smiled and her insides melted. "Then you'll think about it?"

She looked back to Brock. Could Brock make her feel like this? She had to find out before she made the decision that would affect the rest of her life. "I will."

***

Daniel wasn't sure how to feel as he listened to the cheery Christmas music and watched Eileen and her guests hang ornaments on the tree. Throughout the evening, Brock stayed close to her, and Daniel could tell Eileen was pleased by his attention. She seemed to be avoiding Daniel, and it was eating him up inside.

She'd said she'd think about his proposal. Part of him had felt hope surge like a tidal wave. But, he'd also felt keen disappointment that she'd had to think about it at all. As he watched her he couldn't help rehashing his proposal and wondering why she wasn't in his arms right this minute. He'd asked her to marry him and hoped that alone would make her realize they belonged together. Hell, he'd even shocked himself by admitting he'd be willing to give up the job in Washington just to be with her. What more did she want?

He felt Mirabelle tug on his jacket sleeve. "Dear, I brought you some bubbly." She handed him a glass of champagne. He preferred beer, but took the glass.

"Thanks," he said.

"Daniel, don't be blinded by appearances. Believe in what your heart sees, not your eyes." She nodded toward Eileen and Brock who had their heads close as he helped her hang an ornament.

Taking a swig, he found himself surprised to taste beer instead of the expected sparkling wine. He looked at the glass. The clear, bubbly liquid looked like champagne. He shot Mirabelle a questioning smile.

She said, "Open your mind and heart to all possibilities. Looks can be deceiving."

He raised his glass to the little woman, wondering, not for the first time, what she was all about. "I'll keep that in mind."

Daniel's beeper went off. He recognized the illuminated number as that of the police station. "Excuse me, Mirabelle. I need to make a call."

He left the party and went to his apartment. The detective he spoke to asked if Daniel wanted to further question Alyssa that evening or wait until the next day. Daniel told him that unless Alyssa wanted to confess everything, he would wait until tomorrow.

Then, a man on a mission, he headed back toward Eileen's. She'd had all evening to consider his proposal. And he wanted— no, *needed*—an answer.

But he didn't get more than two steps into the shadows of

his patio when a movement on Eileen's stoop caught his eye, abruptly halting his footsteps. Looking toward her apartment, he could just make out two figures standing close together. The only lighting—the Christmas lights over the arch—made it difficult at first to make out who they were.

Then he recognized the tall figure of Brock Van Buren. The woman he now took into his arms was Eileen, and she didn't look like she was resisting.

Daniel heard one of the tenant's clocks striking twelve, sounding like a death-knell.

A vise-like ache tightening his chest, Daniel watched the two kiss. He found himself clenching his jaw so hard, he thought his teeth might break. Her arms went around The Jerk's neck.

What an idiot he'd been! It took watching the two together to realize Eileen was never going to let go of her illusions about Van Buren. Daniel called himself every kind of fool to have ever harbored the belief she cared for him the way he cared for her.

He had to hold himself in check and not give in to the urge to storm across the courtyard and rip her from The Jerk's arms. What he wanted to do was force her to see what they could have had together, to tell her the pathetic substitute for love she would have with Brock Van Buren couldn't compare to what Daniel felt for her, and what he knew in his heart she felt for him. But you couldn't force something like that. He just stood there, feeling sick.

Daniel's beeper went off again, but at first he only heard it as a distant buzz. Finally, the fact that the humming came from his jacket registered with his numb brain. He took the thing out of his pocket, seeing the police detective's number. Alyssa must be ready to talk.

Turning his back on the torturous scene, he walked to his car, the suddenly frigid night seeping into his soul.

***

Eileen put everything she had into the kiss. But try as she might, she felt nothing. She gently pushed away from Brock's arms, standing away from him.

Nothing. She'd felt absolutely nothing. No fireworks.

No bells ringing. No magic. She smiled as the spell shattered into a hundred tinkling pieces. She didn't love Brock. She loved Daniel. A sudden chill wind raised goose bumps on her arms, forcing her to hug herself.

Brock's look was dubious. "What does that smile mean?"

She knew her expression showed wonder. "I don't love you, Brock." She quickly corrected with a giggle, "Oh, I do love you, only I don't *love* you. I love you like a wonderful brother." She remembered the kiss. "Or distant cousin." She was being silly, but she didn't care. She felt giddy.

He smiled with regret. "I'm too late, aren't I?" She could see his breath in the icy air, and she shivered, rubbing her bare arms. Surely this would go down as the coldest December in LA's history.

Feeling oddly removed from Brock, she nodded, whispering, "Too late."

She looked around the courtyard as if seeing it for the first time. The colorful lights, the splashing fountain and the magical Mediterranean setting, all seemed wondrously bright and alive. Stars above twinkled with a vengeance, and the snap in the air felt exhilarating.

Daniel was the man she loved. And he loved her. Eileen realized her fears had dissipated, just like the condensation of her breath in the cold night.

She was ready for the adventure of a lifetime. Ready to work with Daniel. Ready to be with Daniel. Ready to love Daniel. She wondered where he'd gone when he'd slipped out of the party shortly after proposing to her. Nancy said she had noticed him heading toward his apartment. But when Eileen looked over, she saw that his lights were out. Where was he? Surely he'd be back soon.

"I love Daniel," she said, almost to herself as she got a sinking feeling something was terribly wrong.

Fourteen

Mirabelle looked at Gus who sat beside her at her computer as she logged onto Wishmaker's Website. It was the morning after Eileen's party, and Mirabelle knew she could no longer put off the inevitable.

Mary came on the screen. "You don't have to tell me. We all know. Reports of strange weather and unusual cosmic anomalies have come in from far and wide. It must be over."

Mirabelle sighed, feeling for the first time an aching march of the ages in her bones. "I'm afraid so. Eileen kissed the wrong man on the most critical of nights. From the way the evening began, I was sure she would be kissing Daniel, but that didn't happen. Our power would have fared better if she hadn't kissed anyone at all. It's as if the powers of darkness have been plotting against us."

Mary shook her head. "It would be easy to blame it on a mythical pretext. But we have to accept our own failure."

"My failure," Mirabelle said.

"No," Mary's voice insisted. "This was a collective effort. You were just implementing our policies, and you did as well as anyone could. Time has been short from the beginning. Why, we've only given Eileen three weeks to do what usually takes months to accomplish. Eileen hasn't granted because she hasn't completed her last two steps. She still hasn't stated—with belief—what her intent is. And she repeatedly refuses to acknowledge her gift to mankind, even though it is right in front of her nose."

Gus looked confused. "I thought you—Eileen—had until midnight New Year's Eve, when some kind of cosmic power shift was going to take place."

Mirabelle repeated his question to Mary who was linked through a headset.

"She does have until midnight, New Year's Eve," Mary explained. "And if Eileen hadn't kissed anyone on this particular Solstice, she might still have a chance. But she kissed the wrong man, and that weakened the granting power to a mere spark. I know it sounds complicated, and it is, but I'll try to explain. With our universal power exhausted, and the granting power only a glimmer, you can see how hopeless it is."

"If we can get Eileen back on track and help her through her last two tasks, is there a chance?" Gus asked.

Mary's reply was succinct. "Not without Daniel, and he's gone."

Gus looked confused. "Gone? Gone where? I just saw him last night."

"He left some time during the night," Mirabelle said.

"For good?"

"I'm afraid so." Mirabelle's heart felt like it was going to break, but she swallowed back the lump in her throat.

"I'll issue a bulletin to our members, but I'm sure everyone can feel what's happened." Mary added, "Keep me posted if anything changes. We at Headquarters will begin making arrangements to disband."

"Yes, Mary." Mirabelle disconnected, swiveling around to face Gus. "I'm sorry this is happening just when you joined Wishmakers. With a couple centuries' training, you would have made one dynamite Granter."

Gus stood up and walked the length of the sofa. "Well, I'm not giving up yet. It can't be that difficult to get Daniel back. I know the guy loves Eileen."

"Yes, he does. But he doesn't think she loves him. There's nothing else we can do, Gus."

His response was a squint of determination.

***

Eileen woke up on the sofa at six o'clock the morning after her party, her Victoria's Secret satin providing little protection against the early morning chill. She'd tried to reach Daniel for the better part of the night and at some point had fallen asleep. She still had the phone clutched in her hand.

Grabbing the afghan, she wrapped it around her and got up to turn on the heat. But when she peeked out through the curtains, the scene before her had her doing a double-take. Snow! Impossible.

Shocked, she opened the drapes wider to get a better look. When she'd gone to bed the sky had been clear. What the heck was going on? She got a creepy feeling California was under some kind of magic spell.

Two men in blue jumpsuits with the block word "Movers" on their backs walked across the courtyard toward Daniel and Mirabelle's common patio. Suddenly, what she was seeing registered with her sleepy brain. Movers!

Eileen punched Daniel's number, hoping desperately to hear his usual sleepy, gruff early-morning response. Instead she heard an electronic voice telling her, "The number you have dialed is no longer in service. If you—" She disconnected and tried again, thinking she must have misdialed, but she got the same message.

Flipping through her phone book, she found the pager number he'd given her and dialed that. Her heart raced erratically. The message this time said the customer could not be reached. "Please," she said out loud. "Don't let this be happening!"

Dashing to her bedroom, Eileen threw on jeans and a sweater. She didn't bother with socks, instead shoving her naked Popsicle toes into running shoes. Quickly, she checked her reflection in the mirror, and finding it tousled but not too alarming, headed for the door. She had a sick feeling something was very wrong.

She had to walk gingerly across the icy courtyard to avoid slipping. What she saw once she reached Daniel's apartment froze her breath in her lungs. The apartment was nearly empty.

She grabbed the arm of one of the moving men, trying to stay calm. "Where's Daniel?"

The man shrugged. "Daniel who? All I know is, I got orders to box up all this stuff. Don't know no Daniel."

He started to walk away, but she held tight. He stopped, giving her an impatient glare.

She said, "Who ordered these things moved?"

His smile was more like a grimace. "Can't say. Now, lady, if you don't mind, I'm freezing my butt off." He went inside the apartment.

Hugging herself against the chill, Eileen followed, looking around for any clues as to where he might have gone. Other than several boxes marked, *Storage Unit 495*, not one scrap of paper remained.

She hurried back to her apartment and dug through her purse for Daniel's business card, finding a number listed for the FBI's LA office. She remembered Daniel telling her the office was staffed seven days a week. But when she called she was told Special Agent Manatucci was no longer with the Agency and no forwarding information was available.

She hung up, grabbing the Yellow Pages to look up the LA police department's number. He'd been working with them on the investigation. Maybe they'd know where he was. As the phone rang, she said out loud, "Calm yourself. He didn't disappear off the face of the earth. You'll be able to find him. Then you can find out what made him change his mind, and you can straighten out this whole mess."

After being transferred at least six times, she was informed by the detective in charge of Alyssa's case that they had no knowledge of either a Daniel Collins or a Daniel Manatucci working with the department.

Setting the receiver back in the cradle, Eileen looked around her apartment. The beautiful tree had lost its magical appeal, and her apartment felt lonely and hollow.

She hurried to Mirabelle's door and knocked. Maybe Daniel had left word with her. Gus opened the door and immediately pulled her in. The sudden warmth caused her to shiver violently.

He shook his head. "Lucy, you got some 'splainin' to do."

She took a shaky breath. "Do you know where Daniel is? Do you know what's going on?"

Mirabelle said from the kitchen, "I'm afraid Daniel's gone."

Eileen said, "But why? He said he loved me. He wanted to marry me. Someone doesn't say things like that one minute, then take off without a word the next minute."

"Something," Mirabelle looked over her glasses, "must have happened to make him believe you love someone else."

Her heart sank as she remembered the many occasions she'd told Daniel she loved Brock. But she'd been certain Daniel had come to understand how her feelings had changed. Daniel acted like he knew she cared for him, but was just waiting for her to realize it, too. Well, she had. So what happened to change *his* mind?

"Did you and Daniel have a fight last night?" Mirabelle looked like she was searching for an answer, too. "Did you tell him anything to make him believe you didn't love him? Or *do* anything that might make him think that?"

She remembered Brock's kiss. Had Daniel seen? It seemed the only answer. She put her fingers to her lips. "What have I done?"

Mirabelle said gently, "For one thing, you didn't follow directions."

"I did everything you said to do. I found balance, I learned to love unconditionally, I—" She stopped short, taking a deep, ragged breath before she continued. "I didn't follow my heart, and I allowed my fears to make decisions for me."

"Sit down, my dear." Mirabelle came in with a teapot and cups on a tray, setting them down on the coffee table. They all seated themselves.

Mirabelle looked at Eileen with such intense sadness that Eileen felt her chin quiver. The older woman said, "My dear. You still have yet to state your true intent. The universe can't help you if you don't know what you want."

"But I did." She took the tea Mirabelle offered, putting her cold fingers around the warm cup.

"Were you one-hundred-percent sure who your true love was at the time?" Mirabelle was shaking her head.

"No. I messed up big time, didn't I?"

Gus and Mirabelle gave each other a significant look.

"And now it's too late, isn't it?" Eileen put her fingertips over her quivering lips.

"I don't know for sure," Mirabelle said. "The magic may not have been completely diminished. If you complete all the tasks before the beginning of the New Year, you might have a chance. After that, I'm afraid *granting* is out of the question."

"You must discover what gift you have to give mankind," Gus pointed out.

She felt her shoulders slump. What could a computer geek do to help mankind? Maybe she was meant to be with Brock after all. Was this Fate's way of telling her she'd been on the right track from the beginning? So what if she didn't love Brock with the same passion she felt for Daniel? They did have a lifetime of history in common, and that had to count for something.

Eileen looked at Mirabelle and Gus. "I've got some thinking to do. I'm sorry if my not Granting has caused you or your organization any trouble."

The look of sadness she saw Gus shoot to Mirabelle gave Eileen an uneasy feeling. Mirabelle just took Gus's hand and patted it. "You don't worry about us. Like you said, you've got some thinking to do."

***

Daniel spent Christmas as a removed observer with his family. He'd thought getting back to his hokey roots would validate his independent lifestyle, but it didn't. The noisy, chaotic house filled with his brothers, their wives and their kids only made him see what he was missing—what he would never have—with Eileen.

"Hey, bro." His older brother Colin plunked down across from him on the sofa, saying in a hushed voice, "You haven't said two words since you came in yesterday. You get fired or somethin'?"

Daniel didn't feel like talking. He didn't feel much like doing anything. "Nah, I quit."

Colin's jaw dropped. "No way! You leave the Agency? I don't believe it. Man, you ate, drank and slept the Agency."

Daniel shrugged. "It lost its appeal."

"So what now?"

They watched Colin's three-year-old twin sons wrestle across the floor.

"I've got something else lined up." He knew his answer was non-committal, but his new job seemed like a distant image.

Their mom came into the room, wiping her hands on an outlandish Christmas apron. Daniel wondered how many elegantly beautiful women like his mother would wear the monstrosity just because it was a gift from one of her grandkids. The thing was cut from dyed-red bib overalls and had ornaments haphazardly glued all over the front.

"Now, boys," she said, scolding the twins. "You're going to get hurt. Don't get so close to the fireplace bricks!"

Of course the boys ignored her, just like Daniel and his brothers had when they were little.

"They're fine, Mom," Colin said.

His mother had just retreated to the kitchen, shaking her head, when siren-like wails came from the two boys as their heads simultaneously made contact with the bricks.

Without batting an eye, Colin went over to scoop them up and do a cursory examination. "Oh, you're fine."

He put them down and they ran into the kitchen, Daniel assumed, for someone who might be sympathetic. Daniel knew from experience they would get an "I told you so," along with the kisses and unnecessary Band-Aids from Grandma Catherine.

Colin smiled as he sat back down, "Katie's got another bun in the oven."

Daniel felt a smile tug at his mouth. "I was wondering what the politically correct term was nowadays."

His brother brushed him off with the wave of his hand. "It's a girl this time. We've already had the sonogram. You got any names to throw into the hat?" Their family tradition was to have each member put their choice of a name into a bowl and the mother draw from the bowl.

Daniel said, "Yeah, Eileen."

Colin nodded, a suspicious look in his eye. "Any particular reason?"

Colin was digging, Daniel could tell, but he still didn't feel like talking about losing the love of his life. "No, I just like the name," was all he said. His mind went to images of a dynamite little girl with Eileen's auburn curls and her gray-blue eyes. Of course, Colin and his wife both had brown eyes and black hair, so the chances of ever seeing the little girl he'd imagined was pretty much out of the question.

Colin's wife, Katie, came in and sat in Colin's lap. "It's good to have you home, Daniel. We've missed you these past couple Christmases."

Colin's tone teased. "Yeah, having the Grinch around always livens up our holidays."

Maybe he shouldn't have come home. His bummer mood only brought everyone down. Daniel smiled at Katie, "Sorry, I've been in kinda a bad mood lately. I really am glad to be home."

Just then all five grandkids, ages three through eight, came into the room, dragging Daniel's mom by her apron. Darlene, the eldest, picked up the guitar from where it stood next to the Christmas tree and handed it to Daniel's mom.

The rest of the family came in and sat down, Daniel's dad grabbing an armful of giggling kids and sitting in his easy chair.

Catherine began singing the lyrics to "The House on Pooh Corner "in the same sweet, folksy voice of his childhood.

He found himself clearing his throat several times during the song, remembering Eileen telling him about her mother singing the same song to her.

***

Eileen spent Christmas morning with Brock at his parent's house. He seemed to be intent on convincing her that she had been right all along and they did belong together. He even agreed to go with her that evening to her father's house to help with her mother's things. Jeannette and Alyssa had informed her they would be spending the day with Miles Catchum. She was sure to avoid facing her after what Alyssa had done.

And now, during the quiet afternoon as Eileen and Brock walked up the wide staircase leading to her father's attic, she took what she knew would be her last look at her childhood home. "You know," she said to Brock, "I don't remember ever feeling like I belonged here."

Brock smiled. "What would it have taken to make you feel like you belonged?"

"Two parents who loved me, maybe."

"Your parents did love you." He put his arm around her as she opened the attic door. "Remember, our mothers used to be good friends. I remember my mother saying how devoted your mother was to you."

Eileen tried to think back, but only a few isolated images came to her. "I don't remember." She turned on the light.

"I never did like attics," Brock said. "They creep me out."

"Thanks for coming. I didn't want to do this by myself." What she really wanted was Daniel's strength beside her.

The cold, musty room smelled of old wood furniture and decades of dust—as if generations of people had left behind a bit of themselves—and it felt unexpectedly comforting. She even fancied she smelled the hint of her father's vanilla pipe tobacco mingling with the faded scent of rose petals. Her mother's name had been Rose, and Eileen wondered if she'd worn rose-scented perfume.

"Hey, look over here." Brock stood next to an old cedar chest with the name 'Rose' on it.

Eileen knelt down next to the chest, running her fingers over the etched name. "Rose," she said aloud. Her mother had been twenty-nine when she died—only one year older than Eileen.

She opened the lid, her previous fears about what she might find evaporating. She'd been afraid she would confirm her worst fears—that her mother really didn't love her. But, as she knelt, looking down at the boxes and photo albums, she realized those fears went back to her childhood and the mistaken belief her mother had abandoned her, that she'd *let* herself die.

"Well," Brock said, picking up a diary and handing it to her. "This is as good a place as any to start."

Eileen looked at Brock's encouraging smile. She opened the diary.

It began in beautiful calligraphy script, *To My Daughter, Eileen.* Eileen felt tears sting her eyes. Why hadn't her father ever shown her this? True, it had always been up here, waiting for Eileen, but her father never even discussed her mother or allowed a picture of her in the house after she died. Eileen realized that ignoring her mother's memorabilia had been just one more attempt to win her father's approval and love. But it hadn't worked.

She concentrated on accepting her father for the part he'd played in her life and forgiving his indifference. A lightness filled her heart as she opened the book.

Two hours later, feeling like the dust of centuries coated her hands, Eileen replaced the last photo album in the chest, stood up, and looked down at the stack of her mother's memories.

"Brock, I feel like a different person."

He stood behind her, his arms companionably around her. "You seem like the same wonderful woman I've known most of my life."

She didn't correct him. She wasn't about to fool herself into believing he'd ever really looked at her until her makeover. But she found she could easily forgive him. Brock was just, well ... Brock. And after seeing the truth of her childhood, she knew he wasn't the kind of man she wanted to spend the rest of her life with.

"Brock, I think I finally understand my father." She picked up a photo of her mother and held it out to him. "Who does this look like?"

The quizzical look on his face as he gazed at the picture was comical. "Jeannette!"

She nodded. "A softer, more natural version of Jeannette."

"You think your father married Jeannette because she looked like your mother?"

"Yes. And I think he felt guilty about it."

The creak of a floorboard from behind them startled them both. They turned to see Jeannette. Eileen saw her through new eyes. Is this how her mother would have looked if she had lived? Maybe not so harsh, not so overly-made up, but similar all the same? Maybe Jeannette had good reason for being so angry. Eileen knew she'd be angry—and hurt—if she found out her husband had only married her because she reminded him of his first wife.

Jeannette said, "Are you about done up here? I have guests coming at eight."

"Yes," Eileen said. Then, as Jeannette turned to go, she asked a question she'd been dying to ask most of her life. "Jeannette, did you ever love my father?"

She saw the woman's sharp chin quiver. "Yes. If you must know, I did. At first. I thought he would be my ticket to security." She added in a strident voice, "And I was a good wife." She shrugged. "At first."

Remembering what Daniel had told her about Jeannette, Eileen went on. "But, you weren't divorced from your first husband, were you?"

The shocked look on Jeannette's face mirrored Brock's. "I can't believe he told you that. He swore to me he never would."

"He knew?" Eileen asked, astonished. Could she believe this woman?

"Of course he knew."

"But, that's bigamy. You could go to jail."

"Don't be silly. I didn't legally marry your father. There is no marriage certificate. We just went through the motions." She smiled, and her face was momentarily transformed.

Eileen could see the resemblance to her mother.

Jeannette went on. "I couldn't very well divorce an invalid in a convalescent home, could I? My husband had a severe stroke twenty-five years ago and has been in a home ever since. A very expensive home."

Eileen found herself shaking her head. Had anyone in her childhood been who she'd imagined them to be? "Then, what about the will? Is it valid?"

"It should be. Your father said he would make sure I was taken care of. I put my life into that man, knowing all along he only pretended to marry me because I looked like," her voice turned snide, "his one true love, Rose." She straightened her shoulders. "I didn't have his love. The least I deserve is his money."

Eileen realized she felt lighter inside than she had in years. "Do you know why he didn't leave me anything in the will?"

"Yes. Do you really want to know?" The woman raised her

eyebrows.

Eileen's heart accelerated. "Yes, I want to know."

Jeannette stood with her hands on her hips. "His decision to leave you out of his will was stupidly based on the same reasoning he used when making any decision about you. He wanted you to be so damned independent and tough that no one could hurt you, that you could survive anything."

She wasn't sure if Jeannette's words were meant to hurt, but oddly, they were comforting. They explained so much. Jeannette seemed the only one hurting. Eileen looked closer at the woman she'd always thought hated her. Jeannette seemed on the verge of tears. Eileen wanted to go over to her and put her arms around her, but she knew Jeannette well enough to know the gesture wouldn't be appreciated.

Jeannette suddenly appeared to deflate, her voice softening. "Eileen, he was afraid you would die, like your mother, if you weren't tough."

"But my mother died of cancer. It's not like she had a choice."

"I got the impression he felt she didn't fight hard enough." Her laugh was mirthless. "And I've been paying ever since. Well, Eileen, it's payback time. The money, the houses, everything belongs to me." With that, Jeannette turned and descended the stairs.

Eileen took in a shaky breath as Brock put his arm around her. Jeannette had so much bitterness in her heart. And having tasted it herself, Eileen knew how it could destroy.

"You know, if you marry me, you won't have to worry about money," Brock pointed out.

She looked into Brock's eyes. "And end up like Jeannette and my father in twenty years? Neither of us wants that. I don't want to lose what we do have, which is a wonderful friendship." She kissed his cheek and went to take the handle at one end of the cedar chest. "I guess it's time to start utilizing my father's lessons. I may get hurt. But I *will* survive. I'm okay as an independent woman."

Brock chuckled. "Does that mean I don't have to help you with the trunk after all?"

Her laughter bounced off the slanted attic ceiling. "Okay.

Tomorrow I'll be independent."

When they got back to Eileen's apartment, Brock helped her put the heavy chest in front of the sofa. It worked beautifully as a coffee table.

Before he left, he took her hands and looked into her eyes. "You know I love you, don't you?"

She nodded. "Like a sister."

He laughed. "Like a distant cousin." He lightly kissed her lips. "I just want you to be happy."

"I will." On the way home she had told him she was quitting her job at Wincomp. She'd finally admitted to herself the gift she had for computer security design was worth sharing with the world—or mankind—as Mirabelle had said. It might be too late for her seven tasks to help her get her wish. But by completing them, she knew she would enrich her life. She would start the New Year off by looking for a job in which she could utilize that gift. If she couldn't have the love of her life, she could at least have the job of her life.

Fifteen

Trying not to think about Daniel and what she'd foolishly thrown away, Eileen spent the next week immersed in Wincomp's party plans. Alyssa had only been using the party as a pretext to work on Eileen's computer, so plans had virtually halted where Eileen left off. Luckily, she had long ago booked the hotel and orchestra.

The wild, record-breaking weather didn't help. One day it would lightly snow, the next they would have hail, and the next a freezing wind tried to blow cars off the freeways. She'd begun to wonder if the doomsday groups weren't right after all.

Now she stood in the hotel ballroom making last-minute preparations, thanking whatever lucky stars wanted credit that they had a chilly but comfortable enough evening for the New Year's Eve party. She had the feeling though that tomorrow's Rose Parade was going to be a big disappointment to everyone used to the picture-postcard Southern California weather.

"Gus," Eileen raised her voice so Gus could hear from across the large room. "Did you bring tape?"

She saw him roll his eyes. He held up both wrists, each of which sported what looked like funky bracelets. Tape. He jogged across the room to where she stood among the decorated tables.

Gus handed her the tape. "You almost finished here? Everything on my list has been checked and double-checked."

Securing a wobbly centerpiece, she sighed heavily. "I'm done. We can go."

Gus shook his head. "Not exactly in a party mood, huh, girlfriend?"

The party was the last place she wanted to be. Not even thoughts about the software contest announcement could stir more than a dull curiosity. "I'm fine."

Gus snorted. "Yeah, right. Any more 'fine' and I'd put you on a Prozac drip."

She laughed. "I haven't been that bad, have I?"

Gus threaded her arm through his, and they began walking toward the door. "I can see you're doing great for the most part. Just every teensy-bit-of-a-while I see the sadness in your eyes."

She said, "I feel like I failed everyone. And all because I couldn't let go of my fears."

"What were you so afraid of?"

Eileen chewed on her lip, thinking back. She said, "I can see now that in a strange way, to me Brock has always been a substitute for the caring father I wanted but never had. From the first day I met him, when he took care of me, I turned him into the family I wanted so desperately. I was afraid to let go of that fantasy. Afraid I'd have to face the reality that my father was a self-absorbed man who didn't love me."

Gus stopped and comically glanced around as if looking for someone. He snapped his fingers high in the air. "Check, please," he said as if summoning a waiter. "We're ready for a reality check." Then he smiled at her. "So, what did you discover when you stopped letting your fears guide you?" He put his hand to his chest. "Oooh, I'm getting good at this, aren't I?"

She laughed, but her thoughts were on what she'd discovered. "I realized that I am worthy of love. I don't have to gain my father's love or approval, through Brock or any other father-substitute, in order to be happy. I can be happy all on my own. And just because my father didn't know how to love doesn't mean he didn't care for me on some level."

"You got it, girlfriend." Gus put his hand up for a high-five, and they clapped hands together. Then he grew serious. "Now it's time to let it go, Eileen. Use the lessons you've learned and accept what you can't change. Turn it into something positive for yourself and for others."

"I'm trying."

"Have you stated your intention? And do you know your gift?"

"It's kind of late for that, isn't it. My 'intention' has disappeared."

Gus looked confused. "Huh?"

Eileen straightened, stating, "My intention is to find true love. There, I've said it out loud." She cupped her hands to her mouth and yelled, "Now are you happy, wish granters?" She looked at Gus. "As far as my gift? It's to stop hackers. I'm making it my mission to help people feel their privacy is secure, and that some nut won't hack into government data and start a world war."

Gus acknowledged her statement with a satisfied but sad nod. They buttoned their jackets before they left the hotel. The freaky weather was still frigid.

Eileen said, "I feel a better sense of direction than ever before. I feel happier and more at peace than I've ever felt in my life. But I miss Daniel so much it hurts."

Gus put his arm around her. "I know, honey. I know."

***

Daniel thanked the LA District Attorney Mike Bonner for his part on the hacker case.

Mike said, "Sorry to bring you all the way out to LA on New Year's Eve."

Daniel shrugged as he looked at the clock on the wall. It was already ten o'clock. "I'm the one who put this thing on the fast-track."

"Looks like you're on your way to a party," Mike said, glancing at Daniel's tuxedo.

Daniel thought about Eileen. She must be at the Wincomp party by now. He wondered if she and The Jerk would be announcing their engagement tonight. Daniel intended to go to the local Agency party, not Wincomp's. "Yeah. It's the night for parties, isn't it? Not even the strange weather is keeping people in."

Mike chuckled. "Weird weather. Solar flares. My wife's convinced something weird is going to happen at the stroke of midnight tonight. She insists I come home early."

"Women."

They exchanged a knowing look, then Daniel shook the Mike's hand and headed out to his cab, which would take him to his hotel. In a few hours he'd be catching the red-eye for home, and it was none-too-soon. Every minute he spent in the same city as Eileen was torture. The pull to go to her and try once again to persuade her was so strong he felt it as an ache in his chest. But the image of her kissing The Jerk flashed through his mind. It was deterrent enough to keep him from making a fool of himself.

As the taxi dropped him off at his hotel, he noticed the throngs of people in evening dress, making it seem like every person in LA was attending a party tonight. He decided to check his messages before he went to the Agency party upstairs.

When he got to his room, a flashing red light on his phone indicated he had a message. A recording of Pete Silva's voice said, "This is important, Daniel. Call me at this number as soon as possible. Ask for Room 230." The number Pete gave wasn't one Daniel recognized.

He quickly dialed the number. When an operator answered with the name of a hospital, his stomach dropped. Something must be wrong with Maggie, or the overdue baby. Or maybe something had happened with one of their kids. Pete must be going through hell. The guy loved his family more than anything on Earth. The operator put him through immediately.

"Pete Silva here." His friend sounded exhausted.

"Pete," Daniel said. "What happened?"

"Oh, man," Pete's voice rose with excitement. "We got a beautiful little girl. She's right here in the room with us."

Daniel sat down on the bed, relief flooding him. He hadn't realized just how much Pete's family meant to him. "Great, bud, but you scared the bejesus out of me. You sounded like something was wrong."

"Naw, man, I'm good. Just tired. Magg's labor was long with this one. I was her coach, you know." He sounded proud.

Daniel listened with mixed emotions while Pete described the experience. When they hung up, he was left feeling a void.

He'd heard such awe and happiness in his friend's voice, and he wanted that experience with Eileen. He wanted her to know that the man standing beside her when she had her first child—and every other child—loved and appreciated her for the incredible woman she was. Daniel knew in his heart he was meant to be that man.

The thought repeated itself. He was meant to be that man. But he wasn't. Eileen thought she loved Brock. But could Brock make her happy?

Daniel jumped up and paced, nervous anxiety moving him around the small room. He wanted more than anything for her to be happy. He'd just needed to find a way to accept the fact that she didn't love him. If only she hadn't responded to him with the passion of a woman in love when he'd kissed her. If only she hadn't told him with her eyes that she loved him. If only—

He realized he had to see her again, just one more time, even if it meant a repeat of the pain he'd experienced seeing her kiss Brock. He grabbed his coat and headed out the door.

He would just drop in on Wincomp's party, reconfirm for his peace of mind that Eileen truly loved Brock, and then he would leave. He would then be free to start the New Year and his new life without looking back. What was the name of the hotel hosting Wincomp's party? Then he remembered. The Royal.

***

Mirabelle's hand felt heavy and her earthly body incredibly tired as she logged off her computer after talking with Mary. It was their final communication through Wishmakers. She knew every Granter in existence would soon begin to fade into oblivion.

Already her own life-force, which the rejuvenating power of Granting had held in check throughout the ages, felt like a flickering candle. It was a candle that would sputter, then go out shortly after midnight. The magic was at an end. Eileen hadn't granted. Gus would be there shortly to spend Mirabelle's last mortal hours with her.

Opening wide the window behind her computer, she looked up at the starry night and the full moon. Its blue glow filled the room, bringing with it a crisp breeze to tingle Mirabelle's skin. She wanted to experience every last sensation of her mortal life.

She wasn't sad for herself. She knew her life force would continue on another plane. Her sadness existed for the millions of people who would face the darkness of an uncertain world alone, without ever having the chance of experiencing magic in their lives. She watched her screensaver's graphic of a glass slipper slowly spin around, sparkling as it moved. If only she could continue to give the hope of Cinderella's glass slipper to mankind.

As she fiddled with the wand she had shown Eileen the day they met, she wondered what she could have done differently. How better could she have moved Eileen toward Granting? The answers were lost to her. In the end, Granting was up to the client. It had been up to Eileen to face her fears, to discover her true intent, and to acknowledge her gift to mankind. Mirabelle knew Eileen had come close. She'd excelled in most of the tasks. Fear had kept the others too elusive for Eileen to grab hold of.

Mirabelle felt the darkness close in, but it wasn't a darkness that could be remedied by turning on another lamp. It was the insidious darkness that fought for dominance against light in mankind's soul. Now it waited outside her window, and outside every other believer's window. It waited for the last spark of hope to go out. Darkness had finally vanquished light and now sat poised like a hungry predator waiting to devour its prey.

***

Eileen went through the motions of getting ready for the party. She checked herself in the mirror. Hair? Wildly in place. Makeup? Just a hint to accentuate her eyes and lips. Floor-length blue velvet dress? A perfect fit. Teardrop diamond earrings? Catching the light just so. Smile? She looked away from the mirror.

The clock in the kitchen chimed eleven. So what if she arrived a little late to the party? It was a party she didn't have the heart for.

A knock on her door brought a heavy sigh. It had to be Gus. He'd probably noticed her light was on and wondered why she hadn't left for the party. Her heart skipped. It might be someone else. Someone who had changed his mind and come back for her. Daniel? She raced through the living room, wrenching open the door.

Gus smiled at her, and she tried not to let on that her heart was breaking. He said, "Can't find a pumpkin? Or are you afraid of mice?"

"Come in, Gus."

"I can't. I'm on my way to Mirabelle's. I just saw your light and wondered why you're not at your party."

She shivered, even though her heavy dress had long sleeves. "I don't feel much like partying."

Gus was unrelenting. "Get your coat, girl. Those people need you. Won't be much of a party without Wincomp's princess."

She forced a chuckle. "Gus, the world's not going to end just because I've lost heart."

Gus looked skyward, an uneasy expression on his face. "I hope not. Still, you should go. You might have some fun, or even brighten someone else's New Year."

She grabbed her coat and purse from the entry table. "I'm going. I know I should at least put in an appearance." Her smile felt stiff. "So I'll be fashionably late."

Gus looked at his watch. "Eleven-fifteen? That's way beyond fashionably late, darlin'. Any later and you'll miss it altogether. You know traffic's going to be one hellacious female dog."

The thought of facing the New Year's Eve traffic made her cringe. She braced herself for the inevitable as she locked the door and walked with Gus into the courtyard.

***

After a three-block cab ride that took half an hour due to traffic, Daniel entered the Royal's lobby at eleven-thirty. Now that he was actually here, he felt an overwhelming sense of urgency to see Eileen. He maneuvered through partygoers to the crowded front desk, thankful he stood head and shoulders above the other people and could easily get the attention of a pretty blonde clerk.

"Wincomp party?" he shouted over the drone of voices.

The harried clerk smiled then checked her computer terminal. When she looked up again, she raised her voice to say, "The Crystal Ballroom." She pointed upstairs. "Top floor."

Daniel sardined himself into one of the elevators and pushed the button even though it was already lighted. Most of the revelers were probably going to one of the ballrooms at the top of the hotel.

The moment the doors opened on the top floor Daniel felt himself taken along in a sea of people. He went along with the tide until he saw the words, "Crystal Ballroom" over a set of double doors. Then he sidestroked his way across stream to finally find himself blessedly free and standing at the entrance to a large ballroom. Two hundred or so people, Wincomp employees and their family and friends, he assumed, filled the room.

He searched for Eileen's short auburn curls, his gut reacting to the fear he would most likely find her with Brock.

He found Brock quickly enough, but saw no trace of Eileen. Brock stood alone, talking to an elderly couple seated at a table.

Ray came up to Daniel. "Hey, man, I didn't think you were going to make it. Glad you came." He looked behind him. "Where's Eileen?"

Daniel's gaze shot around the room. "She isn't here?"

"No. She was in such a funk, I was afraid she might not show up. But then when I saw you, I thought she might have waited for you."

"Me? Why would she wait for me?" And why was she in a funk? She should be the happiest woman on Earth. She had what she wanted. Brock The Jerk.

Nancy, looking like she more than sampled the champagne, came up and took Ray's arm with an urgent tug. "Oh, hello Daniel. Good to see you. Ray, you're needed at the podium. It's nearly midnight."

Ray shrugged. "Loudest voice gets to start the countdown."

Daniel said, "Nancy, do you know where Eileen is?"

As Nancy pulled Ray away she said in a slurred voice, "She should be here somewhere. Just look for a woman in silver shoes. She told me she'd be wearing a blue dress and silver shoes." She nodded as they disappeared into the crowd.

What could have happened to Eileen? Daniel looked back to find Brock heading to the dance floor with a short redhead. And why wasn't Brock concerned about the woman he loved?

Then a sickening thought occurred to Daniel. Brock didn't love Eileen after all. She must be home right now, heartbroken. Suddenly he hated Brock. How could the man throw away something so precious?

He turned and made his way toward the elevators. He would go to her apartment. At least he could comfort her. He knew firsthand what it was like to lose the love of a lifetime.

***

Eileen got on the elevator at the Royal at exactly eleven-forty-five. Traffic had been horrendous, but if she hurried, she could still ring in the New Year with her friends. She said to the person closest to the elevator buttons, "Top floor, please."

The elevator began its ascent, building speed as it went. Then with a sudden, bone-jarring jolt, it stopped. Eileen felt herself being shoved into the man next to her then back to bump into the woman on the other side as the elevator car rocked from side to side.

A woman screamed, "Earthquake!" The car went silent but kept rocking as everyone held their collective breath. Finally the motion slowed to a rattle.

She heard a woman whimper as the side-to-side rocking started up again, accompanied by a resounding noise of metal banging against metal. Eileen braced herself against those around her. The motion stopped, the lights flickered and, miraculously, the elevator doors opened.

She felt the push of panic from behind her as the crowd surged into the hallway. At her first opportunity she grabbed onto a doorframe to dislodge herself from the rush. Her heart hammered against her ribs. *Don't panic*, she told herself. At some time during the crush of people she had lost a shoe. She took the other slipper off, gathered up the train of her dress and went along the corridor to see if anyone needed help.

***

The moment the elevator doors opened Daniel exited and looked around to access any damage or injuries the earthquake might have caused. Nothing caught his attention. The hallways emptied quickly as people who had exited the bank of elevators now crowded into the stairwells.

The Royal was relatively new and, he was sure, up to LA's strict earthquake codes. He was probably as safe here as anywhere in LA. But he wasn't worried about himself.

He had to get to Eileen. *Deviazione* was old and had brick roofing tiles that could be lethal. The time it would take to get across town made the trip seem an impossible task.

Just then a glimmer of silver caught his eye. A lone silver sandal sat in front of the bank of elevators. Nancy had said Eileen would be wearing silver shoes. But, it was New Year's Eve. So might a thousand other women. He grabbed the shoe and headed in the direction of the stairs.

An incredulous, "Daniel?" from behind him as he started toward the stairwell had him doing an about-face and pushing past people to see if his mind was playing tricks on him.

Just inside one of the hotel room's open doorways stood Eileen holding her other shoe.

Relieved laughter erupted from his chest as he rushed to her and scooped her into his arms. "You're okay!"

"I'm fine. Now," came the muffled words from his shoulder.

He released her, realizing he had no right to take her in his arms.

She stood there, looking into his eyes. "Why did you come back?"

Daniel heard the television from inside the room. An announcer's voice yelled the New Year countdown, "Ten ... nine—

"I came back for you," he said.

"Six ... five—" the announcer intoned as another small tremor shook the hotel.

Daniel grabbed Eileen, bracing them both against the doorframe. "I love you."

"Three ... two—"

Tears fill her eyes. "I love you too, Daniel. So much."

A stronger tremor hit, and Daniel crushed his lips to hers.

She loved him! To hell with earthquakes. To hell with end-of-the world predictions. What did anything matter as long as she loved him.

"One! Happy New Year!" came the shout from the television.

Daniel didn't care. He only cared about the woman in his arms.

***

The quaking of the building stopped, but the one in Eileen's chest built until she thought her heart would burst with joy. Daniel loved her. He'd come back.

Her wish had come true after all.

She felt Daniel's lips reluctantly pull away from hers, but he kept her body tight against his, as he said, "I'm not letting you go until you promise to marry me."

"I'll marry you. But I don't want you to ever let me go."

Daniel brushed his lips against hers again. "Never."

Someone standing at the long window at the end of the corridor yelled to one of his friends, "Hey, come here, quick! You gotta see this. What the holy heck is it?"

She and Daniel looked at each other and followed the crowd to the window. Strange dancing bands of light illuminated the sky.

Daniel took her hand. "Let's get a better look." He pulled her toward the stairs.

"Where?"

"The roof." He whispered, his smile conspiratorial.

They ran up the three flights of stairs and burst through the door leading to the rooftop. Fresh air filled Eileen's lungs.

Then what she saw had her staring at the sky in amazement. "Daniel, do you know what it is?"

He stood behind her and, putting his arms around her, pulled her close. "Strange. It looks like the aurora borealis."

"It does." Banners of light danced across the skies, while a temperate breeze ruffled her hair.

She turned in his arms. "It's as though the entire universe is as happy as I am."

"Happy as we are," he corrected before his lips once again found hers.

Epilogue

Mirabelle Saintly had *felt* Eileen's culmination the instant it happened. Fading to the point of perishing, Mirabelle had suddenly been jolted back into existence with an infusion of power as Eileen kissed her true love, Daniel, and finally put all her lessons into play.

Gus had been at her side, and by the startled look on his face, he was stunned by her miraculous recovery.

At that point Mirabelle quickly gathered the surrounding energy and focused on directing the power to Eileen. Being able to say the words, "Your wish is granted," had never felt so good. And although Eileen may have been too far away to physically hear, Mirabelle was certain the young woman's spirit knew the precise moment her wish had been granted. Now, a few minutes past midnight, as Mirabelle and Gus sat before her computer terminal, she could feel her spirit absorb the revitalizing energy permeating the atmosphere.

Although she would love to take a moment to wallow in the glow, she knew Mary and the others would be logging on to mutually rejoice in their reprieve and to hear all the details of Eileen's Grant. What a New Year's celebration they would have!

She logged on to Wishmakers' website, immediately connecting with Mary.

"We're so happy for Eileen!" Mary cried. "And for Wishmakers, of course."

"It was down to the last second," Mirabelle said, grinning

as she looked at Gus. "But true love saved the day." She wanted to dance, and as she watched, Gus got up and did dance. It was a combination football victory dance and moves only Gus knew the origin of.

Mary's tone was cautious. "We're not out of the woods yet, Mirabelle. Eileen didn't grant on the Solstice, so our power reserves are still down."

"Down, but not out."

"We must begin our next assignments immediately. We must proceed with our goal to enlighten the masses without delay. You and Gus will receive your new assignment within the week."

Mirabelle was thrilled to hear those words—next week. And she was certain Wishmakers would survive, stronger than ever.

***

Mirabelle Saintly walked with a light step to her front door to admit more of her holiday guests.

A year had passed since what had come to be known with Wishmakers as 'The Crisis,' and what the media still called, 'a freak atmospheric disturbance.' Thank heavens no one was killed, but earth quakes and freakish weather had caused great concern worldwide. Doomsayers insisted the unusual weather, earthquakes, and lights had marked the beginning of the end. But Mirabelle knew differently. It marked the start of a new era in which each day was a new beginning. Although Wishmakers wasn't out of the woods yet, they were holding their own. A few more grants, and they would be secure for another millennium.

Daniel and Eileen stood before her with jubilant grins on their faces as they shouted, "Surprise!" Eileen patted her swollen belly. Judging by its size, Mirabelle calculated the happy event was close at hand.

"Oh my, my dears, you shouldn't have made the trip! When are you due?"

Daniel said, "Not for two more weeks."

"Don't worry," Gus piped in from behind her. "I'm a trained midwife."

They all laughed.

"Good news," Eileen said. "Daniel and I are moving back

to LA. We've decided to make this our home base since we can do most of our work from our computers."

"Wonderful!" Mirabelle could see that the light shining in their eyes had the spark of true love. Daniel couldn't keep his gaze off his beautiful wife, nor could she keep her eyes off her handsome husband. What a blessing to be able to watch their love grow and flourish.

***

Daniel sat on the floor in front of Eileen's chair as the Manatucci tribe opened presents at his parents' house. Daniel's father had insisted Eileen take the comfortable easy chair since, not only was it was her first Christmas with them, but she was also due to go into labor at any time.

Daniel got up to retrieve a small package. Gingerly he handed it to her. "Honey, it's your turn to open a present."

Eileen gave him a suspicious look. "It's not going to blow up, is it?"

"Just open it," he teased.

The entire family knew what the small box contained, and even the children were still for a change.

When Eileen opened the lid to the box she gasped, then hiccuped back a sob. She carefully lifted out the glass bottle of fairy dust her mother had given her and that Daniel had retrieved after the fire at Wincomp. He hadn't told her it survived the fire because he didn't know how long it would be held as evidence. He'd just gotten it back the week before.

The tears that sprang to her eyes had every woman in the room crying.

"Mommy, why are you all crying?" One of the four-year-old twins asked.

"Happy," came a muffled reply as Katie put a tissue to her nose.

Sniffing back tears, Eileen handed the bottle to Daniel. "I can't see what you wrote on the card."

Daniel took the bottle. "I didn't put one on it."

But there, attached by a pink ribbon from the thin neck of the bottle hung a small card. The swirling calligraphy script was vaguely familiar, but Daniel couldn't place whose writing it was. He did know for certain, though, the card hadn't been there when he wrapped the gift last night.

"Well," his brother Colin said, "we're waiting."

Daniel took a deep, shaky breath and looked up into Eileen's eyes. "It says." He took hold of her hand and started over. "It says, 'May all your wishes come true. Love, Mom.'"

He watched Eileen's eyes tear again as she looked at his mother. "Oh, thank you."

Catherine held up her hands. "Oh, honey. I'd love to take the credit, but I didn't write that card."

The room went silent as Eileen took the bottle from Daniel and took a closer look at the card. He watched a shaky smile join the tears. "It's my mother's handwriting." She stared at the card in wonder.

Daniel realized where he'd seen the handwriting. He'd noticed it when Eileen had showed him the contents of her mother's cedar chest. But that was impossible.

At that moment, he could have sworn he smelled the scent of roses mingle with the pine of the Christmas tree. Colin's hummed theme from *The Twilight Zone* got only a few nervous chuckles.

The twins got Catherine's guitar and gave it to her.

"It's time, grandma. Please," Little Corrine said. "We're all done openin' presents."

Catherine good-naturedly rolled her eyes as everyone voiced their encouragement.

Daniel knew what was coming and didn't know whether the inclination to take Eileen out of the room was because he thought she might fall apart, or because he thought he might. He looked up at Eileen and saw her smile a question at him. He just squeezed her hand as his mother began strumming the guitar to the tune of "House on Pooh Corner."

He swallowed past the lump in his throat as Eileen rested her head against the back of the chair. And although tears streamed from her closed eyes, her smile was radiant.

About the Author

As a Baby-boomer/Scorpio, Rebecca has her feet firmly planted in reality while her mind, spirit and soul wander about in various worlds of fantasy. While she wouldn't blink an eye if an alien, a ghost or Merlin appeared at the breakfast table, she wouldn't let the event stop her from taking the clothes out of the dryer before they wrinkled.

She and her Prince Charming of twenty-seven years have raised three children, a dog, a cat and two birds, and are now surprised to discover that "The Empty Nest Syndrome" is a good thing. Who can complain about having more time and energy for romance, the inalienable right to spoil their grandkids, and the freedom to travel?

A long-time member of Romance Writers of America and her local Inland Valley and Orange County chapters, Rebecca is constantly developing new stories. Her work has placed in the Orange Rose contest and won first place with the Midwest Fiction Writers. Glass-Slipper-dot.com is her debut novel.

Watch for
Rebecca Anderson's

Wizard's Moon

Triplets Jachin, Boaz and Lillith were separated at birth, and never knew about each other. They also didn't know that their strange psychic talents were the very reason their mother separated them.

The now grown tripletsare destined to be the most powerful wizards who have ever lived, and the time has come for them to unite their powers and try save the wizards' world from evil.

Coming in January 2002